The truth sudden

More than anything in share a bond with Luke

Yes, she had gone and done the unthinkable. She had fallen head over heels in love with him all over again.

Scratch that. Since she was being honest, she might as well admit that she had never been *out* of love with Luke.

She had simply fallen further.

Harder.

And deeper.

And one thing she didn't need a crystal ball to tell her.

With a child involved, it was going to hurt a heck of a lot more the second time around.

Dear Reader:

Silhouette Special Edition welcomes you to romance…and aims to warm up your winter! November's books begin with a very special love story, Sherryl Woods's RILEY'S SLEEPING BEAUTY—this month's THAT SPECIAL WOMAN! title. This novel's heroine gets into more trouble than she can handle—but at least she *does* have a sexy adventurer by her side.

This month also marks the beginning of a wonderful new trilogy, MAN, WOMAN & CHILD, from veteran authors Christine Flynn, Robin Elliott and Pat Warren. It all starts this month with A FATHER'S WISH, Christine Flynn's story of a woman who finds her lost love and child.

Reader favourites Marie Ferrarella, Arlene James and Trisha Alexander are back to delight you with their latest books and we wrap up the month by welcoming a new author to Special Edition: A FAMILY FOR RONNIE by Julie Caille is a story sure to touch your hearts.

So don't miss a moment of these wonderful books. It's just the beginning of a season filled with love and romance from Special Edition!

The Editor

A Family for Ronnie
JULIE CAILLE

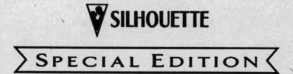

SILHOUETTE

SPECIAL EDITION

*First published in Great Britain in 1995
by Silhouette Books, Eton House, 18-24 Paradise Road,
Richmond, Surrey TW9 1SR*

© Julie Caille 1995

*Silhouette, Silhouette Special Edition and Colophon are
Trade Marks of Harlequin Enterprises II B.V.*

ISBN 0 373 09966 5

23-9511

Made and printed in Great Britain

For Janet Milkovich and Merydith Mathiews,
with thanks for their time and tact.
And for Susan Macias, a.k.a. Susan Mallery,
with sincere appreciation.
Special thanks to the Romance Exchange of the
GEnie network, the best support group in the world.

JULIE CAILLE

was born in England and raised in New York State. She considers herself a left-brained person with right-brained ambitions. She holds a degree in mechanical engineering and spent more than five years analyzing gas turbine engine data for a company in Connecticut.

Despite her analytical mind, Julie has always been a dreamer and a romantic, as well as an inveterate reader. Hours spent with Georgette Heyer paved the way to her next (logical!) career choice. *A Family for Ronnie* is Julie's first contemporary romance. However, she has published several Regency romances, as well.

Her personal philosophy is that all growth is a result of risk taking.

Unkel Luke

me

Chapter One

Oh, Lord, there he was, all six foot two inches of him.

Alicia's heart catapulted into her throat as, across the crowded airport lobby, their eyes locked. Her fingers tightened on her cosmetic bag, and her stomach clenched in a way it had not done since she was eighteen years old.

Ten years, she thought with dismay. After ten years and a failed marriage, she still reacted like a giddy teenager to her first sight of Luke Garrick. It was definitely not a good sign.

Commanding her legs to function, she stepped around a tall woman in a red sundress, watching as Luke bent to speak to the child who clung to his hand. At least two female heads turned as he straightened, which didn't surprise Alicia a bit. Between the cowboy hat, the long, muscular legs in those tight blue jeans and the well-proportioned body, he looked like one of those extremely masculine men advertisers plaster all over their billboards. Not handsome in the conventional sense of the word, but dark and lean and strong and tough.

A dominant male.

He made his way over to her and stopped, his face devoid of expression. "So," he said, amid the babble of voices. "You made it all right."

"Yes." She looked up into his gray eyes and swallowed.

Until this moment she had not really absorbed the fact that she would see him again. They had spoken on the phone twice during the past few days, briefly, and even that had been difficult. Neither had acknowledged the significance of the date she had chosen to travel on; she doubted he even remembered.

Tearing her gaze from his, Alicia looked down at her six-year-old nephew. He had chocolate around his mouth and a dirt smudge across the front of his oversize Oilers T-shirt, but his hair was neatly combed. Maternal anxiety filled her chest. He looked lost, forlorn, a solemn little waif in a sea of noisy adults.

"Oh, Ronnie," she whispered, a lump in her throat. Forgetting Luke, she set down her things and held out her arms to her dead sister's child.

Her nephew.

Luke's nephew.

Their mutual responsibility now that the boy's parents were gone.

No recognition flashed in the child's eyes, for it had been two years since his parents had brought him to visit her in Massachusetts. She held her breath as he studied her, then he stepped forward and allowed her to hug him.

Tears stung Alicia's eyes as she held the small body against hers. He was too young to comprehend tragedy of this magnitude, too young to have to bear such anguish.

"I'm glad to see you, honey," she murmured. "You've gotten so big."

He squirmed out of her embrace. "We saw your plane land."

"Did you? I looked out my window, but I couldn't see you."

"I didn't wave," he replied matter-of-factly. "Uncle Luke didn't, either."

She forced a smile. "Well, I'm glad you came to meet me. I've never been to Houston before so I wouldn't know how to find you on my own."

The man who had once been her fiancé picked up her cosmetic case. "C'mon, Ron, let's take Aunt Alicia to get her luggage."

In subtle ways, he had changed. At twenty, Luke had been appealing, but the past decade had added an intriguing element to his face, an almost daunting quality that had been missing before. To Alicia, he seemed taller and broader, less boyish and more self-assured. Beneath the brim of his hat, his black hair looked curlier than she remembered, probably due to the oppressive southern humidity. And his tan was deeper, though she knew he must spend most of his time in his store.

As they followed Ronnie along the passageway toward the main part of the terminal, Alicia searched her mind for something to say, some remark to ease the awkwardness. "How has he been?" she asked, fighting an urge to double-check the top button of her blouse, which had a tendency to escape its hole.

"He's doing all right," Luke said tersely. "Sometimes something sets him off, and he cries."

"Maybe he's going to need some kind of counseling."

"He's tough. He'll survive."

Unconvinced, Alicia surveyed the child's thin shoulders. "He doesn't look tough. He looks like he'll break in a stiff wind."

Luke glanced down at her, his face a little hard. "Maybe you ought to wait awhile before making assessments."

"It doesn't take a genius to know that child is hurting, Luke. So am I, for that matter. But—" fatigue and worry brought a thin note of accusation into her voice "—you seem to be taking this whole thing pretty casually."

At first she thought he wasn't going to answer, and when he did, his tone was ominous. "So what are you implying, Alicia? That I don't care about Ronnie? That what happened doesn't affect me? You have one hell of an opinion of me, if that's what you think."

Too upset to reply, Alicia returned her gaze to Ronnie, who had already reached the escalator that led down to baggage claim. She saw the child turn to watch their approach, his face so somber that she wondered if he sensed their discord.

They descended to the lower floor in taut silence, a silence that continued while they waited for Alicia's suitcases to appear. Then they headed for the double glass doors and the parking lot outside.

Heat and humidity hit them like a blast from a furnace. "Boy, it sure is hot here in Texas, isn't it?" she said to the little boy.

Ronnie shrugged. "Yeah, but me and Luke don't care," he answered stoutly. "Real men don't mind a little sweat."

While Luke loaded her suitcases into the back of his pickup truck, she swiped a hand over her forehead and studied Ronnie. His straight blond hair and blue eyes reminded her so much of her sister, Caroline, that her heart ached, not only for Ronnie but for herself. She looked away, staring blindly as she remembered all the years of sibling rivalry, all the years of striving to be more than second-best. That it should end like this seemed unbearable.

She pressed her lips together to contain her emotion. She wanted to care for this child, to take him back with her to Massachusetts and raise him as her own. She would love and nurture him as Caroline would no longer be able to do, and, with time, he would come to love her back. It was more than an obligation, more than a commitment.

It was a need, deep-rooted and powerful.

As they climbed into the Silverado, she drew a deep breath, held it, then exhaled slowly and felt some of her tension ease. Then, unwisely, she slid a glance toward Luke and felt a different kind of tension.

During her five-year marriage to Kenny, she'd never mentioned Luke. She'd never dared, for if she had, she wasn't sure she could have concealed the wistfulness in her voice. Luke represented the mystique of her first love, the chance of a lifetime she'd been too afraid to seize.

Or too afraid to believe.

A sudden blare of music startled her, and she realized Ronnie had turned on the radio.

"Got it a bit loud, don't you, partner?" Luke said lazily. He reached over to adjust the volume.

"I like it loud," the child protested. "That's my favorite song."

"They're all your favorite songs."

"When we get home, can I watch the rest of the movie?"

"Maybe later. First we have to get your aunt settled."

"Where's she going to sleep? In with you?"

Alicia's cheeks warmed as Luke sent her an unreadable glance. "I doubt it, Ron. I thought I'd let her use the guest room." His mirrored aviator sunglasses hid his eyes; his tone told her nothing.

"I bet she'd like your water bed better." Ronnie nudged her arm. "Luke's got a water bed. You can't jump on it, though, or he'll yell."

"Uh, thanks for the warning," she mumbled.

"Luke says I can have a water bed when I'm older."

"He does, does he?" Alicia tightened her mouth, wondering how many other promises Luke had made without consulting her. She knew nothing about water beds except that her high-rise condominium did not allow them.

They drove for almost an hour, the scene shifting from the beltway to an area that seemed a strange amalgam of suburbia and country. One minute they would be on a road thick with signs and stores, and the next there would be horses or what she assumed were Texas longhorns grazing in emerald fields that seemed miles from any kind of civilization.

"How far out do you live?" she inquired when the silence had lasted as long as she could tolerate.

"Not too far. We're almost there." A moment later, Luke downshifted, easing his truck onto a narrow road that split off to the left. Within minutes, they turned into a driveway belonging to a white, two-story farmhouse with dark green shutters and gray trim.

Somehow it was not what Alicia had expected. With its steeply pitched roof and projecting angles, it exhibited a charming blend of simplicity and elegance. A covered porch stretched across the front, and a separate double garage perched a short distance from the right rear of the house. The garage door slid up smoothly, and Luke parked the Silverado next to a van emblazoned with the words Garrick and Gunn Electronics.

"Let me out first," commanded Ronnie as Alicia opened her door. "Daffy's waiting for me."

Wondering who Daffy was, she allowed the little boy to scoot by her before she stepped out. As the six-year-old dashed toward the house, Luke came around the back of the truck, his keys jingling in his hand.

"Let me unlock the door for Ronnie, then I'll come back for your things." He tossed the words over his shoulder as he walked away, leaving it unclear whether he expected her to follow or wait for his return.

"Sure," Alicia muttered, standing alone in the sweltering garage. "No problem. Don't mind me."

Perspiration trickled down her face as she went to the back of the truck and hoisted herself up on the bumper. She would get her own suitcases; she wasn't some little old lady who needed a man to do the heavy work. Gritting her teeth, she reached down to grasp the handle of the larger of her two suitcases. She tugged it closer, preparing to lift. Damn, it was heavy. She'd forgotten how much she had crammed into it.

Luke's footsteps crunched on the gravel behind her. "I said I'd get them."

"I can do it," she snapped, still tugging.

"Let me do it, Alicia. You'll hurt yourself." He sounded impatient, as though he were dealing with a child.

"Don't be silly. I am perfectly capable of—"

She broke off with a gasp as an arm hooked around her waist. "Stubborn woman," Luke growled beneath his breath. For a paralyzing instant, she hung in the air, her hips and thighs pressed against the hard male muscle of his torso. A shock of awareness rippled through her, then her feet hit the ground and she was free.

Luke stood very still, his eyes hidden behind the silvered sunglasses. "There's an easier way," he said, his voice sounding a bit strained. He turned and let down the tailgate.

"Oh." Feeling rebuked and rather breathless, Alicia cleared her throat. "I . . . forgot. I haven't ridden in a truck since—" She stopped in midsentence, appalled that she had almost alluded to that long-ago summer when he had courted her.

He set her suitcases on the concrete and pulled his hat lower, an action that caught her attention. A cowboy hat should have seemed a ludicrous affectation on a man born and raised in Connecticut, yet it didn't, even with the sunglasses. Instead, it looked entirely suitable. It also seemed symbolic, as though with this one alteration to his attire, Luke had cast aside his old life—the one Alicia had inhabited—and embraced the new.

"I guess you're planning to stay awhile," he remarked. "It feels like you brought everything you own."

"I like to be prepared," she said defensively.

"So I see." A thread of dryness tinged his voice. "Here, you can carry this." He passed her the cosmetic case and slammed the tailgate shut. "Let's get out of this heat."

Inside the house it was blessedly cool. Pushing back a few damp strands of hair, Alicia paused in the foyer, surveying the natural wood flooring with approval. "This is lovely," she commented. In fact, she thought it had a far more inviting ambience than her own condominium, which was filled with furniture that Kenny had selected.

Luke deposited the suitcases near the foot of the staircase and removed his sunglasses, his expression enigmatic. "Thanks. Want a drink?"

"Some iced tea would be wonderful. If you have any, that is."

"I made some this morning." He led the way down the hall into the kitchen, where Ronnie sat with feet swinging, a half-eaten container of strawberry yogurt on the table in front of him.

"I put Daffy out," the little boy said, wiping his mouth with the back of his hand. "She's probably done by now."

"Thanks, Ron. I'll let her in." Tossing his hat on the table, Luke crossed the kitchen and opened the back door. At once, a large dog of questionable pedigree plunged into the room, took one look at Alicia and headed her way with a deep-throated bark. "Easy, Daf," Luke directed in a warning voice.

Alicia stood stock-still while Daffy sniffed her over with ill-mannered thoroughness. "Is she part collie?" she asked, reaching down to stroke the dog's soft fur with a tentative hand.

Luke took a glass from the cabinet and filled it with ice. "She's all collie. It's just hard to tell because her hair's shaved short for the summer."

"Her real name is Daffodil," Ronnie explained, "but we call her Daffy."

When Alicia arched a brow, Luke made a wry face. "Don't blame me," he said. "She came with the name."

"Can I have a milk shake?" Ronnie asked.

"In a few minutes. Let me take care of your aunt first."

Alicia sat down in the chair next to Ronnie. "You like yogurt, I see."

"Yep. Not all the kinds though. I hate blueberry." He stopped suddenly, and his face crumpled. "Mom hated blueberry too." He stared down at his spoon, his lip trembling.

"I know, darling. I grew up with your mother." Alicia laid her hand over his, but he pulled away, refusing to look at her.

"Do you remember when you came to visit me in Boston?" she said gently. "It was two summers ago. We took you to the Children's Museum."

"No!" Slamming the spoon down, he slid from his chair and raced from the room. Daffy bounded after him, but when Alicia would have followed, Luke caught hold of her arm.

"Let him go, Alicia. He wants to be alone right now. He'll lock himself in his room until he's ready to talk."

Distressed, she stared after the child. "But shouldn't one of us make sure he's all right?"

"It's Daffy he wants right now. She gives him more comfort than you or I could."

As she hesitated, torn with indecision, footsteps pounded up the stairs, and somewhere above them, a door crashed shut. Luke set a drink on the table in front of her and took the chair Ronnie had vacated.

Silence followed.

She poked at one of the ice cubes. "Why didn't you bring him to the memorial service?" she asked suddenly. "Everyone thought it was very odd."

"I don't give a damn what everyone thought," he answered with unexpected harshness. "I wasn't about to drag that kid some fifteen hundred miles so he could stand around and be brave while a bunch of morbid old ladies bawled into their handkerchiefs."

"It wasn't like that," Alicia retorted. "And it wasn't as though the ... the bodies were there." She swallowed hard. "It was a nice service. My parents missed seeing him. He should have been there and so should you."

"Don't tell me what I should have done, Alicia. You did what you thought was right and so did I. Funerals don't do anybody any good. Especially not six-year-olds."

"In your opinion," she murmured, raising her eyes to challenge him.

"That's right, in my opinion." His mouth set in a grim line. "If his grandparents want to see him, they can come to Houston."

"You're being unfair. Remember, they've lost a child."

"And that kid up there—" Luke's finger stabbed the air above his head "—lost a mother and father. As far as I'm concerned, his needs come first. Not yours, not mine. Don't forget, I know what it feels like."

Alicia's mouth opened and shut. "Luke, I—I'm sorry. I did forget. I mean, I didn't exactly forget, but it never hit me until this moment that you were Ronnie's age when..."

"When I got dragged to my old lady's funeral," he finished. He looked away, giving her a view of his profile. "I had nightmares for months afterward. Bad ones," he added, an edge to his voice.

Alicia absorbed this in silence, wondering why he had never told her that. And here she had been thinking him callous. But he'd spoken little of his past during the months they had been together.

"I suppose you're right," she admitted. "It just seems like it must be hard for him to understand what's happened. The service might have given him a chance to say goodbye."

The phone rang.

Uncoiling like a compressed spring, Luke crossed the kitchen and grabbed the receiver, cradling it between his head and shoulder in a pose so familiar it caught Alicia like a blow to the solar plexus. A panoply of unwanted memories flooded her head.

"Yeah?" Though the greeting was curt, his tone warmed with his next words. "Oh, hi, Sharon. Yeah, she got here okay, thanks."

Sipping her tea, Alicia studied him as he listened to a monologue on the other end of the line. Living under Luke's roof was clearly going to be even more difficult than she'd imagined. It was bad enough that her emotions were stirred, but her physical awareness of him was almost painful. His jeans clung to his long legs and molded his hips and thighs almost like a second skin. Why did he have to look so damned sexy? Why couldn't he have grown fat or bald? Ever since she had made her plans to fly south, she'd clung to the conviction that he was just another man, no different from the men she'd had to work with every day. She'd told herself that time had healed her wounds, that avoiding him all these years had been ridiculous, the act of a coward.

Now she knew it had been wise.

For he was different, and had always been different. Even grief and tragedy and time could not annul the fact that he was Luke, her first love. He was the first man she'd kissed, the first to touch her, both physically and emotionally. The first man she'd touched.

If only she didn't remember so clearly. If only time had erased the memory of how his muscled chest felt beneath her palms, of his deep voice whispering words that had made her feel powerful and feminine. And though she had loved her husband when she married him, she had never been able to recapture the heady, tumultuous yearning she had felt for Luke.

But those memories created barriers now. Even if Luke hadn't remembered that this was the tenth anniversary of the day he had proposed, he couldn't possibly have forgotten the rest. Thank God she hadn't given him her virginity. If they'd ever made love, she didn't think she could have survived this at all.

"Okay, Sharon, that sounds great. I'm sure she'll enjoy it. Right. Saturday at three. We'll be there." Luke hung up the phone.

"Who was that?" Alicia asked, trying to keep her voice normal. Heaven forbid he should guess her thoughts.

"Neighbors," he said, turning toward her. "Sharon and Jim Redford. They live a couple of miles down the road. Sharon invited us to a cookout." He studied her face as if trying to gauge her reaction. "I hope you don't mind that I accepted for you. They're good people. They have a son Ronnie's age."

"That sounds nice. No, I don't mind at all." Alicia's fingers eased their grip on her glass; until this moment she hadn't even realized how tightly she'd been holding it.

Luke went to the refrigerator and took out a bottle of beer. "They have a pool," he added, twisting the top off. "Sharon said to bring our suits." He leaned negligently against the kitchen counter and took a long pull of his drink. "You did bring one, didn't you?"

"No. I didn't expect to be swimming."

He scanned her in an assessing manner. "We'd better go shopping then. Sharon's suits won't fit you, and I doubt you'd want to wear one of Nancy's."

"Nancy?"

"Sharon's kid sister. She just graduated from USC. She's going back in a few days to do graduate work." One corner of his mouth quirked up. "She's turned into a real California babe. Runs around in bikinis the size of a postage stamp."

"And of course you think I couldn't wear one like that," Alicia said, and instantly wanted to kick herself. He'd think she was fishing for compliments when all she'd been trying to do was to assert herself.

"I didn't say that." This time his eyes roved over her more thoroughly than they had before, but with no hint of whether he still found her attractive. "I just thought you wouldn't *want* to," he said, a smooth challenge in his voice.

"You were always the conservative type. Have you changed?"

Alicia shifted in her chair, disliking the way the conversation was headed. The conservative type. How was she to interpret that? And why did she find it so irritating?

"Not that much," she said shortly. "I still don't find it appropriate to run around half-naked in public."

"Sharon's backyard isn't too public."

"You know what I mean."

Alicia's mouth went dry as their gazes fused, then Luke broke the contact by taking another swig of beer. He seemed so much more relaxed than she was, so much more in control of himself than she remembered. At twenty he had been moody, intense. A lone wolf in search of a mate. Could he have changed so much? It was possible. His successes in life could have altered him, just as her lack of success, at least with marriage, made her defensive and on edge.

"Okay," he said. "I'll take you to one of the malls and you can pick out something modest. You'll be uncomfortable if you can't go in the water. The sweat factor is about a hundred percent this time of year."

"It certainly is," she agreed, looking down at her fingers. "Speaking of which, I could sure use a shower."

He put down his drink and straightened, his strong features set in a neutral expression. "I guess I should have shown you up to your room first. Sorry."

"I wasn't trying to criticize." Alicia stood and cleared her throat, feeling absurdly self-conscious. "I enjoyed the ice tea, Luke. It was perfect."

She didn't know what she expected him to say. *I remembered how you like it, baby. One teaspoon of sugar and three drops of lemon...*

In contrast, his curt nod seemed almost a slap in the face. "I'll get your suitcase."

Feeling like a fool, Alicia followed him out of the kitchen. Obviously she meant nothing to him now.

Which, of course, was exactly the way she wanted it.

He hadn't wanted her to come to Houston. He'd tried to think of a way to prevent her, but he couldn't, not with the way Caroline and Richard's will was set up. She had as much right to be here as he did and maybe more, since she and the boy were blood kin.

Luke didn't dwell on the thought. The fact that he was adopted had ceased to matter to him years ago. Being taken in by the Garricks had been the best thing that ever happened to him, the zenith of his crazy childhood. If it hadn't been for them, he'd probably be sitting in some prison cell right now, surrounded by bars and concrete walls. That was another thought he didn't dwell on.

As Alicia disappeared into the upstairs bathroom, he lured Ronnie out of his room with promises of milk shakes and videos. The kid had moped long enough; despite what Luke had told Alicia, he didn't like to leave Ronnie alone for more than a short while. Luke had spent enough time by himself to know that solitude was only healthy in moderate doses.

Trying not to think of Alicia standing naked in the shower, he settled Ronnie on the couch and switched on the VCR. They had watched the first half of *Star Wars* the previous evening, and Ronnie had been begging all day to see the rest. As Darth Vader filled the screen, wheezing evilly, Luke sat down next to Ronnie and pulled off his shoes. Slumping into the cushions, he closed his eyes and considered the present situation.

Seeing Alicia again had been a whole lot more stressful than he'd anticipated. He'd almost managed to forget how attractive she was, how powerfully she had drawn him with her wholesome good looks and ladylike charm. She no longer wore her blond hair long; now it was cut in a crisp, sassy style that suggested success and sophistication. Yet despite her career-girl image, she had somehow managed to retain that air of innocence that had caught at his gut the first time.

Damn.

She might call herself a city woman now, but in his eyes she was still the girl from the small New Jersey college town. The shy eighteen-year-old who had stood across from him at his brother's wedding.

The girl in the dusky rose maid-of-honor's dress.

Luke's jaw clenched at the memory. The one thing he did not intend to do was to fall for Alicia Brant all over again. No way was he going to get his head messed up a second time. Yes, he understood the reason for her visit; after all, he and Alicia had been named Ronnie's joint guardians. If she considered it her duty to visit for a couple of weeks, then fine. He understood her decision and even agreed with it. He also appreciated her offer to help him dispose of Caroline's personal possessions. But once duty was satisfied, she had better get that cute little butt back out of his life or he wouldn't answer for the consequences.

"Hey, Uncle Luke." Ronnie's nudge roused his attention. "Can I have my milk shake now?"

"I forgot to get it for you, didn't I? Jeez, I'm sorry. What kind do you want?"

"Chocolate?"

Luke got up, affectionately rumpling his nephew's hair. "Okay, squirt. One chocolate milk shake coming up."

Entering the kitchen, he found Daffy gazing mournfully into her empty water dish. Her food dish was empty, too, and it was past time for her dinner. Annoyed with himself, Luke refilled both bowls and added a couple of ice cubes to the water. How could he have forgotten the dog's needs? Just having Alicia in the house was already making him nuts.

Retrieving the blender from the pantry, he threw in some milk and vanilla ice cream, then added a hefty dollop of chocolate sauce. As he plugged the cord into the outlet, he heard the upstairs shower shut off.

Immediately his imagination conjured up images. She would have one of his bath towels wrapped around her beautiful wet body, only it wouldn't be large enough to cover more than the bare minimum. Cursing his choice of words, he punched the button on the blender.

Get a grip on yourself, Garrick. She's going to be here for a while so you'd better get used to this.

He switched off the blender just in time to hear her light footsteps move from the bathroom to the guest room above his head. His mouth compressed, he filled a tall glass to the brim, grabbed his half-empty can of beer and went back to the living room.

Ronnie cuddled against him while they polished off their drinks and watched the movie. At least Ronnie watched the movie. Luke stared in the right direction and pretended to be interested while his thoughts prowled around in the past.

Alicia entered the room just as Luke Skywalker was guiding his X-wing fighter into the trench of the Death Star.

"Hi," she said awkwardly. "Sorry I took so long."

As her gaze shifted to Ronnie, Luke took silent stock of her apparel. The slacks and blouse she had worn earlier had been replaced by white shorts and a turquoise tank top. Through the thin cotton, he could see the faint lines of her bikini panties. They were of the high-cut variety, very enticing and very skimpy. His eyes wandered over her, taking in the heightened color in her cheeks and her long, beautiful, bare legs.

"Use the Force!" squealed Ronnie.

"Do you think that's an appropriate movie for him to watch?" Alicia asked.

"Why not?" As she moved closer, Luke caught a flash of lacy pink bra at the edge of her neckline. "It's a great movie," he added, wishing irritably that he could say something intelligent. She was used to being around cerebral white-collar types, not guys like him. Heck, she had even married one. A dentist, for crying out loud.

"Yes, it is, but..." She stopped, her eyes still on Ronnie. "Could we talk in the kitchen?"

He wanted to say no. He didn't want to be alone with her in any room, at any time. "Sure," he said with a shrug.

Scooping up Ronnie's empty glass and his beer can, he followed Alicia out of the room, his gaze riveted on the enticing sway of her hips. At eighteen, she'd been modest and virginal. He had never seen her completely naked, never buried himself inside her as he had ached to do. And it seemed ten years hadn't erased that ache. Even now, it tightened his gut as he mentally undressed her, peeled off the top and shorts and that sexy pink bra. His hands itched to touch those legs, to slide up their smoothness until he reached the most secret and feminine part of her.

Annoyed with himself, he set the glass and can in the sink and turned. "Well?" He crossed his arms over his chest, deliberately assuming an aloof posture.

Her blue eyes met his. "Did it occur to you that at the beginning of that movie, Luke Skywalker loses his parents?"

"Actually it was his aunt and uncle."

"Whatever," she said with an impatient gesture. "It's close enough to be a reminder. I think we should be more careful, don't you?"

"I fast-forwarded through that part last night while he was letting the dog out. He didn't even notice."

"I see. Well, I'm glad about that." She reached out, her hand gripping the back of a chair as if for support. "But, Luke, you shouldn't have promised Ronnie a water bed before you talked to me about it. I don't want him to be disappointed."

"Why should he be disappointed?" Luke asked in bafflement.

She hesitated, then sat down, her face tense. "Look, there's a lot of things we need to discuss. I know it's awkward, but we have to do it. I don't know why Caroline and Richard—" she paused and drew a deep breath "—I don't know why they chose to make us both guardians, but that's what they did."

"Yeah, it was a damned weird thing for a couple of lawyers to do," he agreed, a guarded note in his voice.

"You didn't know about it, either?"

Heck, no, he hadn't known about it. If he had, he'd have wrung Richard's neck.

He shook his head. "When they made the first will," he said shortly, "they asked me to be Ronnie's guardian. They never mentioned any changes."

Alicia looked down, her face pale. "You would think they would have warned us," she said, her voice quivering. She covered her eyes with her hand, her soft lips distorted in her effort not to cry.

Dropping his arms to his sides, Luke thought of his brother and sister-in-law and felt the dull ache of grief grind in his stomach. Their second honeymoon to a romantic South Pacific island had ended in catastrophe. He would never forget his own agonized disbelief when he'd learned that the small sight-seeing plane they'd hired to tour the area had gone down in the ocean.

No bodies recovered. Nothing left but memories.

He stared down at a tiny crack in the tile, keeping all signs of emotion from his face. Grief wasn't a thing he shared, not with anyone, and certainly not with Alicia. He couldn't cry; he hadn't done so since his mother died. He had never even expressed sorrow aloud—not when Alicia had shattered his life, and not when his adoptive parents had passed away. And he sure wasn't about to change his habits now at the age of thirty.

But standing by, watching another person's pain, was something else again. As a choked sob escaped Alicia, it took an enormous amount of self-restraint not to stride forward and take her in his arms. Luke's hands knotted into fists as he grappled with the urge.

"I'm sure they thought there was no point," he said gently. "Nobody expects something like that to happen."

A single tear trickled down Alicia's cheek. "I suppose you're right." Pulling a tissue from her pocket, she wiped her face and blew her pinkened nose. "I'm sorry. I didn't mean to bring this up now. I wanted to talk to you about Ronnie's future."

"There's plenty of time for that. You ought to use today to get settled. Tomorrow I'll take you for a tour of the area. We can shop for a bathing suit and drive past Ronnie's school—"

"What?" Her head jerked up.

"Brown Elementary," he explained. "It's only a couple of miles from here. I registered him for first grade the day before yesterday."

Alicia's reaction caught him off guard. Her blue eyes blazing beneath the wet fringe of her lashes, she surged to her feet and glared at him with fury.

"How *dare* you do such a thing?"

Chapter Two

Alicia's hands curled into fists as outrage jackknifed inside her chest. "How could you? And why?"

"Why?" Luke's eyes narrowed. "School starts next week. I didn't want to wait any longer."

"So," she grated, "you're assuming Ronnie will live with you, is that it?"

"Well, where else would he go? You're not suggesting he live with you?"

"Of course I'm suggesting it! I think it would be logical and fitting."

"Fitting maybe, but where do you get logical?"

She could hear the skepticism in his voice, the flat note of mockery that, even at such a moment, produced a ripple of old, bitter memories. This was not the boy she had known, she reminded herself. Luke was a successful business owner now; he was used to calling the shots.

"Children Ronnie's age need a mother," she insisted. "He's my sister's child, Luke. Of course I want to take care of him." She was not about to go into it any further than that; she owed him no soul-baring explanation.

He gazed steadily at her. With black stubble shadowing his jaw and faint age lines framing the corners of his mouth, he looked as grim as a pirate, and just about as intimidating. "And what about that fancy job of yours? You know, the forty-hour-a-week one? What about the neighborhood where you live? Is it a good place for kids, Alicia? Is there a place where they can run and play? Is it safe?" He sounded so reasonable, so smugly certain he knew best that she wanted to hit him.

"Of course it's safe," she retorted. "Do you think I'd live somewhere that wasn't? There's even a playground a block and a half down the street. And if we're talking practicality, who's going to take care of Ronnie if he stays with you? You have a store to run, which I bet takes a whole lot more than forty hours a week of your time."

"I have five employees and a business partner," he countered. "I can come and go as I please. Sharon has agreed to watch Ronnie after school every day except Tuesday. And on Tuesdays, I'll bring him to the store to hang out. He loves it there."

Alicia opened her mouth to protest, anger roiling inside her, then she shut it again. They needed to discuss the situation like rational, intelligent adults, not like bickering children. Indulging her temper would achieve nothing.

"Look," she said, sinking back into her chair, "we have to come to some agreement on this. We've got to consider what's best for Ronnie, and we've got to decide soon, because of the school issue." She paused and drew in a breath. "What kind of school did you enroll him in?"

Luke dragged a chair around the corner of the table and straddled it backward. "A damn good public one," he said. "If you don't believe me, you can ask around. Brown Elementary is just three years old, with great facilities. They've got two rooms chock-full of computers for the kids."

"And the test scores compared with other schools?"

"High. I've got all that information upstairs. I knew it'd be the first thing you'd ask."

His sardonic tone reminded her of one reason they'd split up, the wedge that had shattered their relationship into irreconcilable pieces. But whether Luke liked it or not, they both knew that when Caroline and Richard had come to Houston to start their own law firm, they had planned to enroll their son in a private school.

"No matter where he lives, I think we ought to consider private schooling," she said in a low voice.

"This is a good school, Alicia. Ronnie wants to go there because that's where Brian goes."

"Brian?"

"Sharon's son."

"Ronnie can make other friends. Caroline and Richard sent him to a private kindergarten—"

"Because of where they lived. It's different here. This school system is one of the best."

"The schools where I live are also among the best."

He regarded her narrowly, the piercing gray of his eyes reminding her that he, too, had a temper. "Personally, I think we should consider Ronnie's wishes."

Her eyes widened. "Are you suggesting we should let him choose between us?"

"Why not? The question seemed flippant, calculated to wound.

"Because it's not a choice that a little boy should have to make! Besides ..."

"Besides what?"

It was all she could do to keep the desperation from her voice. "Well, it wouldn't be fair! He knows you better than he knows me, so of course he'd pick you."

"And whose fault is that? You couldn't be bothered to come visit him, could you? Not until now, of course, when you feel obligated and guilty."

Alicia flinched. His very tone was an insult, but before she could defend herself, the VCR in the other room shut off. Ronnie came around the corner into the kitchen.

"You missed the end, Uncle Luke. Luke Skywalker blew up the Death Star."

"Did he, squirt?" Luke's hostility vanished in the blink of an eye. "Guess we'll have to rewind and watch it again."

"Right now?"

"No, right now I want you to spend some time with your aunt. Maybe you could show her your artwork."

Ronnie looked up at Alicia. "You want to see it?" he asked, sounding doubtful.

"Of course I do," she said with a composure she did not feel. "What kind of artwork do you do?"

"I've been drawing dinosaurs. Luke got me a book on how to draw 'em."

"That sounds like great fun."

Avoiding Luke's eyes, she rose and held out her hand, but Ronnie was already turning away. "You have to come up to my room 'cuz I've been taping 'em to my walls. Luke said I could," he added quickly, as if expecting her to disapprove.

Ronnie's room overflowed with toys. There were toys on the dresser, on the bed, on the floor. Bits and pieces of unidentifiable items were strewn across every available surface. Luke must have transferred every plaything the child had ever owned, she thought, stepping carefully through the obstacle course.

Ronnie picked up a plastic sword and began stabbing the air. "This is my lightsaber," he said dispassionately.

Alicia cleared a spot on the bed and sat down, watching him slice at an imaginary enemy. After a few moments, she reached for a black-and-white stuffed dog near her feet. "Who's this?"

The child glanced over his shoulder. "That's Snoofy." Dropping the sword, he took the dog from her and hugged it. "Daddy bought him for me when we went to Galveston."

"He must be very special then," she said gently. Tenderness welled up inside her as he kissed the dog on the nose. Ronnie was so sweet, so young and helpless and innocent. Of course they must do what was best for this child—anything else would be unthinkable. "I see some of those drawings you were telling me about," she said, glancing around at the walls. "They're wonderful, Ronnie."

He turned and surveyed his handiwork. "That's Tyrannosaurus Rex," he informed her, pointing at the one over his bookcase. "And that's Allosaurus, and that's Brontosaurus, and that's..."

She watched the fluctuations of his features while he identified each reptile. He might have inherited Caroline's fair coloring, but he had his father's expressiveness and gestures. Without warning, the throbbing ache in Alicia's chest returned. *Oh, Caroline, why? Why did you have to go?*

"Guess which one is my favorite," Ronnie said.

"I don't know. That one?" She pointed to Tyrannosaurus rex.

"Right. How'd you know?"

"Because," she teased, "he has the biggest teeth."

He stared at the drawing. "Sometimes," he said slowly, "I dream that he's coming to get me. Then he's not my favorite."

"I should think not. What a scary dream!" Alicia hesitated, unsure of what to say next. "Do you wake up when that happens?"

Ronnie's shoulders rose in a slight shrug. "Sometimes. Last time, Luke let me get in bed with him." His voice wobbled slightly. "No dinosaurs can get me there."

Without an instant's hesitation, Alicia gathered him into a hug. "They can't get you no matter where you are," she told him. "Dinosaurs are extinct, Ronnie. You understand that, don't you? You understand you're safe?"

"Yes." For a fraction of a second, he allowed her to hold him, then he wriggled free and retrieved his sword.

Just then she heard Luke coming up the stairs, and immediate tension swept through her, tying her stomach into knots. Damn. Was it going to be this way every time she saw him? She had to get her emotions under control or living here, even temporarily, was going to be a nightmare.

A moment later, Luke's broad shoulders filled the doorway. His gaze touched on Alicia, wandered over the mess, then returned to her face. "We need to find a place for all this stuff," he commented. "I'm planning to build some shelves in the closet."

Alicia's chin lifted. "That's an excellent idea. It will be so much nicer for Ronnie to have his things organized." *While he's here,* she added silently.

As if he'd read her mind, Luke's jaw tightened. "Good. You can help. You might as well make yourself useful."

While you're here, was the implication.

She smiled sweetly. "I'd be glad to. I have no intention of sitting around with my feet up."

If possible, his expression grew even more surly. "Good," he repeated. "Because I have no intention of treating you as a guest."

Muttering a string of colorful curses beneath his breath, Luke stomped back downstairs. He didn't even know why he'd bothered to go up there. The confounded woman had been in his house barely two hours and he already needed a stiff drink. How did she manage to make him feel in the wrong so damn easily? That had always been the problem with her. She'd made him feel wrong, unreasonable and selfish when all he'd ever tried to do was to plan for the future.

Their future, once upon a time.

Ha. Thank heaven the only future they'd shared had been separate. With the passing of years, he'd gained enough maturity to realize that her views had had merit, but he was in no mood to acknowledge that at the moment. Right now, he was just plain aggravated—with her and himself and this whole situation.

It had never even occurred to him that she would want the boy. He didn't know why he hadn't thought of it; he just hadn't. Heck, she'd been married for five years and never had any children of her own. He'd assumed it was because she hadn't wanted them, that she'd considered her career too important to allow pregnancy and motherhood to interfere. As far as he could remember, she'd never shown any sign of wanting kids. Not his kids, anyway. He'd mentioned it once, the summer they had dated, but to his disappointment she hadn't expressed any interest.

Scowling, he walked into the living room and threw himself into an armchair. *Dated.* The word sounded too tame to describe the sizzle he remembered. He should have known better than to get involved with the daughter of two univer-

sity professors. He should have known that their romance
was doomed from the start, that their destinies lay in different directions. He could never have lived up to Alicia's
expectations of him, any more than he could have borne for
her to know his secret.

The best thing he could do was forget the past. He should
concentrate on getting along with Alicia so they could help
Ronnie get through this difficult period in his life. One of
them would have to take on the role of parent. Was Alicia
up to that kind of responsibility? He knew *he* was. In fact,
he had a pretty accurate idea what he was getting himself
into.

Luke stared at the wall, the events of the past two years
unfolding like a movie through his head. First there had
been his brother and sister-in-law's move to Houston to start
their own law firm. Richard and Caroline had been ambitious people, and both had worked almost constantly toward the fulfillment of their goal. Although they had
unquestionably loved their son, Luke had often felt that the
needs of the law firm had taken priority over the needs of
the child. All too often it had fallen to Luke to see that
Ronnie lived a normal childhood. On countless weekends,
Luke had transported Ronnie from Richard's house to his
own home on Friday afternoons and then returned him on
Sunday evenings. He'd played with Ronnie, taken him
swimming and fishing and camping, let him hang out at the
store. Until three weeks ago, when the tragic accident had
changed everything, Luke had functioned almost as a third
parent. Was it really so unreasonable of him to expect to
continue in that role?

He jumped up and started to pace. What it boiled down
to was that he loved the kid. He would make him a good
father—at least he'd believed that until Alicia had arrived.
Somehow her presence reminded him of his lack of educa-

tion, his difficulty with the written word. Even now, so many years after he had learned the name for it, he was still unable to talk about his problem. The ridicule from his childhood had eaten into his heart, turned him into a loner, made him wary.

Made him strong, he reminded himself quickly.

Self-sufficient.

He needed nobody, but that didn't mean he couldn't give of himself. He didn't need a wife or a family of his own, but a tragedy had occurred and he was ready to do what must be done. He could care for Ronnie, help him develop into the man he would someday become. The only thing he couldn't do was read to him, at least not without effort.

Not without the letters turning inside out, tricking him, changing into a meaningless jumble before his eyes.

Not without the knowledge that sooner or later his humiliating secret would have to come out. Someday Ronnie would have to be told the truth... but not yet.

Luke heaved a sigh and went to the window. He gazed at the distant tangle of trees at the rear edge of his property. Despite his handicap, he had made a success of himself, and he was proud. So why had he been discontent all these years?

Damn it, he *had* been content!

Most of the time.

When he hadn't been in bed at night, alone. Or cooking dinner for one. Or sitting on the porch with the stars gleaming down on his bleak, empty yard.

Man, he was really losing it. It was seeing Alicia again that had undermined his confidence and stirred the dissatisfaction in his soul. Ten years ago today, he had been crazy enough to offer her marriage. Ten years ago, he had believed that the disparity in their educational levels wouldn't matter. Well, love hadn't overcome a damn thing. In fact, their engagement hadn't survived her first semester at college.

Forget it. It's ancient history. Who cares?

Luke raked a hand through his hair. Bachelorhood suited him just fine, and self-pity wasn't his style.

The only problem was, he still wanted her.

Recalling that Luke wasn't much of a cook, Alicia offered to help with supper, but he declined her offer and fixed them a spaghetti dinner as good as any restaurant's. Afterward, he loaded the dishwasher while she took Ronnie upstairs and read him a bedtime story. That done, she helped the child locate his Superman pajamas and put his soiled clothing in the laundry.

While Ronnie brushed his teeth, Alicia leaned against the door frame of the bathroom, watching him wistfully. How easily she had fallen into the role of mother. It was a role she had longed for desperately, and Caroline had known it. Had she also known of all the resentment her little sister had bottled up inside? The jealousy and the envy? Alicia prayed not. She was not proud of those feelings, but they had existed. Even now, when Caroline was gone forever, they were still writhing around in her chest like tiny demons.

"I'm done." Ronnie wiped his mouth and surveyed her, his eyes questioning. "How long are you gonna stay here with us?"

"Well . . ." Alicia hesitated. "As long as it takes."

"Takes to do what?" He walked out of the bathroom and stood looking up at her, his piquant face filled with something that grazed her soul.

Setting her hands on his shoulders, Alicia leaned down and looked him straight in the eye. "As long as it takes to decide where you will live, and who you will live with," she explained in a soft voice.

To her dismay, his eyes instantly filled with tears. "I want to stay here with Luke," he said mutinously.

Her heart sank. "And so you may, but that's something we have to decide. Don't worry, sweetheart. Uncle Luke and I will try to do what's best. We want you to be happy."

"I'll be happy with Luke! I don't want to live with you!"

"I understand," she soothed. "You and I don't know each other, do we? That's why I came, Ronnie. So we could become friends."

"You're not my friend," he sobbed. "Brian's my friend. And Daffy and Uncle Luke. They're my only friends." The child fell to his knees beside the dog, who had fallen asleep on the upstairs landing, and pressed his face to the animal's fur.

Uncertain how to handle the situation, Alicia hesitated, her hands curled into helpless fists. "Ronnie," she said at last, "I just remembered something. I haven't seen that water bed yet. Want to show it to me?"

Silence greeted her question; the little boy did not move.

"I've never seen a water bed," she coaxed. "I can't imagine what they look like."

Still no response.

"Do you get wet when you sleep?"

A choked little laugh. "No."

"No? I thought you did. I thought Uncle Luke had to wear his bathing suit to bed every night."

The child lifted his tearstained face. "Really? You really thought that?"

"Isn't it true?"

"No." Ronnie scrambled to his feet. "Come on, I'll show you." He hurried down the short corridor and flung open the farthest door. "There it is," he announced with the aplomb of a game-show host.

Feeling like a trespasser, Alicia stepped into Luke's bedroom. Her gaze swept the room. She had an impression of neatness and restraint, of masculine furnishings in shades of beige and blue, but it was the queen-size water bed that drew her attention.

It dominated the room, as Luke himself had so often dominated her thoughts for the past decade. How many times had she regretted not giving herself to him fully? How many times had she wondered what he was doing and with whom?

Ronnie hurled himself through the air and landed on the bed with a bounce. "See?" He rose to his knees. "Isn't it awesome?"

Alicia smiled and moved closer. "Awesome," she agreed. "But I think I'd get seasick."

"No, you wouldn't," said a cool voice behind her.

She whipped around, her heart knocking against her rib cage. Irrational as it was, she felt like a child who'd been caught with her hand in the cookie jar.

"Go ahead, sit on it," Luke said. "You'd be amazed how comfortable it is." He leaned against the door frame and cocked an eyebrow, his expression calm and rather amused. Like before, he seemed in control of himself, while her poise slipped the moment he entered a room.

"Oh, all right." Alicia shrugged, determined not to let him know how much he rattled her.

Pinning an unconcerned expression on her face, she perched on the edge, cursing because she was too damnably aware that this was where Luke slept. Where, without doubt, he had made love to other women.

"Very nice," she mumbled. Anxious to escape, she started to rise, but a small pair of hands grabbed her shoulders and pulled her off balance.

"Wheeee!" cried Ronnie as she toppled over backward. His tribulations were temporarily forgotten as his imagination took over. "We're on a raft, and there's a big storm, and the waves are big as dinosaurs, and there's sharks all around us, ready to eat us up, and..."

As the mattress undulated wildly, Alicia's stomach lurched from a combination of nerves and the slight motion sickness that had afflicted her in recent years. She shut her eyes. Ronnie's storm swirled inside her, strumming her nerve endings, sending her shattered emotions spinning.

"And jellyfish and stingrays and piranha fish and moray eels and—"

"That's enough, Ron," Luke said. "Get off now, before your aunt loses her dinner." Alicia opened her eyes just as Luke plucked the child off the bed.

Ronnie hung on his uncle's arm. "She thought you wore your bathing suit to bed," he said with a giggle. "Isn't that silly?"

"Very silly," Luke agreed. He turned back to Alicia and extended his hand. "It really is comfortable," he added. His expression was as indecipherable as water, yet she knew darn well that he was thinking what she was thinking.

Alicia could feel a blush creeping up her neck. "Yes, I'm sure it is," she muttered. She shoved herself up and straightened her tank top, but a streak of self-preservation prevented her from accepting his help.

Luke's arm fell to his side. "Go get in bed," he told Ronnie. "We'll be there in a minute to tuck you in."

"Oh, okay." Ronnie shuffled from the room.

Reluctant to remain with Luke in the intimate confines of his bedroom, Alicia started to follow, but Luke's voice stopped her as effectively as a hand on her arm.

"So what do you think?"

She swung around to face him. "About what?"

"This." He made a sweeping gesture. "My humble do-main."

"I think it's lovely, Luke. I told you that. It wasn't quite what I expected—"

"You thought I'd live in a dump," he cut in. "You're surprised, aren't you?"

"No, of course not."

"Don't pretend." His eyes bored into her, yet his voice remained bland, even indifferent. "No doubt it's not what you're used to. I'm sure the dentist gave you a big, fancy house."

She planted her hands on her hips. "No, Kenny didn't give me a fancy house. We lived in a condo. And it was my earnings that paid the mortgage, at least in the beginning while he was setting up his practice. Does that satisfy your curiosity?"

He ignored her question and moved closer, so close she could feel the warmth of his body. "Sounds like you picked a real loser, Alicia. I heard he cheated on you."

Alicia flinched. His words hurt, largely because she had heard something similar—though more elegantly phrased— from her parents. *Really, Alicia, where men are concerned, your judgment appears to be remarkably faulty. Caroline found a nice young man. Why can't you?*

"Attracting losers seems to be a habit of mine, doesn't it?" she said with bitterness. "But you can bet I won't make the same mistake again."

"Are you putting me in the same class as Farrell?" Luke's tone lacked any hint of real interest, as though he was merely asking an academic question.

Unable to believe they were discussing this, she struggled to formulate a reply. Somehow she'd thought they'd main-tain a facade, tiptoe civilly around the subject of their failed romance for the entire length of her visit. On the other hand, maybe she should have known better. Luke could be evasive at times, but he could also be direct.

"No," she said, forcing the word out. "But you were another of my mistakes, weren't you?"

As Luke stared down at her, the planes and angles of his face seemed to change, grow harsher and more unyielding. "We were the mismatch of the century," he said in a clipped tone. "Like oil and water. No wonder your parents disapproved."

For some odd reason, these words hurt even more. Pain lanced through her, as fresh as the day she had returned his ring, as lacerating as the moment he had shoved it into his pocket and walked out of her life. Yet somehow she managed to school her features into an uncaring mask.

"Well, it was all so long ago, wasn't it? I can't even remember what brought us together in the first place."

"Can't you?" He gave a short laugh. "What brought us together was simple, doll. It was this." And he bent down and kissed her.

Shocked, she simply stood there, utterly frozen as his lips traced the stiff contours of her mouth—stroking, rocking, caressing as though he really cared whether or not she enjoyed the experience. When his hand pressed at the back of her neck, exerting a firm pressure, the familiarity of it flung her back to another time and place. Old emotions raged alongside current sensations; snatches of the past swirled in her brain. Yet she forbade herself to respond, to part her lips and encourage him, because then he might know how much he still affected her. He might realize that she had never forgotten him. He might even guess that her marriage to Kenny had never stood a fair chance because of her memories of Luke. And that was something she couldn't bear for him to know.

What brought us together was simple, doll.

As the outrageous statement rebounded in her mind, she tore her mouth free. "Don't call me doll!" she said fiercely. She rammed her fists against his chest, her breasts heaving beneath the thin cotton top. "I'm not a doll, Luke Garrick. I'm a woman—an intelligent, capable human being. And this woman has had it up to here—" her hand slashed across her neck "—with men like you." She started toward the door, then wheeled around once more. "I'm going to kiss Ronnie good-night," she informed him in as steady and cool a tone as she could muster. "Please allow us a few minutes alone."

Luke watched her stalk from the room, his body rigid as a fence post. So what the heck had he accomplished? Not a damned thing. Fury swept through him, but his surge of self-loathing chased it away. He'd acted like a real jerk and he knew it. Yet he'd learned the only thing that mattered.

She still saw him as a loser.

Chapter Three

She was dialing her parents' telephone number, but she'd made a mistake. She tried again, missed the seven, hung up, started again, missed the five, tried again, got a busy signal, wanted to cry. She had to get through, had to tell them something important, but she couldn't get through, couldn't get it right.

Someone screamed.

Alicia jolted upright in the strange bed, the sheet bunched in her sweaty hands, her heart flipping back and forth in an erratic pattern. It took a moment to get oriented, to remember that she was in Texas, not in Massachusetts or at her parents' home in New Jersey.

Then Alicia heard the sobbing. Muted by walls, it held a childlike terror that sent her sprinting across the floor. Alicia yanked open her door just as Luke disappeared into Ronnie's room. Without hesitation she followed, her hand thrown up to shield her eyes as he switched on a light.

In the doorway, she stopped short, for Luke wore nothing but a pair of briefs. The sight reminded her of her own state of dishabille, and for a handful of seconds, she considered a swift retreat. Then she straightened her shoulders. Damn it, what was wrong with her?

"Easy there, pal." Luke sat down beside the whimpering child. "It's only a dream, Ron. Everything's okay. We're right here with you."

Alicia moved to the foot of the bed. "Was it the dinosaur dream, Ronnie?" she asked softly. "Is that what scared you?"

A small, frightened face peeked out from beneath the sheets. "Rex," Ronnie whispered. Eyes brimming with tears, he crawled out and onto Luke's lap.

As the child huddled against his chest, Luke looked up. Until this moment, he had paid Alicia no heed, but now his eyes flicked over her, paused, then moved over her again with a thoroughness that brought heat rushing to her cheeks.

She folded her arms over her chest, then immediately felt ridiculous. "Uh, is there anything I can do?"

"How about getting him a drink of water?" Luke suggested.

"Sure." Alicia hurried into the bathroom, chancing a peek in the mirror as she reached for a paper cup. Filling it with water, she made a slight grimace. The two thin layers of her aqua chiffon nightgown revealed more than she'd realized.

Pushing her embarrassment aside, she returned to Ronnie's room with her chin raised high, wrapped in dignity if not in the concealing folds of the bathrobe she had forgotten to pack. But this time, Luke barely glanced at her.

"Thanks," he said. He took the cup from her hand and held it for Ronnie. "I'll keep him with me for the rest of the night."

Alicia nodded, a tiny lump in her throat. She ached to hold the little boy, to whisk him into her bed so she could kiss and cuddle his fears away. But she hadn't earned the right yet. To Ronnie, she was still a stranger.

She returned to her room and lay in the dark, Luke's near-naked image floating in her mind. It was idiotic, of course, but the memory of all that bronzed male skin did queer things to her stomach. Sexual need curled inside her, as real as her frustrated desire to nurture and love.

Okay, so she was still attracted to Luke, but it meant no more than that outrageous kiss. It was just that she had been lonely for so long. It had been two years since her divorce, and two years before that since she'd let Kenny touch her. The physical side of their marriage had ceased the moment she'd found out about his affair with Tracy, his red-haired hygienist.

Even so, it had been months before she'd been ready to admit that divorce was necessary. For as long as possible, she'd pretended her marriage was as happy as Caroline and Richard's. She hadn't wanted her parents to know that Kenny had used her, chosen her for her high salary and susceptibility to his charm. That in misguided gratitude, she had paid off his student loans and supported him while he set up his dental practice. That he had probably never loved her at all.

Depressed, she glanced over at the glowing digital numbers of her travel alarm clock. Wonderful. Here it was two o'clock in the morning and she felt wider awake than ever. She might as well give up and get up.

After pulling on a pair of jogging shorts and a Save The Whales T-shirt, she padded quietly downstairs and headed for the kitchen. She flipped the light switch and waited for her eyes to adjust, reflecting that she might as well find something useful to do. Unfortunately, the only thing that seemed to need attention was the floor.

She soon located a pail and detergent, but decided against using the mop. Working on her hands and knees would take longer, fill more of her night. With luck, it would also make her tired enough to sleep.

She swept the floor first, her thoughts wandering to the photo she'd seen on Luke's dresser. Though she'd caught no more than a quick glimpse, the image had frozen into her brain.

The woman in the picture had been quite beautiful. Alicia recalled every detail—the ebony hair, the perfect nose, the smiling violet-blue eyes.

All right, so Luke was having a relationship with someone. Someone gorgeous. So what? She didn't care. It was none of her business. She was having a relationship, too, if her friendship with Nick Easton qualified for the term.

Two pails of water later, her knees throbbed and her shoulders ached. As she refilled the bucket for the last time, she wondered if Luke would notice the difference in his floor. Reflecting that Kenny had only noticed the things she had left undone, she shut off the tap and lifted the pail.

"What the hell are you doing?"

Alicia started so violently that water sloshed over the edge and down her leg. "Damn it, Luke, are you trying to give me heart failure? What does it look like I'm doing?"

"Sorry." He didn't sound sorry.

Flustered, she set down the pail and reached for the dish towel, shooting him a look as she swabbed at her leg. At least this time he was decent, if wearing a pair of short, very frayed cutoffs rated that description. One thumb hooked into a belt loop, he leaned against the doorjamb, his frowning gaze following her movements.

She tossed the towel aside, complaining, "This is the third time in twelve hours you've sneaked up on me."

"You want me to wear a bell?" he asked dryly.

I want you to wear more clothes, she almost snapped. Instead she gave him a look of lofty dignity and hefted the bucket over to the last dirty section of floor.

As she recommenced work, Luke came over and hunkered down beside her, perfectly balanced on the balls of his feet. "Alicia, when I said you could make yourself useful, I didn't mean this." Now his voice held an irritating trace of amusement.

"Don't expect me to make a habit of it. I just couldn't sleep."

"Me, neither." He paused, still watching her. "I wondered what you were doing down here."

"Well, now you know." Without conscious intent, her eyes zeroed in on the curly dark hair of his chest. Below, his midsection was hairless and ridged with muscles, but another thin line of hair began at his navel, arrowing straight down into his shorts. Unsettled, she looked away. "You left Ronnie alone? What if he wakes up?"

"He won't. Listen, I appreciate what you're doing, but it's not necessary. I've got a woman who cleans for me. She comes in every other week."

Alicia sat back on her heels. "That's all right. I needed something to make me tired."

"Forget the rest of it. Go back to bed."

"It won't take long. Besides, I don't like to leave things unfinished."

As he rose to his feet, she rinsed the sponge, not daring to look up. The silence lengthened, heightening the tension between them.

"I'm sorry about your marriage," Luke said suddenly.

Alicia stiffened. For a split second, she'd thought he was apologizing for kissing her, so this caught her unawares. "It doesn't matter now," she said with a shrug. "It's over, and I'm doing just fine on my own."

"Are you?"

Partly because he sounded skeptical and partly because of the picture she'd seen on his dresser, Alicia found herself elaborating. "That's right. In fact, I've met someone else. His name's Nick." She scrubbed hard at something sticky, keeping her tone bright and cheerful. "Nick Easton. I gave him your number, by the way. I hope you don't mind if he calls."

Luke didn't answer.

"Mother and Daddy adore him," she went on in a rush. "He's the director of marketing at Crandon Industries."

"A man with big bucks." Sarcasm tinged the remark, but she ignored it.

"I guess you could say that. He's very successful." She gave the last tile a final swipe. "Did you know I was made a manager? It happened last year. I'm the manager of business systems development now. I have fifteen people working for me, most of them men."

"Congratulations. Sounds like you enjoy being the boss."

She carried the pail over to the sink and dumped the water down the drain. "I do, actually. I've worked hard. I deserved the promotion." She paused, then answered what she sensed was his unspoken question. "As for Kenny, I don't miss him. It was just one of those things."

Several seconds passed, then she felt Luke move nearer, his presence a quiet and solid warmth. "It's late," he said. "You'd better get some sleep."

Alicia nodded and turned to face him. The top of her head just reached his chin, and for an insane moment, she yearned to lean on him, to twine her arms around him and draw upon his strength. "Look," she said awkwardly, "I hope I didn't offend you by washing the floor. I guess if someone walked into my house and started cleaning..." Her voice trailed off as his gaze settled on her mouth.

"Don't worry, I'm not offended," he said slowly. With unexpected gentleness, his hand brushed down her arm.

Alicia's knees turned to pudding. If he kissed her now, she wouldn't be able to push him away. A part of her wanted him to do it. Her clenched fingers trembled with the need to touch him, to slide up the textured surface of his arms, to explore the hard male muscle beneath the skin. Knowing she was crazy, too tired to care, she waited for him to make his move.

But nothing happened. Nothing.

"Good night, Alicia" was all he said.

She stared in stupefaction as he turned and walked away from her. It was as though nothing had passed between them, as though the yearning had all been one-sided. With a stab of sick jealousy, she remembered the woman with the violet-blue eyes. Of course it had all been one-sided—that was her specialty, wasn't it? Loving and not being loved in return? Wanting and not being wanted?

At the door to the kitchen, Luke paused. He didn't turn, didn't speak, but she saw his hand tense on the door frame. And then, like an echo from the past, he was gone. Only emptiness and silence remained.

Alicia stared out the window of Luke's truck as it bowled along the highway, thanking every saint she had ever heard of that the morning's light had brought a return of her sanity. Last night's hunger for Luke's touch had been but a passing weakness, fostered by stress, exacerbated by fatigue. With any luck, her face hadn't betrayed her and he hadn't known.

She glanced down at Ronnie, who sat wedged between them, his face pale and remote. She could scarcely believe this was the same child who had taken such delight in the rocking of a water bed. Remembering his exuberance, her eyes stung with unshed tears.

She'd thought a great deal about Ronnie during the days before she had come to Houston. She'd visited schools, both private and public. She'd made arrangements for after-school child care with Gail White, a trusted friend and neighbor with two children of her own. She had even cleared out her spare room in the expectation that it would soon have a little blond-haired occupant. Yes, Ronnie needed a mother, just as Alicia needed someone to love. Someone who would return her love and fill the gaping void in her life.

"Here we are." Luke pulled the truck into a strip shopping mall and eased into a parking space. "You'd better come in," he added impassively. "I'll be a while."

Alicia studied the front of Luke's store as she and Ronnie climbed out. The words Factory Authorized Service had been inscribed across its plate-glass windows, which, like the door, were reinforced with steel bars.

Ronnie slipped by her and went inside, but Luke waited and held the door just as he'd always done in the past. As she stepped past him, she caught a faint whiff of his after-shave. The scent evoked unwanted memories, fragments of the past that tumbled through her head in an instant.

Thrusting them aside, she took a deep breath and looked around. Televisions, stereos and VCRs were shelved from floor to ceiling everywhere she could see.

"Luke, it's wonderful," she said. "My goodness, I'm impressed." Her voice sounded queer to her own ears, as though it were someone else speaking. As though she were standing at a distance, watching herself play a role.

The set of Luke's mouth made her wonder if he thought so, too, but he only took her over to the counter and introduced her to two of his employees, Dave and Woody. Then he led her toward the back.

"This is the big-screen TV area," he explained. "And back here is where we do most of our small-appliance work."

"Hey, Luke!" A short, heavyset man in a worn blue T-shirt waddled around the corner, his ruddy cheeks creased in a smile. "Ronnie told me you were— Oh, jeez, is this the aunt from Boston?"

For the first time, Luke's hand touched the small of her back. "Yeah, Joey, this is Alicia. Alicia, this is my partner, Joey Gunn."

Alicia extended her hand. "Hi, Joey. Nice to meet you."

The chubby man grinned and bowed with old-fashioned gallantry. "Nice to meet you, too. Very, *very* nice," he added, looking her up and down.

Almost imperceptibly, Luke seemed to relax. "Don't mind Joey," he advised, "but don't stand with your back to him, either. He thinks being half-Italian makes it okay to pinch women's rears."

Joey slipped a pudgy arm around Alicia's waist. "Now, honey, don't you listen to a word this guy says. He wouldn't know the truth if it kicked him in—"

"Joey," Luke warned.

"The shins," Joey finished innocently. He patted Alicia's arm and let her go. "So what d'ya think of the place, eh?"

Very conscious that Luke was listening, Alicia smiled. "It looks like you two have really built up a flourishing business."

"Yeah, we do a lot of TV repair. We do everything— stereos, microwaves, computer monitors. You name it, somebody here'll know how to fix it." Joey winked. "Got anything that needs fixin'?"

"Not at the moment," she said lightly. "Where did Ronnie go?"

Joey jerked a thumb. "In the back office playing one of those computer games Luke bought him. Says he's got to get to level five, whatever the hell that means. The kid'll be putting me out of a job before I know it."

"Listen, Joey, can you entertain Alicia for a few minutes?" Luke interrupted. "I've got to pop a couple of chips into an IF circuit."

"Entertain?" Joey waggled his brows. "Hey, no problem. Take as much time as you need."

"And mind your manners, okay?"

"Hands off, huh?" Joey bellowed a laugh. "You gettin' territorial in your old age?"

Alicia waited uncomfortably for Luke's reply, but as usual his face gave nothing away.

"I won't be long" was all he said.

By the time they left the store, Alicia had garnered an earful of Joey's opinions on a variety of topics, including his business partner. According to Joey, on a scale of one to ten, Luke rated about a twelve and a half. A smart woman would hang on to a guy like that, Joey had told her in a forthright tone. Alicia had maneuvered the conversation into other channels, but not before Joey had managed to slide in one more remark. Luke, he had disclosed, needed a wife to look after him.

"Joey's got a good heart," Luke remarked as the three of them piled back into the Silverado. Then his tone sobered. "Actually, it isn't so good. He had a heart attack last fall. It was a real mild one, but he smokes and he's overweight so the next time could be fatal. His wife wants him to retire, but he won't do it."

"Is his work strenuous?" Alicia inquired.

"We don't let him lift anything heavier than a pencil. He used to do repair work, but he gave that up."

"So what does he do?"

"Management stuff. He keeps the books, places orders, schedules service calls." Luke backed the truck out of the parking space and shifted gears. "Brain work and advertising," he added. "He sends out coupons and flyers. I do the hiring and firing."

"You do a lot of repair work, too."

"It's what I do best." His quick look held a trace of defiance. "I like to work with my hands."

She gazed down at her fingernails, reminded that he had once called her a snob. He hadn't understood her desire for a college education, hadn't understood that she'd had no other choice, that the risk was too great. In her family, people went to college. They didn't quit in their first semester to run away and get married. God, if she had done that, she could never have faced her parents.

But she might have, she thought with the crystalline clarity of hindsight. If Luke had made her believe that he loved her, if she had known for sure that his feelings involved more than hot, physical attraction. If he had let her understand him. If he had invited her to step beyond the shadowed wall, to glimpse the hidden corners of his soul.

At Willowbrook Mall, she suggested they split up, for the idea of shopping for a swimsuit with Luke seemed too stressful to contemplate. "It'll be boring for Ronnie," she explained lamely. "Why don't we meet back here in an hour?"

Ronnie tugged on Luke's sleeve. "Can we go to the toy store?"

"Sure, Ron." Luke took the child's hand in his large one, his inscrutable gaze on Alicia.

She waited until he and Ronnie were out of sight, then started off in the opposite direction, frowning as she considered what type of suit she wanted. It couldn't be too revealing because that simply wasn't her style, but it couldn't be too modest because it irked her to be called conservative. She wasn't conservative, not exactly, but she didn't intend to flaunt herself, either, as this California Babe person apparently did.

Fifteen minutes later, she was heading for the dressing room in one of the large department stores, a half-dozen suits draped over her arm. Ironically, the skimpiest suit of all—a halter-top bikini in a tropical print—was the one that most became her. It came with a matching sarong, which made her feel both glamorous and exotic.

Turning sideways, she scanned her reflection and, for a satisfied moment, imagined Luke's eyes gliding over her, passion and tenderness in their slate gray depths. Then the fantasy shattered and her shoulders slumped. What good were fantasies? She'd never yet had one come true.

She bit down hard on her bottom lip, willing herself to be strong, to be thankful for what she had. Yes, she had felt lonely and unloved, but her problems were insignificant compared to Ronnie's. She had to stop feeling sorry for herself. And she had to stop thinking about Luke.

She paid for the suit and was halfway back through the mall when she recalled her promise to call Nick as soon as she was settled. Maybe it was a promise she shouldn't have made, since their so-called relationship didn't seem destined to develop into something that could last a lifetime. Maybe this separation would have been a good way to end things between them. Still, a promise was a promise. Nick was a good and decent man, and he didn't deserve to be forgotten.

No matter what, she would call him tonight.

Luke studied the jagged line of pine trees silhouetted against the night sky. His elbows propped on his knees, he forced himself to sit motionless on the hard wooden bench, his restless energy held rigidly in check. His instinct was to pace, but that would have drowned out the sound of Alicia's voice on the other side of the wall.

He couldn't make out most of the words, so he wasn't exactly eavesdropping. He was just relaxing on his back porch, breathing in the muggy night air, listening to the hum and chirp of the night insects.

And Alicia's phone conversation.

The kitchen phone wasn't portable, but it had a long cord; he could tell she'd taken it around the corner into the living room. He guessed that she was sitting in the overstuffed chair, located just a few inches away on the other side of the wall behind him. If he were a gentleman, he'd move away.

He didn't budge.

Closing his eyes, he strained to hear what she was saying. A few minutes ago he'd caught the words, "I hope you weren't worried," but since then he'd grasped only tone and inflection and a few disconnected phrases.

His teeth clenched as he thought of Nick Easton. The guy probably owned a Cadillac, wore designer suits and read *The Wall Street Journal* over breakfast. He'd have lily-white hands and a salesman's smile and muscles like limp rubber bands. He'd also have money, more money than Luke would earn in a lifetime.

When he heard her say goodbye, he still didn't stir. He didn't want her to know that he knew she was finished. He didn't want her to think he was interested because then she might think that he cared. And he didn't care, not one damned bit.

His lip curled. Heck, if she wanted to get involved with another arrogant, overpaid, overeducated turkey, it was her business. On the other hand, if she thought she and this Easton guy were going to take Ronnie and waltz off into the sunset as a threesome, she had better think again.

When he was certain she had gone upstairs, he rose and headed for the road. Out of old habit, he picked out constellations as he walked—Ursa Major and Cassiopeia hugging the horizon, the North Star winking from its perch at the tip of the Little Dipper. Years ago, he'd been able to recognize a lot more—Andromeda, Draco, the twelve signs of the zodiac. Richard had taught him during the summer between his freshman and sophomore years at Harvard. Luke had been thirteen at the time. Still a troublemaker. Still struggling to come to terms with his legal adoption into the Garrick family. Still hostile and suspicious.

God, how he missed his brother. Richard's death had left a hole in his heart like a vast, desolate crater on some far-distant moon. Luke considered the comparison with twisted lips. No, it didn't fit. A lifeless thing shouldn't be able to ache as he ached. He had to accept. Richard was gone. Caroline was gone. And nothing could bring them back.

He hadn't felt like this since the day Alicia had returned his ring. The day she'd announced in a quavery voice that he'd be better off without her. Of course, he'd known what she'd really meant was that *she'd* be better off without *him*. He'd understood that she'd been trying to spare his feelings, but it hadn't worked. She'd seen him as a loser, just as three sets of foster parents had seen him as a loser. And now she was back in his life. Haunting him.

Damn her.

He'd taken her to the store for one purpose only—to watch her face when she saw that it was a thriving business, not some two-bit repair shop. His mouth tightened. Okay, so she'd seen it. She'd even said she was impressed. So why wasn't he satisfied? For years he had wanted to shove his success in her face, to let her know she'd been wrong about him. But now that he had done so, the victory seemed hollow.

Frowning a little, he slapped at a mosquito buzzing near his cheek. Maybe it was just that he was past all that now. Like Alicia, he'd grown and matured. Changed. He understood why he'd been so slow as a child, why he hadn't been able to read the way the other children could read. He accepted that he was different rather than dull witted. He knew his strengths. But while understanding helped, it had never quite chased away the shadows, the sense of inadequacy. The knowledge that he couldn't do what came so easily to most people.

He thought then of his father, the father who had abandoned Luke's mother, then refused to send money even when she was ill. The father who had failed to come to his wife's funeral, failed to come and claim his children. The father he now knew was long dead and buried.

He could do better. He *would* do better.

With Ronnie.

Chapter Four

"I can't tell you how glad I am that you're here," Sharon Redford confided as she separated Alicia from the group standing around the swimming pool. The two children were already splashing in the water, and the noise level was rising. "Come on, we can chat while I get things ready."

Put at ease by Sharon's friendly manner, Alicia followed the attractive, dark-haired woman into the kitchen, where the unmistakable signs of children and family were everywhere. A twinge of envy assailed her, the same twinge she always experienced when entering her friend Gail's house. The similarities were obvious—a dozen childish drawings tacked to the refrigerator by "Sesame Street" magnets, crayons and cookie crumbs on the table, toys and shoes scattered on the floor. Tangible reminders of motherhood's rewards, duties and pleasures.

"Is there something I can do to help?" Alicia asked.

"Just keep me company while I do a couple of things. Thanks to my husband, most of the food's prepared. Did Luke tell you Jim is a chef?"

"No, he didn't."

Sharon removed several containers from the refrigerator and set them on the counter. "He works for one of the big hotels out by the airport. It's a long commute, but Jim insists we live near my job rather than his." She threw a grin over her shoulder as she rinsed three ripe red tomatoes. "He knows how much I hate to drive."

"What do you do?" Alicia asked curiously.

"I'm the local school librarian. I love kids, and it works out great as far as my son, Brian, is concerned since I'm always around when he needs me." She picked up a knife and started slicing. "I guess you know that Luke asked me to watch Ronnie after school."

"Yes, he mentioned that," Alicia replied with more coolness than she intended.

Sharon cast her a shrewd look. "You're not happy with that arrangement."

"It's nothing personal," Alicia explained. "It's just that we haven't yet decided who Ronnie will be living with. I'd hoped to take him back to Boston with me, and Luke would like to keep him here."

Sharon's pretty brown eyes filled with sympathy. "It's a tough decision, isn't it? Poor little kid. I couldn't believe the news when I heard. I'm so sorry, Alicia."

"Thank you. Did you know my sister?"

"I met her once. She was a lovely woman, very pleasant to talk to." Sharon hesitated. "I had the impression she worked most of the time."

"Caroline was always a very hard worker," Alicia agreed. She glanced toward the window, but the only man she could see from here was Sharon's brother-in-law, Michael. "What about Luke? How long have you known him?"

"Oh, more than a year now. Gosh, hasn't that man told you anything? My tire went flat right outside his house on one of the hottest weekends of the decade. Brian was with me, and Ronnie was there in the house with Luke, so the two kids played while Luke changed my tire." She set down her knife and arranged the tomatoes on a platter. "Of course, I can change my own tires," she added impishly. "But if I can get a big, strong man to do it for me, why bother?"

Alicia couldn't help smiling. "Men do prove useful at times."

"They sure do. Anyway, after Luke finished with the tire, I invited him and Ronnie over for a swim. He accepted." Sharon gave a chuckle. "Jim was a little surprised when he came home and found a strange man in our pool."

Alicia laughed. "Were you in trouble?"

"Nah, Jim hasn't got a jealous bone in his body. He and Luke hit it off right away, though they really don't have a whole lot in common. Luke is Mr. Fixit, and my husband has never been able to fix anything but gourmet meals. However," Sharon added with a twinkle, "they're both big Rockets fans. When it comes to men, sports seem to be the universal glue."

"It must be wonderful to have a husband who can cook."

"Oh, it is. It's just that sometimes I wish he wasn't such a big klutz. My poor darling can barely change a light bulb on his own. I'll tell you one thing. The woman who marries Luke Garrick is going to be one lucky lady."

"So you think Luke will settle down someday?" Alicia made sure the question sounded casual, as though she hadn't any real interest in the matter. Which she didn't, of course, except where it pertained to Ronnie.

"I sure hope so. I'd hate to see him go on the way he is. He seems to lead such a lonely life."

Alicia thought of the photo she'd seen on Luke's dresser. "But surely he must have a girlfriend," she said, her tone as offhand as she could make it.

"I suppose he must. There was a woman named Margie for a while. And I think there was a Sue and a Lucy, but they didn't last long." She shot Alicia a penetrating look. "I don't blame you for being interested. He's a fine man."

Alicia lowered her gaze to the ringless fourth finger of her left hand. "I'm not interested. In fact, the last thing I'm looking for right now is a romantic relationship."

"Too bad. You and Luke together would have been the perfect solution."

"You mean because of Ronnie?"

"I guess that's what I meant." Looking embarrassed, Sharon put a handful of dirty silverware into the dishwasher. "Forgive me for being so pushy. Jim says I sometimes think with my mouth instead of my brain, and he's right."

"I wasn't offended." Alicia looked down at the floor, then something made her blurt out, "Actually, I was once engaged to Luke, but...it didn't work out."

"You were?" Sharon swung around in surprise. "No kidding?"

"No kidding. When we were much younger. I was just starting college and he was getting ready to move to Houston." Alicia's chest felt hollow as it always did when she thought of that period of her life.

"Wow." Sharon leaned back against the counter, her elbows resting on the edge. "Wow," she repeated, shaking her head. "So it's really awkward for you now, I guess."

"Yes, rather. You won't mention it, I hope."

"You mean I can't tell Jim? Darn!"

Alicia glanced out the window again, making sure Luke was still where she thought he·was. "That's up to you. But I'd prefer that Luke doesn't know I told you. Not that it could matter to him after all this time, but . . ."

"I understand." Sharon's conspiratorial smile contained an element of speculation. "Believe me, I understand."

Before she could say anything more, a door slammed shut somewhere toward the front of the house, and a distant female voice called, "Yoo-hoo, I'm home! I gotta go shower and change and then I'll be down!"

"That's my sister, Nancy. She's been out riding horses all morning." Sharon pulled a pair of trays out from under the sink. "Let's take this stuff out to the patio, then we can change into our suits."

Ten minutes later, Alicia stood in Sharon's bathroom, wondering why in the world she had bought a bikini. In the store, she had felt right about the suit, but now that she had it on again, it seemed too revealing, too bold. As she tied the sarong around her hips, she strove to breathe evenly, to rein in her stampeding emotions. She must be strong, cool, detached. This was just a cookout, and Luke was just a man.

Yet the butterflies in her stomach still fluttered when she stepped out onto the patio. Luke had just come out of the water and was sitting on the brick-lined pool edge. As usual, his eyes were hidden behind sunglasses, but his head lifted ever so slightly when he saw her, and his lean, hard, glistening body straightened just enough to suggest a reaction.

Sharon was already in the pool astride a purple-and-green plastic dragon. "There you are," she called, waving her hand. "Come on in—the water's almost ninety degrees. Oh, and help yourself to a drink. There's beer and soda in the cooler."

"Thanks, I will." Affecting indifference to Luke's scrutiny, Alicia bent and searched out a bottle of her favorite brand of light beer. After unscrewing the top, she lifted it to her lips and took a long swallow, enjoying the cool flow of liquid down her throat. From the corner of her eye, she saw that Luke's head was still turned in her direction when she set down the bottle and removed the sarong. Pride made her give him a blithe wave as she walked over to the steps at the far end of the pool, where the two boys were playing with diving sticks. "Hi, there," she said to Brian, as his coppery head bobbed up a few feet away.

The child flashed her a toothy smile. "Hi-bye," he responded and dived again, his small feet kicking water straight into her face.

"Come on down here, Alicia," Luke suggested in a lazy voice. "We banished the kids to the shallow end for a while. They splash." His pectoral muscles flexed as he reached for his drink.

"So I see," she said ruefully. Circumventing the kids, she waded into the water and swam over to the deep end. The best way to handle this was to pretend that she and Luke had never been anything more than friends. Unfortunately, she suspected that such a pretense would prove difficult.

Luke slid back into the water and came up beside her. "Feels good, doesn't it?" he said softly. "Maybe a little too warm, but—"

"Hello, everybodeeee!" interrupted a sunny female voice. "Sorry I'm late!"

Braced for her first glimpse of the California Babe, Alicia looked around. Immediately her heart sank. She'd half expected it to be the woman with the violet-blue eyes, but it wasn't. Nevertheless, this was just as bad.

If she had considered her own bathing suit skimpy, Nancy's was almost indecent. No, that wasn't quite true. The crucial areas were covered.

Barely.

Alicia had never seen anything like it outside of a magazine. Not only did Nancy have the bleached blond hair and clean, pure features of the stereotypical surfer girl, but her figure was sensational. The tiny, crocheted triangles of material stretched across her voluminous breasts did little more than hide her nipples. As for the rest of the bikini, it was half the size of Alicia's.

"I told you so," Luke murmured in her ear.

While Sharon called out introductions from her dragon's throne, Nancy bounced over to the point of the pool edge closest to Luke. "Hi, Alicia, nice to meet you. Luke, honey, I need you to put some lotion on my back. I gotta watch out for those ultraviolet rays."

Alicia felt a prick of annoyance as Luke hefted himself from the water and dried his hands. She didn't quite see why he had to perform this service. Though Jim was busy with the barbecue, Michael lay sprawled on a towel not ten feet away.

As if reading her thoughts, Nancy flashed her an artless smile. "I can't ask Mike. He hates getting this slime all over his hands. And I know—" she playfully removed Luke's sunglasses and set them on her own nose "—that Luke doesn't mind."

Gritting her teeth, Alicia kicked her way over to the opposite side of the pool while Luke squirted lotion onto Nancy's shapely back. As he started to rub, the blonde shut her eyes and gave a sensuous wriggle. "Mmm, that feels wonderful," she purred. "Luke, honey, you do that soooo well. I just love a man with good hands."

To Alicia's disgust, Luke seemed amused. "Shameless hussy," she heard him drawl in Nancy's ear. Without looking up from his fascinating occupation, he added more loudly, "How about you, Alicia? Do you have sunscreen on?"

Alicia gaped at him, unable to believe her ears. Could he possibly believe she would allow him to do that to her? "I'll put some on later," she answered, barely keeping her temper in check. Turning toward Sharon, she smiled and asked, "Got any more toys?" with a gaiety designed to cover her annoyance.

Sharon yielded the dragon with a laugh. "The boys put a hole in our crocodile, so this is all we have left. Go ahead, try him. We call him Puff."

Alicia surveyed Puff, unable to recall a single instance during her childhood when she had had a chance to play with a float. Neither of her parents could swim and both disliked water sports, so family vacations had centered on academics and learning. Alicia had always longed to go where there was water, but instead she and Caroline had been dragged to every museum, battlefield and historical monument the northeast could offer. Of course, Caroline had been temperamentally suited to it all, the perfect child for her erudite parents, but Alicia had been silently resentful. She had always been odd man out, the brooding rebel, the child who couldn't please.

Determined to make up for lost fun, she placed one hand on the dragon's neck and the other on his flank. One, two, three and up... and back down with inglorious rapidity as the dragon flipped over and landed on her head.

The two six-year-olds howled with laughter. "Oh, Aunt Alicia, that's not how you do it!"

Alicia wiped water from her eyes and pretended to glare at her nephew. "Okay, smarty, then how?"

"First you have to take him over to the steps."

Following Ronnie's instructions, Alicia managed to gain a precarious perch on the dragon. Hunched over Puff's neck, she paddled triumphantly to the center of the pool, only to discover there was a trick to balancing. The mo-

ment she sat upright, Puff dumped her again, this time in
deep water.

When she bobbed to the surface, coughing from the unexpected dunking, a strong arm looped around her waist.
"Are you all right?" Luke asked. Seemingly without effort, he held her against him, his other arm treading water
while his powerful legs kicked hard enough to keep them
both afloat.

"Of course," she snapped, and coughed again. "I just
got water up my nose, that's all."

Ignoring her efforts to push him away, he hauled her over
to the side, his arm like a steel band beneath her breasts.
"Time for sunscreen," he murmured. "I'd hate to see all
that gorgeous skin get fried."

"No." Alicia gripped the pool edge, intensely aware of all
the places where their bodies touched. "I'll put some on
myself in a few minutes," she told him, her voice as frosty
as the contents of Sharon's cooler.

Knowing she must seem unreasonable, she looked around
and caught Sharon watching them with an interested expression. At least Nancy had wandered over to the grill,
presumably to flirt with her brother-in-law. The blonde,
Alicia noticed, still wore Luke's sunglasses.

Luke hoisted himself out of the water and sat staring
down at her, his jaw set with clear disapproval. "This Texas
sun is nothing to toy with, honeybun." Softly, so no one else
could hear, he added, "And most of you happens to be exposed to it."

Knowing he was right, Alicia swam to the deep end and
climbed out. As she walked across the pea gravel, the
scorching afternoon sun beat mercilessly upon her back.
Why was she behaving like a quivering teenager? So what if
Luke touched her? She wouldn't allow herself to respond

because, quite simply, it wasn't worth it. She'd had enough pain without adding to it.

Toweling off, Alicia peeked at him, feeling light-headed and cornered, as though some invisible force was thrusting her toward the inevitable. How could she pretend he meant nothing to her? It wasn't true. He represented so much—past hopes and shattered dreams and nameless longings that had haunted her even when she'd been married to another man.

As luck would have it, Luke chose that moment to look up, and for a frozen moment their gazes locked in a connection as potent as the fiercest kiss. Then Sharon touched her arm and the spell broke.

"You really should do as he says," the other woman whispered. "With that fair skin, you could get a wicked burn. We put some on the kids before you came out."

Alicia blinked with dismay. How could she have forgotten Ronnie? Of course he would burn; he was as fair as she was. Stricken with guilt, she watched him leaping and shrieking in the shallow water, his small face innocent and, at least for the moment, free of sorrow.

"Don't feel bad," Sharon added kindly. "You're just not used to looking out for kids, that's all. It'll come."

Alicia nodded. Feeling subdued, she went over to Luke. "Are you sure Nancy won't mind if I use some of that?"

"She doesn't care. Come on, sit down."

Alicia complied, and for a short while, time rolled back and the setting blurred. She was in New Jersey on a hot Saturday in July, one of the many weekends Luke had made the trip from Connecticut to visit her. Eager for each other's company, they had spread beach towels on the grass in the backyard, beyond sight of the house in the most isolated spot they could find.

She shut her eyes, remembering how Luke had massaged coconut oil over every part of her body that hadn't been covered by her modest two-piece swimsuit. Eventually she had daringly unfastened the top to her suit. With love in her heart, she had let him touch her breasts for the first time, watching the way his eyes grew dark and hungry, reveling in the discovery of her own female power. Soon he had grown bolder. He had slipped his fingers inside her suit bottom and stroked her just long enough to make her wet and aching. He had wanted her to take it off, but of course she had refused.

Now she sat facing the diving board, wondering if he remembered that day. The muscles in her back were rigid as he spread the warm puddle of lotion across her shoulder blades in unhurried circles, gliding over her sensitized flesh as though he had a right to touch her. As though she was his woman, which of course she could never be.

Yet he made no effort to prolong the moment. Once finished, he practically shoved the bottle into her hand in his hurry to escape her company. And then he was doing laps, up and down the length of the pool, his arms and legs thrashing as though he were in an Olympic race.

For Luke, it was therapy. Therapy and salvation. Alicia in a bikini was torture enough, but touching her had been excruciating. He knew it was his own fault, but he'd wanted to test himself, to prove he could resist her this time.

Well, he'd blown it. Badly.

Forget her, forget her, forget her. The words hammered in his brain, synchronized with the rhythm of his pumping limbs. But she was so beautiful, so provocative—even more so than she had been ten years ago. The sight of her had undone him, the feel of her skin, its softness and texture. Her musky female scent had called to him, pulling him into

a net of his own making. Damn, damn, damn. He wished
the water were colder. A lot colder.

When he emerged from the pool, Jim was loading ham-
burgers and barbecued brisket onto a platter and Sharon
was beckoning him to come eat. In the ensuing confusion,
he ended up sitting with Nancy, who sent him one of her
sultry smiles and offered him a beer.

Luke purposely avoided looking in Alicia's direction; instead his gaze fixed on the two children sitting cross-legged
on a beach towel. Ketchup dripped down Ronnie's fingers
as he held his hamburger close to his chest, his blond head
bent toward Brian as the other child giggled something in his
ear.

Watching Ronnie's face, he thought of the little boy's
terror the other night. To Luke's knowledge, the dreams had
only started since the accident, just as his own had started
after *his* mother had died. He thought of the dreams he had
had as a six-year-old orphan, nightmarish excursions into an
eerie, mist-filled world, a world where his dead mother
walked, where whispering voices commanded him to kiss the
cold slab of her cheek. And, remembering, he shuddered.

He still believed he had been right to keep Ronnie away
from the funeral, but Alicia's assertion that it might have
helped the kid work through his pain had been nagging at
him. His own nightmares had tapered off gradually, and he
had survived. But it hadn't been easy. Of course, he hadn't
had a loving aunt or uncle to help him adjust. He hadn't had
anybody.

"A penny for those thoughts of yours."

He turned his head to find Nancy studying him.

"Only a penny?" he quipped. He reached for a pickle,
reflecting that it would be a long, cold day in hell before he
took Nancy into his confidence. He never took anyone into
his confidence. Except, sometimes, Joey.

Nancy angled her head toward Alicia, who sat beside Sharon, a short distance away. "How come she never came to Houston before?"

"She's been busy with her career."

Looking thoughtful, Nancy took a bite of potato salad and chewed it. "So are you going to keep Ronnie or is she?"

Luke shrugged. Trust Nancy to drive right to the crux of the matter. "That's still under discussion."

Nancy fell silent, and after a few seconds, he inquired about her plans for graduate school. As Nancy rambled on about the courses she'd be taking, his eyes drifted back to Alicia. God, never in his wildest dreams had he thought she'd buy a suit like that. She looked fantastic. She also hadn't glanced his way once since he'd come out of the water. In fact, she seemed oblivious to his presence.

But that was what he wanted, wasn't it? What he expected of her? Except that *he* wasn't indifferent, not by a long shot. Yes, he could pretend, but he was ready to admit that it was probably beyond his capacity to be indifferent to Alicia Brant. Not that he had any intention of letting her know it.

A little while later, he noticed she had disappeared, but he assumed she had gone to the powder room. Yet as the minutes passed, he grew uneasy. Lighthearted conversation floated around him while he waited for her to return.

When she didn't, he set down his beer and went to look for her. Listening intently, he stopped in the kitchen, but all he heard were the voices drifting in from outside. Then, just as he was about to step into the living room, he heard a low sound, like a repressed sob.

He found her in the front foyer. Her back faced him, and her head was bent as though the weight of the world's problems rested on her slim, bare shoulders.

"What's the matter, Alicia?"

She started and spun around, but at least this time she didn't accuse him of sneaking up on her.

"Luke." She cleared her throat, one finger flying up to touch the outside edge of her eye. "Nothing's the matter." She recovered quickly, and if her voice had not held that faint, betraying quiver, he almost might have believed her.

"You were crying," he said as he moved closer.

"Not really. I was just thinking about Caroline and Richard. I mean, here we are at a party, swimming and laughing and eating and—" Her lovely face crumpled. "And I suddenly felt so disloyal, so treacherous."

"You're not being disloyal." He reached out and smoothed back a damp curl that had fallen over her brow. "You've got to go on living your life. That's what Caroline would have wanted." Platitudes, he thought in frustration. Yet what else could he say? And who was he to offer comfort?

"I don't know what Caroline would have wanted," Alicia said brokenly. "I never really understood her." She blinked hard, her eyes luminous with tears. "She was so different from me, Luke. My sister was s-so perfect."

"The hell she was." Dismissing the statement as foolishness, he caught hold of her shoulders. "She was as human as the rest of us. Don't make her into a saint just because she's gone."

Alicia's head shook. "You don't understand." As if in invitation, she swayed toward him, her head tilting back, her hands coming out to rest upon his naked chest.

A fire ignited inside him, sheeting through his gut in a hot, shimmering wave. Unable to move, to tear himself away, he could only stare mindlessly down at the fullness of her lower lip. Such a sweet, kissable, stubborn mouth. He'd been fascinated by its shape ever since the first time he'd set eyes on her.

"Please," she whispered. "Someone might come."

"Let them," he said hoarsely. His control stretched to its limit as he stood there, waiting for her to tell him to take his hands off her and go away. She hadn't wanted him to kiss her the last time, so why should now be any different?

Damn it, why didn't she say it? She had always been an enigma to him. Even now, when he should have been able to figure her out, he wasn't sure what it was that she wanted. On the other hand, he didn't much care, because her time had run out. Whether she liked it or not, he was going to kiss her again. One more time, he promised himself. Just to get her out of his system.

As soon as their lips touched, he realized the magnitude of his mistake. Man, oh, man. Desire slammed through him with the force of a knockout punch, spinning his brain so that he forgot where he was, forgot everything but Alicia. This time he sure wasn't kissing a statue. She was warm and willing and alive in his arms, as eager and responsive as a man could want. Her hair, her taste, her voluptuous female scent—it all captured him, held him in thrall.

He drew her against him, hard, so that every inch of their bodies touched. His hands went around to cup her bottom, while his tongue ran up the line of her jaw to her ear, nipping gently before returning to cover her mouth. The delicious feel of her breasts crushed against him brought back old memories, old yearnings that had never really left him. She responded as though she remembered them, too, her tongue stroking against his with the same fervor, the same delirium.

Yet amid the haze, his thoughts gathered, grew sharp and focused. Nothing had changed. Their lives, their needs and goals, were as disparate now as they had ever been. She couldn't possibly want him. And he shouldn't want her, either.

She stared wide-eyed when he released her and stepped back. "Damn," he muttered through gritted teeth. He clenched his hands and repeated the curse, watching the way she winced at the word. Knowing he'd hurt her, he felt a sharp pang of remorse drive deep into his chest, but he said nothing, uttered no apology.

Pain shone in her eyes. "We shouldn't have done that." Her voice came out low and husky, trembling with an emotion that could only be regret.

"No," he agreed flatly.

"We're both involved with someone else."

He opened his mouth to ask what she meant, then shut it again before he could make matters worse. She must think he was dating Nancy. Fine. If it would keep her away from him, let her think what she liked.

"Right," he said. "So let's forget this happened, okay? I wanted to comfort you and things just got a little out of hand."

The door at the back of the house opened and closed.

Like a startled fawn, Alicia jumped and ran, her arm grazing his as she hurried away. Luke stayed where he was for another minute, then strolled into the kitchen, where his ears told him someone was refilling the ice bucket.

"There you are." Nancy shut the freezer door and scrutinized him, one eyebrow cocked. "I was wondering where you'd gone. What's the matter with Alicia?"

Luke searched his mind for a coherent answer. "She's a little upset. Uh, about her sister, I mean."

"Oh, yeah. I guess it takes a long time to get over a shock like that." Looking solemn, Nancy came over and touched his arm. "You upset, too, Luke, honey? Is there anything I can do?" Her eyes roved over him a little too thoroughly for his comfort and when she added, in an innocent tone, "Anything at all?" he wanted to groan. Obviously his wet bathing trunks hadn't quite hidden the waning effects of his encounter with Alicia. "Just kidding," Nancy added. "Hey, I know what you need."

"What's that?" he asked her sardonically.

Setting down the ice bucket, she removed several ice cubes and dropped them into a paper cup. With a straight face, she held it out to him. "Here. It's quicker than a cold shower."

Luke snatched it from her and gave her a light swat on the behind. "Someday, young lady, you're going to turn some poor sucker into a raving lunatic."

"Hmm," she murmured, looking pleased at the idea. "Just like somebody's making you crazy, hmm?"

"Nobody's making me crazy."

"Right." She reached for the ice bucket, her smile mocking. "Just keep telling yourself that, sugar. Maybe you'll start to believe it."

Chapter Five

"I don't wanna go to any stinkin' school."

Across the top of Ronnie's head, Alicia's gaze linked with Luke's. The class lists had been posted yesterday. Until then, Ronnie had seemed, if not enthusiastic, at least reconciled to the fact that he would soon be starting first grade.

Alicia slipped an arm around Ronnie and gave him a reassuring squeeze. "Just because Brian's not in your class doesn't mean you won't see him. And it doesn't mean you won't have fun, either. You'll make lots of new friends."

"No, I won't." Ronnie's lower lip thrust out.

Luke put a hand on Ronnie's knee. "Your aunt's right," he said gruffly. "So let's go on in."

Together they urged the child out of the truck and across the parking lot toward the entrance to Brown Elementary. Ronnie dragged his feet, his head tucked low, while Luke carried Ronnie's backpack—jammed full with the requisite school supplies—slung over his shoulder.

Alicia followed, a small frown furrowing her brow. If it was this difficult for Ronnie to go to Brown, how much harder would it be for him to go back with her to Boston? The timing was incredibly bad. If only the Texas schools didn't start so early, if only she had an established emotional relationship with her nephew. But she didn't, and even if Ronnie grew attached to her, would he be willing to change schools? By then he would be accustomed to his teacher. He would have made new friends, established a routine. Yet the alternative was to force a decision now, and that just didn't seem right.

For some reason, Alicia had expected to be able to walk Ronnie straight to his classroom, but instead they were directed to the cafeteria, where the children were sorted according to grade level and teacher. At first glance, pandemonium seemed to reign inside the large room, but it soon became apparent that the system worked.

Nine boys and girls were already queued behind the sign reading Grade 1, Mrs. Glover, lunch boxes and backpacks strewn around them. Alicia led Ronnie to the end of the line behind a little brown-haired girl with a French braid.

"I guess you've got to sit here, sweetie."

The girl swiveled around to stare at Ronnie. "Where's your name tag?" she demanded.

Ronnie eyed her with hostility.

"Where does he get it?" Alicia asked quickly, noting that the girl wore one pinned to the front of her dress. It proclaimed her name as Tara.

"From the teacher. She's the lady next to my mom." Tara pointed at a short, plump woman in a lavender shirtdress. She had tight silver curls and gold-rimmed glasses, and at the moment was immersed in conversation with a slim brunette in a white tennis skirt.

"That's Mrs. Glover?"

"Yep."

Alicia glanced at Luke. "Do you want to talk to her?"

Luke nodded and set down Ronnie's backpack.

They made their way over to the teacher, dodging little feet and bodies as they went. The woman in the tennis skirt blew Tara a kiss and gave Luke an appraising look before she walked away, her hips swaying just a wee bit more than necessary.

"Hello." Mrs. Glover blinked owlishly at them.

Luke shook her hand and introduced himself, adding that he and Alicia were Ronnie's aunt and uncle.

Mrs. Glover shuffled through a stack of colorful name tags until she found Ronnie's. "Oh, dear, I do wish the parents could have been here. The first day is so important."

"Ronnie lost his parents in an air crash," Alicia said. "Three weeks ago."

"My Lord, the poor angel." One plump hand pressed to her heart, she peered past them at the line of children. "Which one is he?"

"Blond hair, red shirt," Luke indicated. "I think you should know he wasn't too crazy about coming here today."

"His best friend is in a different class," Alicia added, "so that's made it even harder. You might want to call if any problems develop." She held out a slip of paper with Luke's home and work number written on it.

The teacher tucked it into her pocket and patted Alicia's arm. "I know you and your husband are worried, Mrs. Garrick, but I promise I'll take good care of him."

"Oh, I'm not—" Alicia stopped and flushed. "I mean, I'm not Mrs. Garrick. We're not married."

Mrs. Glover's brows arched very high. "Oh?"

"We're just living together," Luke said flippantly.

Alicia frowned at him. "His brother was married to my sister," she explained. "I'm only visiting."

"Oh, I see." Mrs. Glover's brows resumed their proper position, though she still looked a little doubtful. "So Ronnie will be residing with you, Mr. Garrick?"

"That's the plan for now."

"The arrangement may change," Alicia added.

The teacher adjusted her glasses, her eyes shifting back and forth between the two of them with an air of faint disapproval. "Well, I trust that at least *one* of you is willing to provide this child with a home."

Luke's gaze slid over to Alicia. "Yeah," he agreed. "*One* of us will."

Haunted by the memory of Ronnie's pale face and wretched expression, Alicia walked back to the truck in silence. He hadn't let her kiss him goodbye. He hadn't responded to her hug. Instead he'd stared over her shoulder at Luke, as though Luke was the only one who mattered.

As Luke inserted the key into the ignition, she looked over at him. "You didn't hug Ronnie," she said accusingly.

Luke didn't glance at her as he started the engine. "He didn't want me to."

"Are you so sure?"

"Yeah, I'm sure. He was trying to make me feel guilty for sending him to school, that's all."

"That's *all?*" she echoed. "What about the pain he's feeling? He had that nightmare again last night, didn't he?"

"Yes." Luke didn't speak again until he'd negotiated his way out of the busy parking lot. "He'll get over it, Alicia."

"You act like you don't care about him."

Luke pulled the truck into a side street so fast her heart got a shot of adrenaline. Shifting into Park, he angled his body toward her, his face dark with forbidding anger. "You don't understand anything, do you? You come down here all self-righteous and start making pronouncements—"

"Damn it, Luke, I'm just concerned!"

He stared at her for a long moment, then drew in a harsh breath. "I know that. But don't start analyzing me, Alicia. I know Ronnie pretty darn well. He's spent a lot of time with me the past couple of years. A lot of time," he repeated with emphasis.

Suddenly his words sank in. "What do you mean?"

"You don't know?"

She shook her head. "I know Caroline sometimes worked on the weekends—"

"She and Richard worked every weekend. All day long and into the night. Ronnie hardly ever saw either of them."

Disbelief washed through her. "Are you saying my sister neglected her child?"

He turned his head to gaze out over the steering wheel, his mouth hard, his profile boldly defined against the clear morning sky. "I don't know. I guess she thought it was worth it. But she and Richard were all caught up in this success thing."

"There's nothing wrong with wanting to be successful. Even you play that game, Luke."

"But not," he said, "at the expense of my kid."

Emotion clutched at Alicia's insides, twisting until all she could feel was pain. "You don't understand Caroline. I can't believe she would have been anything but a dedicated mother. Caroline was—" she struggled for words "—amazing. She could do anything, literally. My mother used to say I should try to be more like her."

Luke's lip curled. "Your mother was talking a lot of bull. Look, I've got to get to work."

They drove in silence, and as the minutes passed, Alicia felt more and more confused. How could Luke say such things? The fact that Caroline had gone to the trouble of bringing Ronnie to Luke showed how conscientious she was. She could have hired a nanny instead of making the long drive from her home in West University to Luke's part of town. Surely that demonstrated that Caroline had cared. After all, hadn't Caroline entrusted her most precious possession—her child—to no one but her brother-in-law, a family member? No fault could be found in such an action, could it?

When they arrived back at Luke's house, he drove into the garage and handed her the keys. "You're sure you can handle the truck?"

"I'm sure," she answered coolly. They had agreed that he would take the van and leave her the Silverado so she could pick up Ronnie from school.

"You remember how to drive a standard transmission?"

"More or less." Of course she remembered. He was the one who had taught her.

"Maybe I'd better go over it with you just in case."

"That won't be necessary." Alicia opened the door and stepped out, and after a moment, Luke did the same.

"So." He altered the tilt of his hat, his gray eyes watchful. "You'll be okay on your own?"

"I've been on my own for quite a while now," she said tartly. "I can take care of myself."

"Yeah." His eyes swept over her, not in the appreciative way he had studied her at the cookout, but in an overt, assessing way nevertheless. "I'll call you later."

Without another word, he strode toward the van, his easy masculine gait sexy enough to draw any woman's eye. Even when she was still upset, Alicia found she was not immune to his virile magnetism. Her eyes trailed after him, unconsciously admiring his physique until she realized what she was doing. Then she hurried to unlock the front door, determined not to stand and watch him drive away as though powerless to resist catching a last glimpse of him. As he backed the van down the driveway, she went inside and gave a sigh of relief. She looked around, and then the queer feeling hit.

She was alone in Luke's house.

Luke's *home*.

How many times had she tried to imagine this place? Dozens, perhaps hundreds. She had tried to connect with him across the miles, tried to envision what it would have been like to share his life. But never once had she imagined a place as warm and homey and inviting as this. He had created this place on his own. He had gone on without her, probably without a backward glance.

Canine toenails tapped across the hardwood floor and a moist nose prodded her hand, distracting her from this thought. Alicia looked down and smiled.

Not quite alone after all.

"Hello, Daffodil." She stroked the collie's head, then on impulse knelt down and wrapped her arms around the animal's body. Accommodating and patient, Daffy sat on her haunches while Alicia took comfort from their closeness. "Pets are supposed to be great stress relievers," she murmured. "So how about it? Can you do for me what you do for Ronnie?"

As if in answer Daffy started to lick Alicia's face.

Alicia allowed this to continue for almost a minute before she pushed the dog away with a laugh. "Okay, that's enough. Thanks, I feel better. Whoa, girl!" Daffy's licking subsided, but her soulful brown eyes continued to regard Alicia with gentle puzzlement. Touched, Alicia rubbed her cheek against the soft, shorn fur of the collie's neck. "You're so beautiful," she whispered. "I wish you were mine."

In the mood for music, she headed for the living room, where Luke kept a CD and tape player in a low, built-in cupboard. She bent to examine the collection of compact discs stored there and discovered, to her delight, that Luke's taste had expanded over the years. In the old days, rock and roll had been all he'd listened to, but now an array of classical selections stretched along the upper shelf. In addition, a large number of books on tape occupied space on a second shelf, a variety that ranged from literary classics to modern popular fiction.

After a brief debate, she chose Vivaldi's *The Four Seasons,* then went to make a cup of tea. By the time the caffeine had wrought its magic, the rich dramatic strains of "Summer," filled her ears. Filled her soul, too, with tendrils of longing so intense it made her ache. Good music always did that to her, made her feel things that at other times she kept buried. Her chin on her hand, she wondered if Luke ever felt this way—lost and lonely and afraid, waiting and yearning for a completion that bore no name. A completion that might never come.

She finished her drink and set down the mug, her fingers stiff and tight on the handle. Then, in an abrupt movement, she released it and jumped up. Enough brooding. It was time to do something constructive.

She headed for Ronnie's room, taking the stairs with such energy that Daffy leapt to her feet with a bark. Outside Ronnie's room, Alicia stopped. To her left, down the hall, Luke's room beckoned. Its pull wrapped around her like an invisible arm. Slowly, as if in a hypnotic trance, she turned and looked. His door was ajar.

Her pulse quickened. This was crazy. She'd already been in there, seen the bed, the furniture, the photograph.

The photograph.

That was what called to her. The woman with the violet-blue eyes.

Alicia glanced around as if to assure herself that no one would see. Then she walked down the hall and pushed open the door.

Except for a few scattered items of apparel, the room looked the same. Luke's cutoffs hung on the closet door-knob, a T-shirt fell carelessly across a wooden chair.

Guilt trickled through her, but she ignored it. The picture was still there, still positioned so it could be viewed from the bed. Without thinking, she raised a hand to pick it up, then froze in midair. Touching was far more invasive than looking. She would not touch.

Her hand fell limply to her side, but her eyes stayed pinned to the woman's face. Those bewitching eyes, fringed by their long black lashes, seemed to stare back as though equally entranced by Alicia. The mouth curved up in a tantalizing smile, the kind of smile a woman might give to her lover. And Vivaldi's music played on in the distance, muffled but audible, winding its way around corners to embrace her soul with its majesty.

A message had been scrawled across the bottom right corner of the photo. *To Luke with love. Christina.*

Alicia cleaned and sorted and organized things in Ronnie's room until midmorning, when the phone rang. There were two telephones in the house—one on the table next to Luke's bed, the other in the kitchen. Unwilling to reenter Luke's room, she raced downstairs and grabbed the receiver on the fourth ring.

"Hello," she said breathlessly, half-expecting the caller to be Ronnie's teacher.

"Alicia, it's me. I'm calling from the hospital."

"Luke, what happened?" Her heart skipped a beat as visions of accidents streaked through her head. "Are you all right?"

"I'm fine. It's Joey."

Her heartbeat returned to normal. *Thank God. Nothing had happened to Luke.* With a mental shake, she forced herself to pay attention to what he was saying.

"... started feeling lousy as soon as he got to work. Nausea and cold sweats, a tingling in his right arm. They've got him plugged into a bunch of monitors over here in the chest pain observation unit."

"Gosh, I'm sorry. Is his family with him?"

"His wife's here. His son and daughter-in-law are on their way." Luke paused. "Look, I need to ask a favor. I rode with Joey in the ambulance, so now I'm stuck here at the hospital. Any chance you could come get me? I'd ask Woody," he hastened to add as though fearing her refusal, "but he's alone in the store. One of the guys called in sick and the other two are out on service calls and—"

"Of course I'll come," she interrupted. She tore a sheet of paper from a small pad on the counter and jotted down the directions he gave. "I'll be there as soon as I can."

Minutes later, she tossed her purse onto the seat and climbed into the Silverado, her eyes on the gearshift. Luke's lessons stood out sharply in her memory when she touched it, and she could feel his hand over hers as though it were yesterday.

Five simple steps, just like he had taught her. Let up on the gas, push down on the clutch, shift gears, let up on the clutch, give it gas. Easy as pie. Except she suddenly wasn't sure about the gear pattern.

"Just use the Force," she muttered as she turned the key. Luckily the Force cooperated, and by the time she hit the main road, she was driving like a pro. Pleased with herself, she hummed the *Star Wars* theme beneath her breath, watching for the street signs and landmarks Luke had mentioned. When she pulled up in front of Houston Northwest Medical Center, Luke was waiting near the front entrance.

"Thanks for coming," he said, sliding into the passenger seat. "Any trouble finding the place?"

"Nope. Your directions were great. I assume you want to go back to work?"

"I have to." He buckled his seat belt and sat back. "Any trouble shifting?"

"Not after I figured out where reverse was," she said lightly. "I hope you have insurance on your garage."

A full three seconds passed before he turned his head. "You're kidding, right?"

She smiled and accelerated, then shifted smoothly into second. "Yes, I'm kidding, but I'd rather drive an automatic. Any update on Joey?"

"His son got here just before you did. Other than that, nothing."

Something in his voice made her throw him another quick glance. "You look exhausted."

"I am." The brevity of his answer told her he didn't want to talk, so she said nothing more for several minutes.

"Make sure I don't miss the turn," she remarked, scanning the signs. "I have a feeling we're almost there."

"It's right after the next light. On the left."

A few seconds later, she pulled up outside Luke's store. "Do you need anything else?"

Luke hesitated, his hand on the door handle. For a long moment, he said nothing, then he turned and looked her in the eye. "I might need another favor. I'm not sure yet."

"What is it?" she asked curiously. Her instinct told her something was troubling him, something other than Joey's illness.

"Never mind for now." He opened the door and got out. "Don't forget to pick up Ronnie," he added.

That night Luke paced back and forth in his room, anxiety eating like acid at the lining of his gut. Murphy's Law had never been more dependable than it had of late. Everything that could go wrong, did. Inevitably. Joey's illness was proof of that.

Luke walked to the window and stared out, but instead of moonlit grass and trees, numbers and dollar signs flashed in his head. Receipts, invoices, unfinished business—everything was piling higher and higher, burying him, suffocating him with worry and frustration.

God knows he'd tried to do something about it. He'd spent the afternoon holed up in the back office, attempting to figure out what Joey had been doing for the past few months. Attempting to sort and calculate and enter figures into the computer's spreadsheet. But the numbers had jumped around, reversed themselves, played hopscotch in his head until he'd literally yanked at his hair. The harder he'd concentrated, the more the numbers had danced. Just like always.

He needed help.

The admission drove a gigantic fist of tension through his chest. Asking for help meant explanations, and explanations meant exposure. And exposure meant humiliation and shame. He had learned that lesson at a young age and he had never forgotten it.

Turning on his heel, Luke gazed around the room as though it held the solutions to his problems. His eyes settled on Christina's photograph, lingering on the warmth of her smile. Her eyes seemed to be encouraging him, urging him to take this thing one step at a time. And the obvious next step was to swallow his pride and ask for help.

He found Alicia curled on the sofa in the living room, her feet tucked under her and an open book in her lap. But she wasn't reading. Her delicately arched brows were drawn into a frown, and she was staring at the carpet.

His heart hammering, he strolled to the sofa and lowered his long body onto the cushions. She shifted as though to make room for him, an unnecessary action considering that more than two feet of space separated them. Her movement drew his gaze to her bare legs, and his throat closed. At that moment, he would have sold his soul for the right to touch them.

"You look worried," she commented. "Is it Joey?"

He propped a foot against the edge of the coffee table. "Sort of," he said evasively. Then, to procrastinate, he added, "Ronnie's finally asleep."

"I wish he had told us more about his day at school," she replied. "He was so quiet all evening." She was silent for a moment. "But that's not what's bothering you, is it?"

He clenched and unclenched his left hand. God, it was difficult to tell her. Sharing had always been hard for him, uncloaking his weaknesses even harder. What made it even worse was that he wanted her to see him as a success.

"As a matter of fact," he said, forcing out the words, "I've got a problem." He stopped, feeling as though he were about to dive naked into an icy pool.

"What kind of problem?" She leaned toward him.

He evaded her gaze, staring instead at the clutter on the coffee table. He was acutely aware of her nearness. "It started when Joey had his first heart attack," he said in a toneless voice. "Before, I could count on him to handle his end of the business. The bookkeeping, the records, the bills." He pulled in a breath. "He was different when he came back. He started reading paperbacks all day—mystery novels, thrillers, those Stephen King horror things. I don't think Joey ever read fiction in his life until his stay in the hospital. Since then, it's become like some kind of addiction."

She drew up her legs and sat cross-legged, her gaze fixed on his face. "Have you said anything to him?"

"No. I figured the poor guy deserved a break. And I thought extra pressure might make him sick again. I thought he'd get his act together before the business suffered."

"And he didn't," she stated after a short silence.

"No." Luke found he still couldn't look at her, and he hadn't even gotten to the hard part yet. "The records are a mess. Joey hasn't reconciled the books in the past two months, and some of the stuff before that looks screwed up. Today I learned that one of our suppliers has been refusing to fill our orders because our payments have been late. We're behind with the rent and utilities." Filled with nervous anxiety, he surged restlessly to his feet and began to pace. "I got a call this afternoon from the bank. Our last loan payment never got paid. The woman threatened to call in the loan if it wasn't paid by tomorrow. To top that off, it looks like I'll soon have the IRS on my back because Joey did a number there, too." He risked a glance at Alicia. "About the only thing he's kept up on is the employee paychecks."

"I don't understand, Luke. Why have you been leaving all this up to Joey? It's your business, too."

He forced himself to turn and face her, studying her upturned face with a sick feeling. He couldn't tell her the truth. Lord, it was bad enough to tell her this much, to watch her good opinion of him go flying out the window. Not, he reminded himself, that she'd had such a hot opinion of him to start with, but this clinched it.

"Because that was the deal," he said flatly. "I'm a repairman, Alicia, not an accountant. Joey was the one with

the business background. We agreed from the beginning
that he'd take care of all that. And don't forget we've been
in business for ten years and it's worked fine so far."

"Pretty trusting," she remarked. "How do you know he
hasn't cheated you?"

"He hasn't," Luke said, irrationally annoyed. "Joey's
honest, I'd stake my life on it. Trust isn't the issue here,
Alicia."

"Isn't it?" she countered. "You're asking me to help you,
and you won't give me the whole story."

"How do you know I'm asking for help?"

Her blue eyes challenged him, then she shrugged. "Why
else would you tell me? I figured you knew I kept the books
for my husband."

"No, I didn't. But I remembered you were planning to
take some business courses in college. Sounds like you did."
He thought of Alicia's ex, and felt a surge of contempt for
a man he had never met—not because Kenny Farrell had let
his wife keep his books but because Farrell obviously hadn't
had the wit to appreciate and cherish the intelligent and
beautiful woman who had been his wife. Instead, the bastard had cheated on her, caused her pain.

"I minored in accounting," she informed him.

Luke shoved his hands into his pockets. "Think you
could help me out for a few days? I'm willing to pay you.
You can name your price." He sensed her puzzlement, her
inability to comprehend why he would make such an offer.

"You don't have to pay me," she said. "If I help you, I'll
do it as a favor."

"If?"

She smiled at him. "I still haven't heard the magic word."

For the first time in years, Luke felt himself flush, but a
smile jerked at the corners of his mouth. "Please," he said
quietly.

"All right." Her expression sobered. "But what are you going to do after that? What if Joey is too sick to come back?"

"He'll come back."

"You don't know that." She uncurled her legs and touched his hand. "Luke, you're going to have to learn how to do these things yourself. I'll teach you—"

"I know how to do them," he cut in. "I understand about credits and debits. That's not the problem."

"Then what is the problem?" she asked.

"The problem is..." *The problem is that I'm severely dyslexic. My brain doesn't process information the way a normal person's does. I can't tell a B from a D. I can't tell if a word is misspelled. I can barely write a check without making a mistake. And I live in dread of making a fool of myself. Of being told I'm stupid, slow, retarded.* But he couldn't say those words. They stuck in his throat, choking him with their taste. "The problem," he began again, "is that I'm swamped with repair jobs. I got a few days behind when...because of Ronnie and what happened. The telephone's been ringing off the hook with customer complaints."

"I see." She chewed on her lip. "Well, I'll be glad to do what I can. When would you like me to start?"

"Right away," he said in relief. "Tomorrow morning."

She bent her head for a moment, then lifted her chin. Her eyes met his. "I'll do it. I'll straighten out your mess for you, Luke. But I've changed my mind about one thing. My services do come with a price."

He stiffened, wondering if she meant to use Ronnie as a bargaining chip. Instead, she surprised him with a smile—a sweet, mischievous smile that reeled him in hook, line and sinker.

"I expect you to buy me the largest, gooiest, yummiest chocolate ice-cream sundae in the state of Texas. I haven't had one in years and I want the works—hot fudge sauce, whipped cream, chopped pecans, a cherry on top. No stinting allowed."

He studied her face, noting the changes, the new maturity, the laugh lines, the tiny scar near the corner of her left eyebrow. "You've got yourself a deal," he said with a grin.

And if his voice held a trace of bemusement, it was because she had managed to turn him inside out again. Without even trying, she'd taken his feelings, dusted them off and carried them into the sunshine. And there they lay, exposed, ready and eager to cause him more anguish and heartbreak.

Thank you very much, Alicia Brant.

Chapter Six

"I expect you have things you want to do with the rest of your day." Alicia forced a bright note into her voice. "I mean, it's Saturday and you've already put in eight hours at the store."

She dipped a spoon into the rich topping on her chocolate sundae and glanced around the sunny ice-cream parlor. The scorching weather had brought families and teenagers to Craig's Creamery in droves. Voices floated around them, echoing off the pale walls.

"I'm doing something I want to do," Luke responded.

Awareness shimmered through her as their gazes met across the tiny table. He still looked tired, but the five days she'd spent at the store, untangling Joey's mess, had chased away the worst of the shadows beneath those deep-set eyes.

"I mean other things." She made a vague gesture with her spoon.

"Like what?" Brows lifted, he removed the cherry from the top of his sundae and held it out. Alicia accepted it without comment. During the past week, she'd grown accustomed to the fact that, far from forgetting her likes and dislikes, her former fiancé remembered a host of details about her. Obviously her passion for maraschino cherries numbered as one of them.

"Like, see your friends," she answered. "Get back to the life you had before...everything happened." She put the cherry in her mouth, self-consciously noting how he followed the action, how his gaze stayed on her lips as she savored the delicious, sweet taste.

"You trying to get rid of me?" He leaned forward, his bare forearms resting on the table, his broad shoulders straining against the fabric of his red T-shirt.

She swallowed. "No, I'm trying to be nice to you. Don't forget I've seen how hard you work. I just thought you might like to—" *To be with Christina.* "To have an evening off," she finished lamely. She tasted her ice cream and added, "I'll be glad to stay with Ronnie if you want to go out."

Luke scraped a hand over his chin, then shoved some ice cream into his mouth. Alicia's stomach knotted as she waited for his reply.

All week they'd striven to keep their conversation impersonal. Her days at the store had been spent poring over numbers and making phone calls, while Luke did repairs and visited Joey at the hospital. Evenings revolved around Ronnie. Typically, Luke would take Daffy for a walk after Ronnie went to bed, then return and watch television. Alicia preferred to read in the evening, but something about being in Luke's home made it difficult for her to concentrate. At the store, she could close the inner office door and shut him out, but it wasn't that simple when they'd shared an evening like a married couple. It was too domestic, too intimate.

"Okay." The sharp word cut across her thoughts. "Maybe you're right. Maybe I should get out."

"You deserve some relaxation time," she agreed, though a disorienting spurt of disappointment shot through her. Had she wanted him to refuse? To insist they spend the evening together?

"But so do you," he went on, his mouth twisting. "So how about we take Ronnie to the zoo tomorrow?"

"Sounds like fun," she said, greeting the suggestion with relief. Anything to postpone spending a whole day together at his house, trying to behave as though she felt comfortable when she didn't. Sooner or later it would have to happen, but by then maybe she'd be ready for it.

"I'm glad you didn't keep his name," Luke said suddenly.

"What?" Alicia's shoulders stiffened.

"Farrell's name. I'm glad you went back to Brant."

Several seconds passed before she summoned a response. "My parents wouldn't agree with you. They blamed me for the breakup."

He frowned. "Why would they do that? He cheated on you, not the other way around."

She picked up a napkin and dabbed at a blob of melted ice cream on the white metal table. "I suppose," she said, her lashes lowered, "because they didn't know all the sordid details. I didn't allow them to find out."

"Yeah, well, even so. They should have supported you, not blamed you."

A trace of bitterness compressed her mouth. The mere idea ought to have been amusing, but it wasn't. She sighed and said, "My mother thought I should have handled the situation better. Kenny was an awfully charming man. She and Daddy both thought he was the perfect son-in-law."

"So they excused what he did?" Luke asked curtly.

"Not exactly." She shook her head, more to clear it of wayward thoughts than to negate his assumption. "But they thought I must have neglected him. Mother still thinks I threw away something wonderful. She says I should have tried harder." Alicia picked up the cherry stem and rolled it between her thumb and forefinger. "Kenny knew how to push Mother's buttons," she added wryly. "He'd compliment her on her cooking, her hair, her intellect. And he'd listen to Daddy talk about the physics textbook he's co-authoring. Sometimes he'd take them out to expensive restaurants or dinner theaters. They loved that."

"Lousy bastard," Luke muttered.

"True, but not for any of those reasons. He really was a very good son-in-law. He was just a bad husband."

"He didn't hit you, did he?"

"No."

"You're sure?" Luke's eyes bored into hers.

"He never hit me, Luke. He was just a very cold man beneath his warm exterior." She shifted in her chair. "He couldn't talk about his feelings, and he didn't want to hear about mine. He couldn't share. But he had the ability to make people laugh and feel happy and...that's what my parents saw."

"So what about this new guy?" Luke growled. "Is he another happy boy?"

She ignored the derision in his voice. "Nick is nothing like Kenny. He's a nice, warm, likable man." Something in the curl to Luke's mouth prompted her to add in a tone edged with sharpness, "Is it so hard for you to believe?"

"That you could attract a nice guy? Not at all, Alicia. I think you could—" Biting off whatever he'd been about to say, he scowled and went back to eating his sundae.

Alicia did the same, wishing fervently that they had brought Ronnie along. Though she might have expected otherwise, the tension eased when the child was around. However, Ronnie had spent the day at Sharon's house while Alicia accompanied Luke to the store. They'd been on their way home when Luke had surprised her with a stop at the ice-cream parlor.

Luke finished first and glanced at his watch. "We'd better hurry. I promised Sharon we'd pick Ronnie up by five."

Alicia reached for her purse.

"Whoa, I didn't mean to rush you. Go ahead and finish."

"I've had as much as I can eat. Anyway, I don't need the calories." She shook back her hair and carried the remains of their indulgence over to the trash can, recalling how Kenny used to hassle her when she ate a dessert. He'd been the type of person who made cruel remarks about overweight people and had often insinuated that Alicia would join their ranks if she didn't abstain from the sweets she so enjoyed.

"You don't need to worry about calories," Luke remarked as they headed for the door.

"Is that a compliment?" She flipped out the question without thought, then regretted it when she noticed his gaze traveled over her, his gray eyes gleaming like liquid smoke in the afternoon light.

"Yeah, I guess it is." As they made their way to the car, his fingertips grazed the small of her back. "You're not as slim as you used to be, but that's immaterial. You look healthy and you look good. Real good."

He unlocked and opened the door of the Silverado, and she slid into the passenger seat, too flabbergasted to answer. She hated to admit that she was flattered, especially since the statement had been uttered as matter-of-factly as a weather forecast.

An hour later, she stood at her bedroom window, her eyes narrowed against the golden rays of the sinking sun. Below, Luke and Ronnie romped on the backyard grass in a mock tussle over a Frisbee. Wearing frayed cutoffs and a muscle shirt, his black hair tousled and his face relaxed with pleasure, Luke had never seemed more blatantly masculine and appealing. Over the low hum of the air conditioner, she could hear the rich rumble of his laughter through the glass.

Alicia's chest tightened at the sight. How many times had she conjured up a scene like this in her daydreams? How many times had she ached for a man who wanted and appreciated children? A fun-loving man who could cut loose and play, not because he wanted to win friends or impress people, but because he was happy and at peace with himself. And how many times had the man in her dreams had Luke's face?

The irony of the situation nearly choked her. She'd told Luke that Kenny had been unable to share his feelings, yet she might have said the same about Luke. During those long-ago weeks he'd romanced her, he'd never let her beyond a certain point, never said he'd loved her as she had loved him. He'd said he needed her. Wanted to marry her. But he'd never spoken the words she'd needed to hear, never revealed the secrets of his inner self. He'd talked only of his plans for what was to come. Always the future and never the past.

As though he'd had a darker side to hide.

It had seemed like enough when she'd accepted his ring. She'd rationalized the problem, promised herself that as time progressed the rest would follow. She'd been so young, so naive. At barely eighteen, where had she found the courage to break things off? Or had it been courage? Perhaps it had only been cowardice.

She looked down at the man and the boy on the lawn, battling insidious tendrils of self-pity. She felt left out, lonely, like Cinderella gazing into the ashes while her stepsisters left for the ball. Yearning engulfed her, not for compliments or flattery or even sex, but for connection and a family of her own.

And, if the truth were to be acknowledged, for Luke.

"No," she whispered, touching the glass. "I won't let you do this to me again, Luke Garrick. I won't let you put another scar on my soul."

Determination gripped her. She had to do something. She needed to move, to get her blood flowing, and this time she wasn't going to wash floors. In a frenzy of movement, she yanked open a drawer and pulled out a pair of jogging shorts and a tank top. She threw them on, her breathing shallow.

Maybe she was suffering from another round of shock from Caroline's death. Heck, this could even be PMS. Whatever the case, she was going to fight it before it disabled her, before it made her turn tail and run back to Boston, to her world... without Caroline's child.

She knew the precise moment Luke became aware of her presence in the yard, for his body stilled and his smile died. He sat up, brushing grass from his arms, wariness replacing the animation in his face. His eyes settled on her, and his arm draped around Ronnie's shoulders in a gesture that seemed almost proprietary.

Alicia approached them, her face set in a careful, cool mask. "What time did you plan to go out?"

"I don't know. Does it matter?"

"Well, if you're going to be here for a while, I thought I might go jogging."

His brows rose as he took in her running shoes. "Since when do you jog?"

She lifted her chin. "Since my divorce. The heat has slowed me down, but I need to get back to it before I lose all the progress I've made."

He gave her a ghost of a smile. "Go ahead, I'm not in a hurry. Just be sure you don't overdo. And drink a lot of water when you get back." He paused, his expression suggesting he couldn't quite believe she did anything athletic. "I hope you did some warm-ups."

"Of course." Transferring her gaze to Ronnie, Alicia reached down and ruffled her nephew's hair. "In a while, you and I are going to spend some time together. So you be thinking about what you'd like to do, okay?"

"Okay," the child agreed without much enthusiasm.

The lush leaves of a nearby magnolia tree rustled as Alicia turned and started across the yard. The sweet scent of honeysuckle drifted on the warm, humid breeze, bringing with it a resurgence of her melancholy.

She glanced back over her shoulder, but neither Luke nor Ronnie appeared to notice. Instead, they were already wrestling again. Laughing. A man and a boy who looked as though they belonged together.

Alicia's shoulders slumped as she started down the road.

"Don't you have somewhere better to hang out on a Saturday night than this place?" Joey grumbled when Luke walked into his hospital room later that evening. "Go on, pull over a chair. This damned place..."

Luke noticed that Joey's voice had gained strength since the day before, and his bed was in a more upright position. Joey was still plugged into a heart monitor, and various wires and tubes connected him to more machines. The room smelled like all hospital rooms—antiseptic and medicinal, with a whiff of human body mixed in. An open Stephen King novel lay facedown on Joey's great mound of a stomach. No roommate occupied the other bed in the room.

Luke settled into the chair and propped a foot against the bed rail while Joey listed his grievances over the blare of the TV. Luke had heard them all before, but he was willing to listen to them again if it made Joey happy.

In the first quiet interval, Luke leaned forward and looked his partner in the eye. "Listen, Joey, I want to talk to you about the business before Nora gets here." Nora was Joey's wife, and Luke expected her to walk in at any moment.

With a grimace, Joey reached for the remote clipped to the sheet near his hand and lowered the volume of the TV. "Hey, I know I'm a little behind with the books, but don't worry about it. As soon as I get back on my feet—"

"It couldn't wait that long." Wishing there was a way to avoid the issue, Luke kept the accusation from his voice. "You've really been letting things slide and the problems got serious. Anyhow, I wanted to tell you it's been taken care of, in case you were worried. Alicia straightened everything out."

"The pretty little aunt from Boston?" Joey looked both surprised and relieved. "How'd you swing that?"

"She used to keep the books for her husband. I asked her to help me out."

"She know about your problem?" Joey knew better than to say the word dyslexia.

Luke shook his head. "She doesn't need to know. She's going to come into the office a couple of times a week from now on while Ronnie's in school. Until you're back, of course."

"It might be awhile," Joey said glumly. "Nora's been on my back about retiring, and the doc says it's a good idea."

Something cold trailed down Luke's spine. "So what are you going to do?"

Joey snorted. "I'm comin' back. I love that place too damn much to let a bad heart keep me away. I've been lying in this bed for the past few days, thinking about the early days when we first opened up. You were just a smart-assed kid back then, but I knew you were the partner I needed." His voice grew low as he reminisced. "Charlie Lucci recommended you. Good old Charlie called me after you fixed his stereo in your parents' garage. I remember he said, 'Joey, this is the guy you're looking for. He's just a kid, but he's smart. Real smart. He understands circuits the way you and I understand food.'"

Luke smiled. "I remember the day you called me. You wanted me to go into business with you and you didn't even want my money. I thought you were a nut case."

"I know. But you wanted in, I could hear it in your voice. You were smart, though. You checked me out, made me give you a mile-long list of references. I liked that. It showed you had brains. I knew you'd own half the business someday and I was right."

Luke was silent for a moment, recalling how excited he'd been when he'd first shared the news with Alicia. His excitement had dissipated when he'd observed her horrified reaction. She'd wanted him to say no, to turn down the opportunity of a lifetime just because it would take him a thousand miles away. She'd been wrong to expect it of him, just as he'd been wrong to ask her to give up her college education and go with him. The only right decision had been their broken engagement, though it had taken him years to believe it. Even now, sometimes, he wondered...

Joey's sigh brought him back to the present. "Hell, Luke, I know I dropped the ball there for a while. I let you down and I apologize. It won't happen again." Looking rueful, he poked at the book on his stomach. "I gotta stop bringing these things to work, that's all. Never knew a guy could get so hooked on stories. I hadn't read a book since I was in high school, when they fed us a lot of literary crap."

"And what about your health?" Luke asked evenly. "I don't want you back if it's going to kill you."

"Bookkeeping isn't going to kill me. Making a few phone calls isn't going to kill me, either. If another attack is gonna get me, it'll happen no matter where I am. That's what I told Nora."

"That's right, talk about me while I'm not here," said a cheerful, feminine voice. A short, dark-haired woman sailed into the room, a vase of flowers in one hand and a sack of paperbacks in the other. Luke jumped up and relieved her of her parcels while she went over to kiss Joey's cheek.

"Sorry I'm late, hon. The phone rang just as I was on my way out the door." Still smiling, she greeted Luke and urged him not to leave on her account.

"Ah, let him go, Nora," Joey razzed. "He wants to get back to A-lee-ci-a." With a weak grin, the large man kissed the tips of his fingers. "I bet you like having her around the house."

Luke preserved an unruffled facade. "I'm going to work out," he said dryly. "It's been weeks since I had a chance."

But this only fueled Joey's teasing. "Going to pump some iron, eh? Any special reason?"

"Oh, leave him alone," Nora chided. Turning to Luke, she added with a twinkle, "Your visit seems to have worked wonders. This is as feisty as he's been all week."

"Feisty?" Luke arched a brow. "I could think of a better word for it. Take care, Joey. So long, Nora."

Despite the warm glow of this camaraderie, Luke left the hospital with a chill in his gut. His brow furrowed, he climbed into the truck and drove to the fitness center, navigating almost unconsciously as his thoughts drifted. What would he do if Joey did decide to retire? He'd need a new partner, someone he could trust. But who? In order to trust someone, he'd have to know them—and know them well. How many people fit the bill? Not many, and none of them were looking for jobs. Current employees? While all of them were trustworthy, he couldn't think of any who could do Joey's job, let alone buy into the business.

But the problem was even worse than that. He'd have to tell whoever took Joey's place about his dyslexia. The knowledge gnawed at him, gave him a sick feeling in his stomach. After all, he hadn't even been able to tell Alicia.

Alicia.

Somehow every avenue of thought led to her. She lingered in his mind throughout the next hour as he sweated through various weight-training exercises. He couldn't get her image out of his head, couldn't forget how beautiful and sexy she'd looked when she'd returned from jogging—her face all flushed, her blond hair mussed and curling, her skin damp with perspiration. It had been an unexpected turn-on. Even now, it embarrassed him to remember the way his body had reacted. His body had wanted to follow her up to the shower, to join her there, to lift her against the tiled wall and make passionate love to her under the spray. His mind had done so, though his body hadn't moved.

He told himself he was a fool.

Wiping his neck with a towel, he wondered if it was too soon to go home. He glanced around the large glass-enclosed room filled with exercise equipment until he found a clock. Ten-fifteen. He didn't know how long Alicia expected him to stay away, but he was tired and he wanted to go home.

Twenty minutes later, he unlocked the front door of his house and stepped inside. The sight of his noble watchdog sprawled on the cool wood floor greeted him. As he dropped his duffel bag, Daffy lifted her head and yawned, as though to suggest he had disturbed her beauty sleep.

"Well, excuse me," Luke muttered. "What are you going to do if there's a burglar? Lick his hand?"

Daffy sat up and thumped her tail.

"I know, I know. You knew it was me." Luke bent down and scratched her ears, listening for sounds that would tell him where Alicia was. He heard nothing. Good. She must have gone to bed.

Anxious to get a drink, he straightened and headed for the kitchen. It almost seemed like the old days, when he could walk through his house knowing it was as empty as his heart. But it wasn't empty, because a little boy slept upstairs, and the woman who had once possessed his soul was... asleep on his living-room sofa.

Luke froze in the doorway, caught off guard by the unexpected sight. She lay on her side, her hair spilling like spun gold over the blue sofa pillow, her legs curled as if to make room for someone else to sit down. She looked like a princess from a fairy tale—fragile and lovely and utterly, heartstoppingly desirable.

A wet nose nudged his leg, as though Daffy were urging him toward Alicia. Without conscious intent, Luke moved into the room, his footsteps muffled by the thick beige rug.

He went as close as he dared, feasting his eyes on the delicate curve of her cheek, her slightly parted lips, the rise and fall of her beautiful breasts. His thirst was forgotten, replaced by a driving, inexorable hunger.

In all these years, he'd never found anyone else who made him feel like this. Just looking at her made him break into a sweat. He wanted to touch her, to lie down with her, to run his palms over the sweet satin of her skin. Most of all, he wanted to hear her cry his name as he gave her the ultimate pleasure.

But that could never be. She was divorced from one man, involved with another. Even if she was not, there was always the past. And her career. And his "problem." As though to reinforce that thought, he noticed a book lying on the coffee table. Tired as he was, he managed to decipher the title: *The World of Pooh* by A. A. Milne. She and Ronnie must have been reading it.

He picked up the book, got himself a glass of cold water from the kitchen and went upstairs. Behind the closed door of his bedroom, he thumbed through the pages, forcing himself to read a few of the sentences aloud. Frustration filled him as the letters and words jumped around. Half the words looked as if they had been misspelled; he had to stop and stare in an effort to make his brain see them as they really were.

The second time he lost his place, he slammed the book shut. He wanted to hurl it against the wall, rip it to pieces, burn it. Instead, he carried it into Ronnie's room and placed it on the table next to the child's bed. His jaw clenched, Luke gazed down at his nephew's face, illuminated by the soft glow of a Donald Duck night-light.

God, how he loved this kid.

For several seconds, overwhelming defeat weighted him down. Maybe he should let Alicia take the boy back to Boston. After all, what kind of father was he going to make? What kind of dad couldn't read to his kid? What kind of a role model could he be?

Then, stubbornly, he shoved aside his self-doubt. "No way," he whispered to the small, sleeping form on the bed. No way am I giving you up."

"Maybe we'll see a woozle," Alicia teased Ronnie while Luke paid their entrance fee to the Houston Zoological Gardens.

"Aunt Alicia!" Ronnie rolled his eyes. "Woozles aren't real!"

"How about a heffalump?"

"Aunt Alicia!" This time Ronnie laughed. "Heffalumps aren't real, either. That's only in *Winnie-the-Pooh*." To Alicia's amusement, he then proceeded to chant, "Help, help, here comes a heffalump," as they strolled toward the tropical-bird area.

Alicia inhaled a deep breath of sultry summer air and smiled to herself. Thanks to *The World of Pooh*—a gift from her to Ronnie—their evening together had gone better than she'd expected. At first the child had been distant and uninterested in the book, but his natural curiosity had taken over when she'd started to read aloud. By the time Pooh had fallen out of the honey tree, Ronnie had been cuddled next to her on the sofa, enthralled. And for the first time in her life, she'd come close to knowing what it felt like to be a real mother.

Displaying the usual energy of a child, Ronnie scampered ahead, peering at the various species of exotic birds with their bright, colorful plumage. "Hey, Uncle Luke, look at this one!" he exclaimed. "Boy, is it funny! What kind of bird is it?"

Alicia moved along the fence to stand next to her excited nephew, who was staring with widened eyes at a peculiar-looking creature with a huge white-and-gold beak. Luke joined her at the child's side, but to her surprise he did not answer the question.

Alicia scanned the small sign affixed to the wire mesh that contained the bird. "It's a Javan Rhinoceros Hornbill," she told Ronnie. "Well, that makes sense, doesn't it? The beak looks like a rhino's horn." As they moved from cage to cage, Alicia continued to read the identifying signs, but Luke remained curiously silent. She glanced at him with a frown. "Luke, are you all right? The heat isn't bothering you, is it?"

"No," he said, not moving. "Is it bothering you?"

She shook her head. "You just seem kind of quiet, that's all. I thought maybe you weren't feeling well."

"I'm fine." His firm tone invited no further inquiries.

Alicia sighed and looked back at Ronnie, who had begun to flap his arms and screech for the apparent edification of a large king vulture. As the vulture stared back in haughty silence, Luke strode over and lifted Ronnie high into the air.

"He says you're hurting his ears," Luke told the little boy. "He says a majestic bird like him would never make a horrible noise like that."

Ronnie giggled. "How do you know what he's saying?"

"I just know."

"Okay, then what's the rhino bird saying?"

"Let's go see." Shifting Ronnie so he rode piggyback, Luke walked back to the Javan Rhinoceros Hornbill and stood very still. "Can you hear him? He's saying, 'Oh, woe is me, woe is me. This big beak is sooo heavy, you should all feel verrry sorry for me.'"

Ronnie found this hilarious, and from then on insisted that Luke put words into the mouths of every bird or animal they saw. Alicia joined in, and for a while they were laughing so hard that passersby turned and smiled, no doubt thinking them a happy family.

After more than an hour in the August sun, they headed for the gaily colored snack bar located near the Hippo House. They'd viewed everything from lions and giraffes to lemurs and tamarins, and even Ronnie was ready for a break.

Bypassing the tables with their red, orange and green umbrellas, they carried their drinks to a shady spot of grass and sat down. As they sipped their sodas, Alicia decided that the excursion had been good for Luke. Stretched out as he was, with the weight of his torso supported by his elbows and his eyes holding a faraway expression, he looked like a man at peace with the world. Yet as she gazed at him, her own peace of mind fled, ousted by a sharp and tingling awareness.

She made a tiny grimace. This had been happening all week, and there didn't seem to be anything she could do about it. One minute she'd be fine and the next she'd be absurdly conscious of him, not only on the physical level, but on an emotional level, as well. And then she'd relive their kiss, replay every moment of it in her mind. She'd feel his strength and heat all over again, remember the urgent way he'd pressed against her and her own answering excitement.

He must have sensed her looking at him, for he turned and looked at her quite suddenly. "What are you thinking about?"

"You." The honest reply just slipped out, and she wished she'd had time to fabricate an alternative.

"Yeah?" His lips curved. "What about me?"

"I was, uh, just wondering if you had a nice time last night."

"It was all right. I stopped by the hospital first—"

"What do I do with this?" Ronnie interrupted, waving his empty paper cup.

Luke gestured. "There's a trash can over there."

"I'm hungry. Can I have an ice-cream sandwich? Pleeease?"

Luke sat up and removed a dollar bill from his wallet. "Make sure you get a couple of napkins."

Alicia watched Ronnie skip over to the refreshment stand, then turned back to Luke. "How is Joey doing?"

"He's getting better. He was cracking jokes left and right. I stayed with him until Nora got there, then I went to work out at the fitness center."

"How long have you been doing that?" Again, he'd surprised her. She'd been so sure he'd have gone to Christina.

"Three or four years," he admitted with a grin. "Ever since I noticed I was getting flabby."

"You? Flabby?" Alicia had to smile. Idly, she glanced back over at Ronnie . . . or at the empty spot where the child had been. "Where's Ronnie?"

Luke's head jerked around, and in a swift movement he levered himself to his feet. "Jeez, I don't know. He was there a minute ago. Wait, there he is! What the—"

Alicia grabbed her purse and scrambled up as Luke started down the sidewalk in a lithe, steady jog that would easily overtake Ronnie's shorter steps. As she tossed the empty cups in the trash, she heard Luke call Ronnie's name. The child did not turn or respond. In fact, he ran faster in the opposite direction.

Bewildered, she hurried after them, her sandals slapping on the hard pavement. She saw Luke reach out to Ronnie, take him by the shoulders, but to her amazement the little boy resisted Luke's attempt to check him.

"No!" Ronnie yelled. "Let me go! Let me go!"

When she caught up to them, Luke was trying to calm Ronnie down. "Hey, stop fighting me, squirt. Tell me what's wrong. Come on, Ron, it's me, your favorite uncle, remember?''

"Let me go! I've got to go after her!" The child writhed and twisted, his legs kicking like small pistons.

Alicia caught hold of Luke's arm. "Better let him go before someone accuses us of kidnapping him."

Looking grim, Luke stepped back, hands lifted in mock surrender. "Okay, you talk to him then."

"Ronnie, love, who do you want to go after? Who did you see?" Alicia put an arm around the child's shoulders. His whole body was shaking with sobs.

"M-Mommy! I saw Mommy!"

Alicia's breath caught with dismay. "Oh, darling, that's just not possible."

"I did, I did!"

"Where did you see her?" Luke cut in.

"There!" Ronnie pointed, tears streaming from his face. "It *was* her! I know it was!"

Across the top of Ronnie's head, the adults exchanged a dismayed look. "Why don't we go take a look?" Luke suggested gruffly.

Docile now, Ronnie allowed them each to take one of his hands. Alicia's heart twisted with pain. Common sense told her they had to do this, but at the same time it seemed so horribly cruel.

"What color was she wearing?" she asked.

"Red. With white dots. She was with another lady."

Side by side, they walked past the rhinoceros area, alert for any sign of a woman in red. No luck. They passed by the bears, then circled around to the big cats. And then they saw her—a tall, slim blond woman wearing a pair of red shorts and a red-and-white polka-dot blouse. She stood in front of the snow leopard's cage, next to a dark-haired woman with a stroller.

From the back, she looked exactly like Caroline.

At once, Ronnie tried to pull away, but just in that instant the woman turned around. Ronnie froze. "It's not her," he whispered in a numb little voice.

Luke scooped up the child and carried him to a nearby bench. Alicia followed and sat down next to them, stroking Ronnie's back as he clutched his uncle, sobbing softly into Luke's shirt.

"That happens to me, too, darling," Alicia murmured. "Sometimes I see someone who reminds me of your mom or dad. When you lose someone, I guess that's bound to happen. And it hurts so much, doesn't it?"

This time she must have said the right thing, for although Ronnie turned his face away, his hand crept out and settled on her shoulder. Alicia took the little hand and held it between both of hers. She and Ronnie had taken a small step forward.

Chapter Seven

Ronnie's bedroom door slammed so hard the walls of the house seemed to shudder.

Anxiety spurted through Alicia as she selected a dress to wear to Brown Elementary's first open house. Things had been going so well since that day at the zoo. Ronnie had seemed almost happy during most of the past two weeks.

But a few days ago that had changed, and today was the worst day of all. From the moment he'd come home from school, Ronnie had been difficult. He'd sulked, refused to talk, played with his dinner and even been mean to poor Daffy.

A large crash followed by a rapid succession of thuds indicated that the tantrum was far from over. Alicia grimaced, dismay feathering down her spine. Something had to be done; it sounded as if Ronnie was tearing his room apart.

Thrusting her arms into the sleeves, she made a barefoot dash for Ronnie's room, one hand clutching the front of the dress together as she sped down the hall. At the same time, the bathroom door jerked open and Luke emerged. Momentum propelled her straight into him, his superior size and weight forming a wall of solid muscle that stopped her short.

Strong hands shot out to grip and steady her. Shirtless, with stray dabs of shaving cream clinging to his face, Luke stared first at her face, then down at the scantily clad length of her body. Transfixed, she stared back, blushing scarlet as his eyes raked over her, his pupils dilating with a recognizable flare of male lust. Somehow she'd lost her grip on the edges of the dress, which now hung open as though she'd intended to display herself for him. No slip shielded her. She felt as naked and vulnerable as she had in the bikini—more naked, in fact, for both her bra and panties were sheer, with only the tiniest swirls of white silk to protect her modesty. Worse, her paralyzed limbs couldn't seem to move, so that the moment stretched into an agonizing eternity.

Another loud crash shattered the spell.

Releasing her, Luke strode down the hall and jiggled the knob on Ronnie's door while Alicia hurriedly fastened the buttons on her dress. "Hey, Ron, let me in. I want to talk to you."

"No," said a sullen, childish voice.

"Why not?"

"I *told* you I'm not going."

Luke tried the knob again. "Come on, we want to talk to your teacher. See the stuff you've been working on."

Alicia came up behind Luke, hoping the flush on her face had faded. "Ronnie, please let us in," she pleaded. "Darling, we know you're upset about something. We're upset, too—even Daffy," she added as the dog ambled over.

"Daffy wants you to open the door. She's unhappy because she knows you're unhappy."

Silence answered her, then reluctant footsteps dragged across the floor. The door opened, and Ronnie stood looking up at them, his face set in a bleak expression. "I don't want Daffy to be sad."

"Then tell Daffy what's wrong," Alicia said in a gentle voice.

Ronnie shuffled over to the collie, who sat patiently, ears pricked, soft eyes puzzled. With a hiccup, he dropped down onto his knees and wound his arms around the animal's neck. "Oh, Daffy, please don't be sad. I'm sorry I made you sad." For long seconds Ronnie said nothing more, then a whispered disclosure tumbled out. "Everybody else's mom and dad are going to be there. But mine won't because they're dead."

The words should not have stunned Alicia the way they did. She should have guessed the problem. Better yet, she should have anticipated it. Berating herself, she looked helplessly at the top of Ronnie's bent head, wishing that something in her limited experience with children had prepared her to deal with this.

Luke's expression told her he hadn't expected it, either. She saw him close and open his eyes; then he went down on the floor and gathered the little boy onto his lap.

"Well, Ron," he said, his voice low and matter-of-fact, "I don't have any words to say that can set things right. I wish I did. But I can't bring your mom or dad back. They're gone from this life, Ronnie. But I can promise you that wherever they are, they still love you and they're still watching over you. And they expect me and your aunt Alicia to do our best for you." He cleared his throat. "That's what we're trying to do. We want you to take us to your open house tonight because we're proud of you and because we love you."

"Very much," Alicia added, dropping down on her knees. She smoothed Ronnie's soft blond hair, filled with tenderness for her sister's child.

Ronnie lifted his face. "I love *you*, Uncle Luke," he said dolefully. "But I don't love Aunt Alicia, and I don't want to live with her."

Alicia sucked in a breath. The brutal words, uttered with such childlike candor, cut into her like a whip. "Excuse me," she said after a shocked instant. "I have to finish getting dressed."

Unable to bring herself to look at Luke, she climbed to her feet and returned to her bedroom. Hands shaking, she leaned against the closed door and pressed her palms to her cheeks.

Since their outing at the zoo, she believed she had breached Ronnie's defensive wall. Except for those first few days at Luke's store, she'd been here for him every day after school. She'd read to him, talked to him, taken him places. She'd demonstrated her growing love for him in every way she knew how. He had seemed to respond.

Fraught with a sense of failure, Alicia sat on the bed and strapped on her sandals. All her life she had tried to please, to be perfect, but it seemed she was never quite good enough. She'd failed as a daughter, as a fiancée and as a wife. And now it seemed she'd failed again, this time as a mother figure. Her lips twisted. She might as well throw in the towel and go back to Boston. She wasn't wanted here.

Yet even as she went to the dresser and picked up her hairbrush, her fighting instinct took over. She couldn't give up. Of course the child didn't love her yet. Love didn't happen overnight, or even in three short weeks. And one couldn't expect a six-year-old to be tactful.

A light tap intruded upon these thoughts.

"Who is it?" Alicia set down the brush.

"Ronnie." The child's voice was barely audible through the closed door.

She walked over and opened it. "Yes?"

"I—I'm sorry," he quavered, his face pale and resolute. As though he had something else to say, his lips moved, but no sound came out. Instead, he spun around and fled down the stairs.

While Alicia watched him retreat, Luke emerged from his room, one hand shoving his wallet into his back pocket while the other hand jingled his car keys. When he saw her, he walked over to her. Dressed in a pair of gray slacks and a plaid sport shirt, his raven black hair curling and damp from his shower, he looked so sinfully attractive her heart somersaulted. "Did he apologize?" he asked, his voice a bit gruff.

She nodded and bit her lip.

"Good." Luke seemed to hesitate, then he brushed a hand down her arm. "I know he hurt you. I could see it in your face. I'm sorry."

Alicia shrugged. "I'll get over it. Anyway, he's the one who's hurting. His needs come first, remember?"

"But he's got to learn he can't say things like that."

"Even if he means it?"

"He didn't mean it. He's become real fond of you."

"Fond isn't the same as love," she noted wryly.

Luke lifted her chin with his fingers. "No," he agreed, his eyes holding hers. "But it's a first step, isn't it?"

Children and parents swarmed like ants along the crowded halls of Brown Elementary. Voices mingled in a babble of enthusiasm, but Luke hardly noticed the noise as he strode along the corridor. Like a film rolling past, he kept getting flashes of the scene that had taken place earlier—Alicia in that incredibly sexy lingerie, Alicia touching Ronnie's hair, Alicia flinching from the child's unwitting cruelty.

She walked silently beside him, her head held high and her face composed. He couldn't help admiring how lovely and fresh she looked, how her pretty, floral dress conformed to her curves and accentuated her femininity. But though her face was calm, her expression had a shuttered quality that disturbed him.

When they entered Ronnie's classroom, she seemed to collect herself and come to life. She smiled and admired Ronnie's artwork and the animal mobile hanging over his desk. She made polite conversation with the mother of the little boy who sat next to Ronnie. But Luke knew it was all an act. She was still hurting and hurting bad. And it bothered him.

A lot.

When Alicia wandered over to a group of pictures mounted on the wall, Luke trailed after her, intending to say something—anything—that would put a real smile on her face. Then he noticed what had drawn her attention—a photograph of a smiling, mustached chef holding a large plate of insects—and knew he had found an avenue.

Moving up behind her, he tried to unscramble the large colored letters titling the exhibit. *Many.* That word he could manage, even though his recalcitrant brain put the "Y" at the front. The next word stopped him. Leopep? Staying calm, he struggled to look at the individual letters, to see them in the order that they really were, but they still fought him.

Then a voice from across the room clued him in. "Many People in the World Eat These For Lunch," a dad with a loud, deep voice read. Luke breathed a sigh of relief and transferred his attention back to Alicia.

"Looks yummy," he murmured, gazing at a picture of some sort of giant beetle held between someone's teeth.

Alicia pointed to one of the captions. "They're good for you and tasty too. An important food source for human-kind." She shook her head, her voice carrying a stunned note. "I have never been so revolted in my entire life."

"Come on, I bet they're great with a little salt. Betcha can't eat just one."

Alicia gave a visible shudder. "I'd rather die than eat one of those things."

Resisting an urge to fit his hands over the curves of her hips, Luke leaned closer, his lips close to her ear. "I bet they wiggle when you bite into them," he murmured. "Then there's that first, satisfying crunch—"

"Luke!" Swinging around with a laugh, she gave him a light slap on the arm. "Ugh! You know, after seeing this I may have second thoughts about this school district."

"Makes you kinda wonder what's on the school menu," he agreed. He grinned, wishing it could always be this easy. A few jokes, a little teasing and, bingo, no more pain, no more sleepless nights, no more gut-gnawing tension be-tween them.

Still smiling, she said, "We'd better get in line to talk to Mrs. Glover. Where's Ronnie?"

Luke angled his head toward the back of the room. "He's busy trying to impress some cute little brunette."

"Oh, it's Tara. I thought they didn't like each other."

They watched the two youngsters interacting. Ronnie had stuck the eraser end of two pencils into his nostrils and was rolling up his eyes to look like a monster from a grade-B horror flick. His audience seemed mesmerized, her face full of reluctant fascination.

Amused, Luke folded his arms over his chest. "Now there's a technique I never tried. What do you think, Alicia? Would that work for you?"

"It would certainly be impressive, but why waste it on me?"

Her tone held humor, but as he glanced down into her gorgeous eyes, he nearly gave her an honest answer. *Because in ten years I've never stopped thinking of you. Because no matter how hard I try, I can't get you out of my head....* "Beats me," he said instead, deliberately injecting a note of dryness into his voice. "I guess it would be pretty pointless, wouldn't it?"

"Yes, it would." Her agreement came quickly, he noticed.

When they went to stand in line, Luke paid no attention to the tall, slim woman in front of them until she turned and gave him a dazzling smile. He gave her a brief, discouraging nod. Tara's mother. He remembered her from the first day of school.

"Hello," the woman oozed with a flutter of eyelashes. "You're Ronnie's uncle, aren't you? Tara has told us so much about poor Ronnie. Such a dreadful tragedy. Do let me offer my condolences."

"Thanks," he said politely.

"By the way, I'm Marielle Howard." Flashing a perfect set of bleached teeth, Marielle extended a hand flaunting several diamond rings.

Luke shook hands with her, responded with his own name and introduced her to Alicia, all the while keeping his face arranged in a disinterested expression.

"So nice to meet you," Marielle cooed to Alicia. At once, her heavily made-up eyes returned to Luke, as though to give another woman even a second of her time was far too great an imposition.

Despite Alicia's presence at his side, Tara's mother flirted outrageously with him until it was her turn to talk to Mrs. Glover. When at last the woman was occupied with the teacher, Luke gave Alicia a sideways look. To his secret relief, her eyes were twinkling.

"And you didn't even need pencils," she whispered. "Now I *am* impressed."

"Very funny," he muttered, his lips twitching.

She moved closer. "Well, it is, Luke. Have you ever considered a career in modeling? I bet you could be on the covers of romance novels like what's-his-name with the long hair."

He pretended to glare at her. "Are you suggesting I have a pretty face?"

"Pretty isn't quite the word I'd use," she assured him. "I was thinking more along the lines of an eye patch and cutlass."

Beguiled by her teasing smile, his brain cells started doing back flips. This was the old Alicia, the one he'd fallen in love with, the one whose sense of humor had woven its delicate magic upon his senses. He had always loved it when she directed her mischievousness at him, given him the laughter and sunlight he needed so desperately. Unfortunately, he found he loved it just as much now, a decade later, when a mere tantalizing taste of it was all he was likely to get.

"Mr. Garrick." Mrs. Glover's imperious voice roused him, and he realized Marielle had moved on. "And Miss—"

"Brant," Alicia reminded the teacher. "It's nice to see you again, Mrs. Glover."

They murmured a few pleasantries, then Mrs. Glover got down to business. "Quite frankly," she said, "I'm glad you both came tonight. If you hadn't, I would have suggested a meeting."

"Is something wrong?" Alicia asked.

Mrs. Glover sighed. "First, I ought to say that Ronnie is extremely bright. In fact—" she lowered her voice "—he's probably my brightest student."

Luke hadn't been aware of his tension until she said these words. Even though he knew Ronnie wasn't dyslexic, a part of him had unconsciously been braced for the worst. He'd been terrified she was going to say that Ronnie was slow, that he couldn't sequence letters or numbers, that he had difficulty rhyming words. The fear was reflexive, a knee-jerk reaction left over from his childhood encounters with teachers.

"However," Mrs. Glover went on, "his behavior is another story. Sometimes he's quiet and withdrawn, but at other times he's unruly. He's been especially uncooperative and disruptive this week. I don't suppose he told you what happened today?"

Luke and Alicia shook their heads in unison.

"He broke a little girl's pencil box. I saw him do it, and I know he did it on purpose."

Alicia spoke first. "Mrs. Glover, this is a very difficult time for Ronnie."

"I know that, and that's why I've tried to make allowances."

"We'll replace the pencil box. But I think I know why he's been so naughty." With a quick glance at Luke, Alicia explained how getting ready for the open house had reminded Ronnie of his loss.

The teacher nodded. "Well, I do understand. And maybe things will improve after tonight. I hope so. Have you two come to a decision about where the child will live?"

Luke could feel Alicia's eyes on his face, and knew she was leaving this one for him to answer. "No," he said. "That's still up in the air."

"Then may I suggest you do so? Ronnie needs stability right now. This uncertainty can only be contributing to his distress. The sooner Ronnie feels settled, the sooner he'll start to adjust."

"I'm sure you're right," Alicia agreed. "And believe me, Mrs. Glover, we both want whatever is best for Ronnie." Her eyes met Luke's for a brief, meaningful instant.

She avoided his gaze as they thanked the teacher for her time, shook hands and went to collect Ronnie from the back of the room. Tara had left, but three other little girls had taken her place.

Luke gave Ronnie a light cuff on the arm. "Come on, Casanova. Let's go."

They made their way through the crowded halls past the library, where Sharon Redford was conducting the annual school book fair. Luke scanned the cattle drive thronging the area, intending to walk on by, but Alicia stopped him with a tug on his arm. "I'd like to buy Ronnie some books. Sharon told me a good percentage of the money goes to benefit the school."

As she guided Ronnie toward the melee, Luke leaned against the wall and watched the sway of her rounded hips. Try as he might, he couldn't stop himself; something about the woman seemed to be linked directly to his pulse. Worse, every time he looked at her, his imagination went wild. He kept remembering their kiss, the smothering, erotic pleasure of her bikini-clad body pressed against his.

Damn.

He shut down that line of thought. A simple case of lust would have been easier to deal with than this unrelenting, bone-deep awareness that had taken up residence in every pore and fiber of his being. Not a minute passed but that he wanted her—in his bed, in his life, at his side. Under him.

But want and need weren't the same thing, he told himself sternly. He didn't *need* her. And he wasn't in love with her.

Or was he?

The idea was so terrifying that again he deliberately shifted his thoughts, this time to Mrs. Glover's advice. He wondered if it might have swayed Alicia to yield her claim to Ronnie. He doubted it. Alicia could be damned stubborn when she decided to be. He knew she still wanted to take Ronnie back to Boston, just as he wanted to keep the child here. They were as much at an impasse as they had been the day she arrived.

Luke's jaw tautened with the knowledge that the impasse couldn't be allowed to continue. As Mrs. Glover had pointed out, they weren't being fair to Ronnie.

One of them was going to have to lose out.

An hour later, Alicia set her drink on a coaster and sat down at her favorite end of the sofa. It had become her own special place in the room, just as the corner behind the overstuffed chair was Daffy's spot. They were both creatures of habit, she reflected, drawn to the security and safety of the familiar.

Luke, on the other hand, was never content to stake out a single place as his own. More often than not, he prowled restlessly, though tonight he had picked a chair across the room in which to plant his long body. Legs extended, he slouched back and looked at her, his face tight and brooding.

Alicia fidgeted under his hooded scrutiny. "Ronnie's asleep," she remarked. "Poor little thing. Between the open house and his emotions, he's exhausted."

Luke said nothing.

Silence stretched between them like a drawn bow. The very air vibrated with mysterious potency.

Avoiding his eyes, she reached for the pile of books she had bought at the book fair. Satisfied with her purchases, she thumbed through them—thirteen paperbacks and two hardcovers, most of them selected by Ronnie. She'd chosen a couple of them herself, one in particular since it featured a story about a child who had beaten leukemia. She'd thought it might help Ronnie to understand that bad things happened to other children and that tragedies could be survived.

Finally unable to bear it any longer, she chanced a peep in Luke's direction. As far as she could tell, he hadn't moved a muscle. She tried to smile even as the tension clawed at her stomach. "Is something the matter? Do I have a smudge on my nose or..."

Her sentence died as he stood up. It had been so easy to joke with him in Ronnie's classroom, but in the confines of his home she found it almost impossible. A wall of constraint stood between them, high and insurmountable, clogging her throat as she tried to come up with a humorous response.

Silent and quick, he came across the rug toward her. His hands reached out, and she gave a small gasp as he pulled her to her feet.

"Luke! What on earth—"

His mouth cut off the rest of her question, taking fierce possession of hers without hesitation or apology. His kiss was hard, demanding, his face rigid with a desire so primitive it sparked an instant conflagration in her blood.

When she tried to pull away, his arms tightened. "Kiss me," he muttered. "Kiss me the way you did last time. Come on, Alicia...please."

This was the danger she'd sensed all along. He was so virile, so sexy, so utterly masculine that a part of her wanted to do as he asked. That part of her wanted to damn the consequences, to thread her fingers through his black hair, to open to him and urge him on. At the same time, another more prudent part of her hung back, appalled and afraid of making an incalculable mistake.

"Why, Luke?" Her breathing ragged, she arched away from him, needing words, needing to understand what was happening between them.

"Because I want you. I want to make love to you so much, it's driving me out of my mind."

As if to prove this, his fingers dug into her bottom, forcing their lower bodies together. She could feel his arousal, rock hard and ready. And oh, how she wanted to give in to him. One word of love, one hint of forever...right now that was all it would take for her to yield.

"You wanted me ten years ago, too," she whispered, giving him an opening, a chance to say something, anything, that would make it all right.

"I want you more now. A thousand times more. I've tried so hard to resist you but I can't." His voice was thick, slurred as though he were drunk. "I've wanted you since the day you arrived. More than you can know. Please, sweetheart, let me show you how much."

Her hope shriveled. She felt silly and naive. She should have known he wouldn't say it. Sex was all he wanted from her, and while she wanted it, too—maybe even more than he did—she also knew she could never be content with that and nothing more.

"Well, we can't always have what we want," she replied, too unhappy to care that she sounded sanctimonious.

"Tell me about it," he grated. "My whole life has been one big compromise."

"Are you expecting me to go to bed with you out of pity?"

"Hell, no. I want you to do it because you want me as much as I want you." Sliding a hand between them, he cupped her breast, his thumb sliding over its peak in a provocative, back-and-forth motion. "You see?" he whispered. "You want me, too. You want me so bad you're shaking. So am I. I'm hot and you're hot. Why not be honest and admit it?"

His explicitness shocked and aroused her in a way she would not have thought possible. Kenny had never said such things; he had been quick and silent and emotionless in bed. Kenny had never held her like this, his body undulating against hers, stimulating her even as he stimulated himself. Kenny had never gazed at her as though he wanted to devour her, body and soul.

She swallowed hard. "Just because I have normal female responses doesn't mean I'm going to sleep with you. You know we have no future together."

"So?" His eyes smoldered. "We have the present. We're living in the same house, damn it. We might as well take advantage of it."

"And what about Ronnie?" she asked, a thin strand of hysteria breaking into her voice. "What kind of example does this set? We're supposed to be role models, not irresponsible sex maniacs. Maybe your other women are willing to behave like this, but—"

She fell back on the sofa as he abruptly released her. He stared down at her, dark and formidable in his icy displeasure. "What other women are you referring to?" he demanded.

She glared up at him. "Nancy, for one."

"Nancy is not my woman." He paused, breathing heavily, a mixture of contrition and guilt flashing across his face. "I know I let you think she was," he conceded in a milder tone. "I thought it would be safer. Smarter. But I was wrong."

"Oh, really? And you're saying there's no one else?" Alicia held her breath, her heart thumping a painful staccato against her ribs. Like a conqueror, he stood over her, his stance reminding her that he was master here, that his strength was superior, that he called the shots.

"That's what I'm saying. Anyway, shouldn't that be my line? Or have you forgotten good old Nick?"

"I don't sleep with him!"

She flushed the moment the words left her mouth, but to her surprise, Luke's eyes seemed to soften. "I shouldn't have said that, Alicia. I'm sorry." He paused, looking intent. "You know, I'm beginning to think you haven't changed at all."

"I don't take sex casually, if that's what you mean."

For a long moment he gazed at her, his mouth curved in a rueful line. "You might not believe this, but neither do I." With those words, he turned away.

The urge to call him back was powerful, so powerful it nearly got the better of her. But he had already crossed the room, snapped his fingers at Daffy and turned the corner into the kitchen. Paralyzed with indecision, Alicia watched the collie crawl out from her corner, stretch and amble off after her master. She listened to the dog's toenails clicking across the kitchen tile, heard the back door open and close. Then there was silence, a silence so complete it enshrouded her.

With a tiny sob, Alicia lowered her head to her hands. Refusing him *had* been the right thing to do. She knew it in her heart.

So why, oh why, did it feel so terribly wrong?

Chapter Eight

"Thanks so much for the lift home. That car of mine is about as reliable as my horoscope." Sharon Redford kicked off her heels and popped open the can of diet soda she'd taken from her refrigerator. "And thank God it's Friday."

Alicia sipped her own soda and raised an eyebrow as Ronnie and Brian hurtled through the kitchen and up the stairs to the second-floor game room. "They're full of energy, aren't they?"

"If I only had half of it. I'm still worn out from last night's book fair. Make yourself at home while I get out of this dress. I'm dying to get in the pool. You brought your suit, I hope."

"Sure did. I'll meet you out there."

As Sharon hurried off, Alicia retrieved her swim wear from the car and changed her clothes in the bathroom. She and Ronnie had become frequent visitors at the Redford home after school when Jim and Luke were at work. Usu-

DOUBLE YOUR ACTION PLAY...

"ROLL A DOUBLE"

Peel off label
place inside

CLAIM 4 BOOKS
<u>PLUS</u> A FREE
GIFT

ABSOLUTELY FREE!

SEE INSIDE..

NO RISK, NO OBLIGATION TO BUY...NOW OR EVER!

GUARANTEED

PLAY "ROLL A DOUBLE" AND GET FIVE FREE GIFTS!

HERE'S HOW TO PLAY:

1. Peel off label from front cover. Place it in space provided at right. With a coin, carefully scratch off the silver dice. Then check the claim chart to see what we have for you - FREE BOOKS and a gift - ALL YOURS! ALL FREE!

2. Send back this card and you'll receive specially selected Silhouette Special Edition romances. These books have a cover price of £2.20 each, but they are yours to keep absolutely free

3. There's no catch. You're under no obligation to buy anything. We charge nothing for your first shipment. And you don't have to make any minimum number of purchases - not even one!

4. The fact is thousands of readers enjoy receiving books by mail from the Reader Service, at least a month before they're available in the shops. They like the convenience of home delivery, and there is no extra charge for postage and packing

5. We hope that after receiving your free books you'll want to remain a subscriber. But the choice is yours - to continue or cancel, anytime at all! So why not take us up on our invitation with no risk of any kind. You'll be glad you did!

NOT ACTUAL SIZE

You'll look a million dollars when you wear this lovely necklace! Its cobra-link chain is a generous 18" long, and the multi-faceted Austrian crystal sparkles like a diamond!

"ROLL A DOUBLE!"

PLACE LABEL HERE

SCRATCH HERE

SEE CLAIM CHART BELOW

11S5SE

YES! I have placed my label from the front cover into the space provided above and scratched off the silver dice. Please rush me the free books and gift for which I qualify. I understand that I am under no obligation to purchase any books, as explained on the back and on the opposite page. I am over 18 years of age.

Ms / Mrs / Miss / Mr _____

Address _____

_____

_____ Postcode _____

CLAIM CHART

		4 FREE BOOKS PLUS FREE CRYSTAL PENDANT NECKLACE
		3 FREE BOOKS
		2 FREE BOOKS

CLAIM NO. 37-829

Harlequin Mills & Boon
FREEPOST
P.O. Box 70
Croydon
Surrey
CR9 9EL

NO
STAMP
NEEDED

ally the two boys chose to swim, but today they'd elected to watch TV instead.

Outside, she settled on the pool edge and applied sunscreen to her exposed areas, her bare legs dangling in the water. For once, she and Sharon would have the whole pool to themselves and enjoy some peace and quiet without splashing and noise. If only some of that peace could find its way into her soul.

"This is the way to live, eh?" Sharon's voice preceded her as she stepped out onto the patio. She plopped down next to Alicia with a blissful sigh. "So how's it going with you and the big guy?"

Alicia passed over the sunscreen, a little surprised by the question. "Oh, all right, I guess."

"Uh-huh. So what's that blush mean? Things heating up between you?"

"No. Not really. It's just that he…asked me to go to bed with him." Confidences had never come easily to Alicia, but with Sharon they just seemed to slip out. She'd even told her new friend about Kenny and Tracy.

"And you didn't," Sharon surmised.

"No."

Sharon's gaze slid sideways. "I bet you were tempted."

"More than you can guess." Alicia studied her toes. "But it would only complicate things. My life is complicated enough without that."

"Did he understand?"

"I'm not sure." Alicia wrinkled her brow, trying to remember exactly what had been said. "Maybe not."

Sharon slid into the water, her hands on the rim of the pool while her legs made slow, lazy kicks. After awhile, she said, "By complicated, do you mean this business with Ronnie?"

Alicia hesitated. Why was it such a difficult question to answer? This was Sharon, for pete's sake, not her mother. Talking would probably be therapeutic.

"It's more than that," she replied. "In a way I guess I'm still getting over my divorce. And my job at Crandon is competitive and stressful. I didn't realize how much I needed a break until I'd been here a few days. I hadn't taken any vacation days in four years."

"Good grief, why not?"

Alicia scooped up a handful of water and splashed it onto her thighs. "I've always wanted to be successful, but after I found out about Kenny's affair, I started to drive myself even more. I suppose it's some sort of defense mechanism left over from childhood." Her lips curved with remembered frustration. "When I was growing up, my parents expected me to excel. I always felt that if I wanted their love, I had to earn it. So I got straight A's and won spelling bees. Now that I'm older, they expect me to have a successful career like Caroline did. So that's what I'm doing."

Sharon's legs stilled, her brown eyes clouded with sympathy. "But since you understand why you do it, why don't you give yourself a break?"

Alicia sighed. "I try, but now it's a habit. Just lately, my career seems to be the only part of my life that's successful. My ego needs that to compensate for the failures."

"And what about Luke? Is that how you see him? As one of your failures?"

Alicia gave a wry smile. "Well, you could hardly call what we had a success. I'm afraid to try again. I think I must have a low tolerance for pain right now. Anyway, he and I...well, we just don't click anymore."

"I'm not so sure of that," Sharon said dryly. "I've seen you two together. There's something there, a connection, a rightness. If you want my opinion, I'd say you've both got it bad for each other.''

Alicia shook her head. "Not a rightness. A sizzle, maybe. Our hormones connect. Not our souls.''

"Jim and I started out with a sizzle. It jump-started straight into love.'' Sharon looked at her. "And what about Ronnie? Caring for him will be tough, especially if your job is so demanding.''

The words were blunt, but kindly meant, and should not have sent a cold frisson down Alicia's spine. "I can manage. I've arranged for a good friend to take care of him after school. She lives close by, two condos over from me. Besides, I've already redecorated. Ronnie's room is ready and waiting.''

"Oh, Alicia.'' Sharon reached over to squeeze her hand. "What can I do to help?''

"Nothing. Luke and I have to reach a decision, and I want that decision to be fair. I don't want my job to be made into an issue. After all, he works, too.''

"Have you considered,'' Sharon asked carefully, "what it would do to Luke if you took Ronnie away from him?''

Alicia lowered her head. "I can't help it. I love Ronnie, too. He's all I have left of my sister. Besides—'' she faltered a little ''—I've always wanted children. The irony is that I married a man who despised them. If ever a man was careful about birth control, it was Kenny.'' Her mouth twisted as she eased down into the water. "Let's not talk about this anymore, okay?''

"All right.''

By tacit consent, they floated and paddled for a while without speaking. Alicia closed her eyes, feeling the soothing, sensual caress of warm liquid against her flesh. It made her think of Luke, of his hard, branding kiss and the look in his eyes when he'd said that he wanted her.

The memory had kept her awake half the night. Eventually she'd climbed out of bed at three in the morning and gone downstairs for a drink. In the end, she'd sat on the sofa in the living room and read all the books she'd bought for Ronnie at the book fair.

Something nudged at her mind. "Sharon."

"Yes?" Sharon glanced over at her.

Alicia lifted a hand, sending a spray of droplets dancing across the water's surface. "Do you remember that book I bought? The one about the child who had leukemia?"

"Yes, of course. We sold sixteen copies."

"Did you realize that the author was the child himself?"

Sharon nodded. "That's what makes it so successful. Children relate well to books written by other children."

"How would a child go about doing something like that? I mean, what if Ronnie were to write a book?"

Sharon narrowed her eyes. "I don't know about getting it published, but there are two or three contests he could enter."

"That's good enough. Do you think you could get me some information about those contests?"

"I think so..." Sharon's head cocked as if something had caught her attention. "Goodness, is that Jim's car I hear?" She sounded as breathless as a girl on the way to her first prom. The back door opened just as Sharon scrambled out of the pool. She gave a little shriek as her husband whipped a bouquet of red roses from behind his back. "Jimmy, you remembered!"

Feeling like a fifth wheel, Alicia climbed out of the pool while Jim Redford laughed and bear-hugged his wife. "Of course I remembered, sweet cheeks. How could I not?"

"Is it your anniversary?" Alicia inquired.

"Not our wedding anniversary," Sharon said coyly.

Jim winked. "Something just as memorable. It was six years ago today that I first set eyes on this gorgeous creature."

"Blind date," Sharon added. "And *he* almost didn't show!"

Alicia smiled and offered congratulations. She truly was glad for the Redfords, but witnessing their joy also reinforced her own feelings of loneliness. She and Kenny had never had that kind of closeness. She and Nick didn't have it, either.

Then the truth hit her.

More than anything in the world, she wanted to share such a bond with Luke.

Yes, she had gone and done the unthinkable. She had fallen head over heels, mind-mushingly in love with him all over again. Scratch that. Since she was being honest, she might as well admit that she had never been *out* of love with him. She had simply fallen further, harder and deeper.

And she didn't need a crystal ball to tell her that it was going to hurt a heck of a lot more the second time around.

Luke came home that night to be enveloped by the mouth-watering smell of apple pie and roast chicken. The wonderful aromas drew him down the hall to the kitchen, where a sight so domestic, so welcoming, greeted his eyes that he had to blink twice. Alicia stood at the sink, paring potatoes, her sweet tush swaying in time to an oldies tune on the radio. Ronnie sat at the table, drawing a picture. And Daffy sprawled like a sultana in the middle of everything.

Still and quiet in the doorway, Luke drank in the scene. He ought to be used to it by now, but he wasn't. Until three weeks ago, he'd never known how good it felt to walk into his house and find a woman and child waiting for him. He'd never known the luxury of having his dinner waiting for him after a long, stressful day. Heaven couldn't be any better than this.

He had to remind himself that it was an illusion, that the woman wasn't his, that the bubble could burst. *Would* burst, he reflected. This wasn't permanent. He needed to remember that Alicia the Career Woman must be bored to death between the tedium of household chores and bookkeeping duties. Still, he might as well enjoy it while it lasted.

Holding that thought, he walked over and set his hands on her soft, slender shoulders. "Hi, I'm home."

"Eek!" Jumping as though he'd stuck her with a pin, she spun around so fast the blade of her knife barely missed his arm. "Luke! For goodness sake, I didn't hear you come in."

"Sorry," he said, his smile rueful. "I guess I really will have to wear a bell, if only for my own protection."

He removed the knife from her hand and set it on the counter, observing the way her expression changed, grew guarded. She probably hadn't forgiven him for the way he'd come on to her. He couldn't blame her if she hadn't. Still, the way she looked right now, with her hair tousled and her eyes all wide and vulnerable, made him feel just as lustful and possessive as he had last night. Maybe more.

Quelling his politically incorrect inclinations, he glanced over at Ronnie. "Hey, squirt. Whatcha drawing?"

"Power Rangers," Ronnie said without looking up.

As Luke removed a bottle of dinner wine from the cupboard, Alicia went back to peeling potatoes. "I fired your cleaning woman today," she said.

Luke nearly dropped the bottle. "Why did you do that?" he asked, staring at her back.

"She doesn't do a good job. You're wasting your money on her."

Lifting an eyebrow, he poured wine into two glasses and set one at Alicia's elbow. "Carmella's all right. At least she's honest."

"Everything she does, I can do better. In half the time."

"That's nice to know, but you're a bit overqualified for the job, aren't you? You're not exactly Susie Home-maker."

To his surprise, Alicia looked offended. "I'm perfectly capable of doing housework. More capable than Carmella, that's for sure. Last time she was here, it took *five* hours for the kitchen floor to dry and it wasn't even clean. And she used steel wool on the kitchen counter. Besides," she added, setting the pot of potatoes onto the stove, "she kicked Daffy."

Luke glanced at Daffy, whose reproachful gaze seemed to confirm this. "Then you were right to fire her." He braced a hip against the edge of the counter. "And I didn't say you weren't capable. I just thought you'd be bored."

"Actually I don't mind it at all."

"Aren't you forgetting something kind of important?"

"What?" Her lashes lifted.

"You'll be leaving soon," he said, more harshly than he intended. "And then I'll have nobody—" he paused for the tiniest instant "—to clean my house."

Something flickered in her eyes, but before he could an-alyze it, the telephone rang. As luck would have it, the caller was good old Nick, the white-collar wuss. With an inward snarl, Luke handed the receiver to Alicia, who took it around the corner into the living room.

Luke carried his wine to the table and sat down next to Ronnie. "So what's new, pal?" he asked, straining to hear what Alicia was saying.

"Nothin'."

"Nothing, huh? How was school?"

"Okay."

"What did you do?"

"Nothin'."

Giving up, Luke sipped his wine and eavesdropped shamelessly. It sure didn't sound like a conversation between two people in love. In fact, it sounded more like a business call. Very polite, very brief. No endearments, no hushed tones, no whispered phrases.

When she returned the phone to its cradle, she looked perfectly composed. No blush, no excitement, no distinctive sheen to her eyes. Amazing, he thought. If she were his woman, he'd have been saying things that put color into her cheeks.

Then his insides twisted. What was he thinking? She *had* been his once. And he'd let her go. And she was never going to be his again. Since he doubted he'd ever get married, Ronnie was his best shot at having a family. Through Ronnie, he could prove to himself that he could be a good father.

Alicia was only an obstruction to that goal.

But it was difficult to think of her as an obstruction when she fitted so nicely into his life. She fitted nicely against his body, too. And he'd bet his entire life savings that he'd fit nicely into hers.

The thought almost made him groan aloud. Damn it, he couldn't go on living like this—being almost perpetually aroused with no hope of physical release. He'd never had this kind of problem before Alicia walked back into his life. Unfortunately, there wasn't much he could do about it short of taking matters into his own hands, so to speak. And that just wasn't going to cut it because the problem was more than sexual. As much as it scared him to admit it, the problem involved his feelings.

And every one of those feelings was coming straight from his thudding heart.

Alicia jogged along the side of the road, perspiration trickling down the valley between her breasts. Maybe she should have skipped the aerobic workout since it was dark now. But Luke had been late getting home from work, so dinner had been delayed. And anyway, she thought stubbornly, this gave him some time alone with Ronnie.

Ignoring the stitch in her side, she gritted her teeth and kept going. During the past year, she'd made great progress toward her personal fitness goal, and she didn't want to backslide during her stay in Texas. If only it wasn't so damned hot and humid. Between the heat and the food in her stomach, she was starting to feel a bit nauseous. Gasping for air, she slowed to a walk, wondering how far she'd come. A mile, maybe less.

Suddenly, a screech of tires tore through the evening air. The glare of headlights accelerated toward her, the car's driver alternately slamming the brakes and ramming the gas pedal as he zigzagged along the narrow country road. Without a second to spare, Alicia dived off the road and into the grass. Uproarious laughter and heavy-metal music blasted the night as a carload of teenagers whizzed by.

For a few seconds, she didn't move, her teeth clenched against the sting of razor-sharp pain. Somehow she'd had the bad luck to land smack on a pile of refuse, most of which felt like shattered glass.

Slowly, unsteadily, she climbed to her feet. It was too dark to see the extent of her injuries, but she could feel the blood trickling from her many cuts.

"Damn," she muttered. "Damn, damn, damn."

Dazed, she started back up the road toward home. Home. How she wished Luke's place really was her home. She didn't want to go back to her condo. She hated it there, hated the memories associated with it.

A slow, steady dribble of blood oozed down her legs. Her nausea increased and her pace slowed. Her breath came in quick, shallow huffs, her lower lip trembling so badly she had to catch it between her teeth.

A lifetime later, she reached Luke's driveway. Feeling light-headed, she limped toward the front door, wishing he would come bursting out to take care of her. Indulging in this fantasy, she imagined the worried look on his face, the strength of his sinewy arms as he swept her tenderly off her feet.

But the door didn't open. She hadn't even been missed.

Self-pity swelled inside her as she turned the knob and hobbled in. No one hurried to greet her. Not even Daffy.

She lifted a hand and wiped away one foolish tear. She didn't need them anyway, she thought with a touch of belligerence. She could take care of herself. Shatterproof, that's what she was.

Without even glancing at her wounds, she started up the stairs. She moved quietly because she could hear Luke's voice drifting out of Ronnie's bedroom and she wanted to reach the bathroom without being seen. Yet, as she neared the top, she came to a dead halt and listened.

Luke was reading to Ronnie. Haltingly. Stumblingly.

As though he barely knew how.

Disbelief spiraled through her as she leaned dizzily against the wall. She couldn't take it in, couldn't understand. He mispronounced words, simple words that anyone should have known. He floundered and stopped, then backtracked and started over. His reading was slow, laborious, painstaking.

It couldn't be true. It had to be true.

The man couldn't read.

Forgetting her physical pain, she closed her eyes, love and self-recrimination merging in her chest. How could she not have known? How could he have hidden something like his illiteracy from her? Somehow, all those years ago, she had failed him. She must have. Otherwise, why hadn't he entrusted her with his secret?

In the next instant, she nearly lost her balance, and that told her she was in trouble. Clutching the banister, she opened her eyes and looked down at her injuries. To her horror, she saw a deep, horizontal slash across the back of her left arm. She'd been losing a heck of a lot more blood than she'd realized.

A shudder ran through her. She'd better get into that bathroom before she bled to death.

Luke went rigid as the bathroom door snapped shut. *Oh, God, she'd heard him. Alicia had heard him. He'd been found out.*

Shock and humiliation and shame crashed down on him in huge, suffocating waves. His numbed gaze flicked to his watch. Lord, she'd only been gone thirty minutes. He'd banked on her staying away for at least three-quarters of an hour.

Ronnie jostled his arm. "Come on, Uncle Luke. Read."

Luke blinked, trying to focus on the words, but adrenaline was kicking its way through his veins. "I...I think we'd better stop now. It's getting late."

"But it's almost the end," the child pleaded. "Pleeease."

Sweat broke out on Luke's brow. He couldn't think, couldn't find his place on the page. His mouth was dry. "I can't, Ron. Not now."

"Why?" Ronnie's guileless blue eyes met his.

"Because I'm tired." Hating himself, he shut the book. "Now give me a hug and let's get you tucked in."

The little arms that wrapped around him were nearly his undoing. "I love you, Uncle Luke."

Luke closed his eyes, emotion tightening his chest. "I love you, too, Ron." That was the understatement of the century.

He left Ronnie and went to his bedroom, passing the bathroom on the way. For once, he didn't picture Alicia under the shower spray even though he heard water running. Instead, he imagined the way she must have looked when she heard him struggling to read. In his mind's eye, he pictured the expressions on her face—the horror, the disgust, the pity.

He lay on his bed and stared at the ceiling fan, watching it spin around and around like the hopeless circle he was caught in. Maybe she hadn't heard. If she hadn't, then no damage was done. If she had, he had to tell her. He had to make her understand that he wasn't stupid or slow or lazy. His pride demanded it. But if she hadn't heard . . .

His jaw tightened. She *must* have heard. Ronnie's door had been open. She knew all right.

Or thought she did.

For a few seconds, he let himself remember how it had felt. To be young, alone, ridiculed for his handicap. Shoved into classes with mentally handicapped children by busy teachers with no time to spend on a child with special needs. He remembered the shaking heads, the low voices, his foster parents' disappointment. They'd wanted to take in a bright child, not a sulky, rebellious little dummy. So he'd been sent on to another foster home and then another. And each time he'd been rejected, it had been like a piece of burning shrapnel exploding in his face, tearing apart the very substance of his human dignity.

Suddenly his brow creased. He could have sworn he heard Alicia calling him. But that was nonsense, surely. Wishful thinking.

And then it came again, her voice so low he almost missed it. "Luke... I need you."

His mind stalled, but his body arched off the bed in an instinctive reaction. He reached the bathroom in time to hear her whisper his name again, faintly, with a quivering little sob that made his insides clench.

He tried the knob. "The door's locked. Alicia, what's the matter?"

She didn't answer, but he heard movement inside, then the pop of the lock release. Then he received his second shock of the hour.

He didn't know what he expected, but the sight that met his eyes was certain to stay with him for a long time to come. Alicia was leaning against the edge of the sink, her face nearly as white as the porcelain bathtub. Unshed tears glistened in her blue eyes and her hands clutched at the skimpy towel that wound around her wet body.

A towel smeared with blood.

There was blood on the floor, too, and on her discarded jogging clothes. His stunned glance took in her lacerated knees.

"My, God, what happened?"

She made a pitiful attempt at a smile. "Glass," she quavered, swaying a little. "Smashed beer bottles, I think. I thought the bleeding had stopped, but then I took a warm shower. I started to get...so...dizzy."

As she spoke, her grip on the towel loosened, and when he saw her arm, he bit back an oath. Savage emotions rocked his soul. He wanted to yell at her for not telling him sooner, shake her for trying to deal with this on her own.

Instead, he sprang forward and slid an arm around her waist.

"It's okay," he murmured. "Shh, sweetheart, I'll take care of you. Don't cry, darling."

As she gave a small sob and drooped against him, he grabbed a hand towel and wrapped it around her arm. Then, supporting her weight, he urged her out of the tiny bathroom.

Mentally reviewing his meager knowledge of first aid, he scooped her up and headed for her bedroom. Of course, a smart man would have made sure the towel stayed put, but rather than doing its job, it pulled loose to hang limply, trapped between his arm and her shapely underside.

"Luke . . ." The choked word contained embarrassment.

"Don't worry about it," he soothed. "I'm not looking." Which wasn't quite true, though he was making a truly noble effort to avert his gaze from her beautiful naked breasts, her satiny stomach and the fascinating cluster of downy blond curls at the apex of her lovely thighs. Affecting clinical indifference, he lowered her to the bed, re-covered her with the towel and made a quick examination of her injuries. "I think that arm is going to need some stitches," he said. "When was your last tetanus shot?"

"I don't know." Her eyes were closed. "Oh, Luke, I feel so strange."

"What's the matter with Aunt Alicia?" Ronnie piped from the doorway.

Luke moved to shield Ronnie's view of his aunt. "Hey, squirt, go into my room and call Brian's mom. Ask if she can come over right away. Tell her it's an emergency."

Ronnie's eyes widened with alarm. "Is Aunt Alicia going to die?"

"No, she's just got a little cut, but I have to take her to the hospital to get patched up. Don't worry, Ron. She's fine, I promise. Do you think you can call Brian's mom?"

"Yes." Ronnie disappeared.

Luke, meanwhile, did his best with antibiotic cream and gauze bandages. By the time the doorbell rang, he had gotten Alicia into panties and a pair of shorts. He had just buttoned her into a cotton blouse when Sharon came into the room.

As he expected, Sharon agreed to take Ronnie back to her house for the night. "Of course I don't mind," she said, her concerned gaze on Alicia's pale face. "You go ahead and take care of this lady. She needs you, Luke." Sharon laid a hand on his arm, exerting a slight pressure that seemed to hold some special meaning.

While Sharon gathered Ronnie's things, Luke shoved a pair of espadrilles onto Alicia's feet and lifted her into his arms.

"Luke, this is silly," she mumbled. "I can walk."

"Right. And pigs can fly."

"I'm too heavy for you."

"Says who?" he asked, making his way down the stairs. In fact, she was light and easy to carry, and the foolish thought came to him that he never wanted to put her down again. "I work out with weights, remember?" he added in an injured tone.

Her shaky laugh rewarded him. "Sorry. I forgot."

And as she nestled her head against his shoulder, he wondered how anything could possibly feel so right and perfect.

Chapter Nine

Alicia pushed aside her cereal bowl and leaned an arm on the kitchen table. The sound of Sunday-morning cartoons emanated from the living room, signposting Ronnie's location. Across the table, Luke sat hunched over his second cup of coffee, his dark hair rumpled and curly, a day's growth of beard shadowing his firm chin.

She studied him from under her lashes. She'd done nothing but think about him since Friday night. She'd thought about how considerate and gentlemanly he'd been while helping her dress. She'd remembered how carefully he'd carried her, as though she was a fragile and precious object to be revered. She'd recalled how masterfully he'd shielded her from the paper pushers at the hospital, how attentive he'd been, how watchful and alert to her discomfort and distress.

No one else had ever treated her like that.

Not ever.

And so she'd given in when he'd bullied her into spending Saturday taking it easy on the sofa. In all honesty, she'd needed the rest. Though the cut on her arm had hit a vein rather than an artery, she'd lost enough blood to require a bit of recovery time. At the hospital, they'd told her that she shouldn't feel much worse than if she'd donated a pint of blood. That had proved true.

To her surprise, Ronnie had insisted on coming home from Brian's so he could be with her. He had hovered over her for most of the day, his blue eyes inquisitive and concerned despite the number of times she'd assured him she was fine.

Even more surprising, Luke had hovered, too. Not in the same room and not in the overt way Ronnie had done but close enough to keep an eye on her. In between mowing the lawn, gathering laundry and replacing an ailing light fixture in the kitchen, he'd managed to check on her far more often than the situation warranted. He'd brought her drinks, presented her with lunch on a tray and made sure that Ronnie wasn't tiring her out.

If things had been different between them, if Luke had been her fiancé, her man, she could have allowed herself to bask in the unutterable joy of being cared for and cherished. But it wasn't true, and as the day progressed, she'd had to remind herself of that with increasing frequency. Over and over she'd told herself that love played no part in his actions, that he was just being kind. And when that hadn't worked, she'd tormented herself with images of Christina until the last delicious crumbs of her fantasy had been dusted away.

The light clunk of Luke's coffee mug brought her back to the present. "So how do you feel this morning?" he asked. "No more dizziness?"

"No, none at all." She made her voice cheerful, hoping her face hadn't given any hint of her thoughts. "All systems are back to normal."

As if he doubted her statement, his assessing gaze moved from her face to her bandaged arm and hands. His mouth flexed, reminding her how angry he'd been at the irresponsible teenagers who'd caused her injury. In fact, she'd discovered that while she'd been napping on the sofa yesterday, he'd taken a trash can to the place where she'd fallen and cleaned up the glass.

But apparently he believed her, for he nodded and said, "Do you feel up to taking a ride?"

Alicia's heart plummeted. Something in his tone told her what he had in mind. She'd been dreading it, had avoided any mention of it, and yet all this time she'd known it was coming. Yesterday she'd been dallying with air castles; today she would cope with reality at its devastating worst.

"Yes," she answered quietly, her reluctance quelled. "I think I'm ready."

"I've boxed up most of Richard's stuff, but I figured you or your parents would want some of Caroline's. We need to start clearing things out." He paused for a moment. "I've got a possible buyer for the house."

A small shock wave rippled through her. She knew it was Luke's job as executor of the estate to liquidate Richard and Caroline's assets and to set up the trust fund for Ronnie. She just hadn't expected the house to sell this fast.

"Already?" she said. "I thought the real-estate business was slow around here."

"It is. I guess we're just lucky. Some doctor made an offer. He came in a little low, so I made a counteroffer."

Alicia traced a finger along the edge of the table. "So—" She cleared her throat. "When did this happen?"

Luke's gaze was steady, his face taut as carved marble. "The agent called Friday afternoon. I meant to tell you. But then you got hurt, and it went out of my mind."

The message came through loud and clear. She'd jumped on him about the school issue, so he'd thought she'd take exception to this, also. However, the last thing she wanted was to be involved in the disposal of her sister and brother-in-law's assets. Visiting the house would be traumatic enough.

"That's okay," she hastened to assure him. "What about Ronnie? We can't take him."

"I'll ask Sharon to keep him for a few hours. I thought we could go after lunch. We can eat out if you'd like."

"That would be nice," she said, her tone automatic.

She looked down at the soggy remnants of her breakfast cereal, wondering if she'd ever be able to eat again. Right now, her stomach churned with the knowledge that today she would walk into her sister's house. What would it be like? Would it be as precise and organized as Caroline? When she trod the floors of the home where her sister had lived her life, would Caroline's presence follow her from room to room?

"Alicia." Luke's hand slid across the table to cover hers. It was a large hand, a hand accustomed to manual labor, tanned and firm and strong. "We don't have to do this today if you don't want. Or I can go by myself. If you just give me an idea what to look for, I can bring back—"

"No," she cut in vehemently. "It's as hard for you as it is for me. I'm not going to let you carry this load alone."

He smiled at that, though his eyes stayed serious. "I can handle it, babe. You don't have to go."

"Yes, I do," she asserted. "Let's face it, Luke. This isn't easy for either of us."

His fingers tightened over hers, conveying a wealth of understanding. "No, but I've gotten over the hump. If it's going to be too tough for you, I think you'd better skip it."

Damn him, he was being too nice. She needed distance, not kindness and compassion. The empathy in his eyes strained the fragile fabric of her self-control. It made her want to lean on him instead of being strong, draw him close instead of being safe. Most of all, it made her want to weep—for her sister, for Richard, for Ronnie. And for her own lost dreams.

Sending him a frown, she disengaged her hand from his. "I'm going with you," she said shortly. "It's not a subject for debate."

She spoke the words with coolness, enough to redefine the line that should be separating them. A little less chumminess and camaraderie would make it a lot easier to cope. She might love him, but she wasn't about to let him know it.

The tactic worked only too well, for at once the good humor faded from his face, replaced by a brittleness that had been missing before. He rose to his feet and reached for his hat. "Fine," he said evenly. "I have to go out and deliver some parts. I should be back around eleven-thirty."

But as he walked away from her, her chest felt as empty and hollow as the echo of his receding footsteps.

After Luke left, time seemed to slow down. There wasn't much for Alicia to do, so she decided to sit in the living room and fold laundry while Ronnie watched Looney Tunes. Carefully, as though to make up for driving Luke away, she smoothed her fingers over the soft cotton of one of his shirts.

How silly to be envious of a piece of cloth. But the shirt had rights she could never have. The right to press against his body, the right to absorb his scent.

The right to belong to him.

The knowledge of her own folly throbbed inside her like a festering sore. Matching pairs of socks together, she thought what a fool she was to be sighing over a piece of clothing. And for heaven's sake, why was she in love with Luke when she could have been in love with Nick? Nick was handsome and predictable and safe, and he came from the same world she did—the world her parents approved. On the other hand, she doubted Nick loved her, either, so perhaps for once she had been wise.

She looked over at Ronnie, stretched out on the rug with his chin on his hands, and tried to imagine taking him back to Boston and installing him in her guest room. But a child wasn't like a light fixture, something to be disconnected from one location and reattached in another. Ronnie was a child, a human being, and as Mrs. Glover had pointed out, he needed stability. Still, the thought of going back alone—without Ronnie—was almost more than she could bear.

As the child giggled over the cartoon, Alicia wondered what Caroline would have wanted them to do. Just the other day she had read an article that suggested it was becoming popular for parents to name two guardians in their wills—one to raise and educate the child, the other to look after the financial interests. But Caroline and Richard had not specified these roles for her and Luke. Apparently they had trusted them to do what was right, and had not anticipated how difficult it would be.

When the program came to an end, Ronnie shut off the TV and came to sit next to her, his curious gaze trailing over her various bandages. "Does it still hurt?"

"No, it's much better, thanks to you and Uncle Luke." She slipped an arm around his shoulders. "You both have been taking such good care of me."

Ronnie accepted the gesture, cuddling against her as he so often cuddled against Luke. "Maybe I'll be a doctor when I grow up," he said pensively. "Or a teacher."

"How about a writer?" she teased, watching his face. "Like the little boy who wrote that book we read yesterday."

"Can we read it again?"

The request took her by surprise, but she was more than willing to comply. As she settled the book on her lap and began the diarylike narrative, Ronnie leaned closer, his expression betraying fascination as he inspected each illustration.

"This really happened," he stated when they reached the end.

"Yes, it did. Tommy got through a hard time by writing about what happened to him and by drawing the pictures. I'm sure it helped him to feel better." Alicia smiled at him. "Maybe you could do the same. I could help you if you wanted me to. And I know you could do the pictures."

"But Tommy's story has a happy ending," the child objected in a thready voice. "Mine doesn't."

"Oh, darling," she whispered, and hugged him again. "I know it's hard to believe, but you'll be happy again. It's going to take a while, but it *will* happen."

"I know," he quavered with a wisdom far beyond his years. "I'm happy sometimes. But sometimes I'm sad 'cuz I miss my mom and dad so much."

Again he surprised her, this time with the suddenness of his movement as he turned his face into the pillow of her breasts. And as his hot, silent tears soaked into her blouse, Alicia rested her cheek on the top of his head and enfolded him with her love.

* * *

"Do you ever miss the climate up north?" Alicia asked.

Luke rubbed a thumb along the rim of the steering wheel as he considered her question. The drive to West University, where Caroline and Richard had lived, usually took about an hour. Alicia had been quiet when they'd left the house, but somewhere around the time they'd hit I-45, she'd started to make desultory conversation. He enjoyed listening to her talk. Her voice was pleasant and easy on the ears, soothing him in a way nothing else could have done. And for the first time since Friday night, he relaxed.

"Yeah, sometimes," he admitted. "But not during the winter. I can do without the snow and ice."

He found himself elaborating, explaining all the things he liked about living in the South. And she listened, really listened, as though what he said mattered, as though he was saying something important and intelligent. As though she had not overheard his humiliating struggle to read, which he knew damned well she had.

The woman confused him, that was for sure. Her coldness this morning had thrown him off kilter, a rejection he somehow hadn't expected despite the conclusions she must have drawn about his inability to read. But when he'd returned, braced for distance and tension, she'd been agreeable, even friendly.

Wacky, that's what she was. Wacky and gorgeous and desirable as all get-out. Just as she had always been.

He glanced over at her, observing her clean-cut profile with a distinct sense of wonder. No, in subtle ways, she *had* changed. Life had left its mark on her, matured her in some ways, hurt her in others, just as it had carved exciting new facets into her personality. Facets he had only begun to appreciate.

For instance, she had honed the ability to draw people out of their shells, a talent that impressed him because he didn't share it. She didn't do it with Sharon's gregarious vivacity, but it happened all the same, quietly, before the person even realized what was happening. All the guys at work adored her, and all had told her their life stories, even Dave, the world-class introvert. Much to her credit, she was sincere. She genuinely seemed to like hearing them talk about themselves—though he'd noticed she didn't reciprocate.

And Luke wished she would—to him—because he wanted to know everything about her, every little detail about what made her tick, everything that had happened to her during the last decade. It wouldn't do him any good. It wouldn't make his nights any less restless. But he wanted to know. He ached to know as much as he ached to hold her in his arms.

He took the Southwest Freeway exit while she turned the conversation to Ronnie. At first, he thought she was leading into the who's-going-to-raise-Ronnie issue, but that wasn't the case. No, she was talking about writing contests and child authors, things he didn't know anything about.

"I got the idea from that book," she explained, her voice solemn and her blue eyes earnest. "The one about the child with leukemia. Don't you think it might help Ronnie come to terms with his loss? Or maybe it's too soon," she added uncertainly. "What do you think?"

What did he think?

She was asking a guy who couldn't read whether he thought his six-year-old nephew should write a book.

He could feel his mouth curling as he glanced at her, wondering why she didn't see the irony. "I think you're pretty optimistic," he said with a shrug. "But I guess it's worth a try if Ronnie wants to do it. What did he say?"

"He said his story didn't have a happy ending. But that's not the point." She sat up straighter, leaning toward him just a little. "Tell me," she said in a soft voice. "What was it like for you?"

"What?" He stiffened.

"When you lost your mother, I mean. Do you think putting your feelings on paper could have helped you?"

As the seconds ticked by, coherent thought eluded him. That part of his life was such a jumble of unhappy memories that he seldom allowed himself to reflect upon it.

"I don't know." He kept his gaze fixed on the blue Mazda ahead of them. "It wasn't an option. I didn't have anyone who cared enough to suggest it."

"Sometimes," she said slowly, "I wonder why we didn't talk about these things when we were...together. We didn't communicate very well, did we?"

"Maybe not," he acknowledged, his mouth thinning. "I didn't talk about it because it was in the past. And at the time, I didn't want to think about that part of my life. I was more interested in the future." He paused. "We're almost there, by the way."

It was her turn to be silent. He let a minute slip by, then he glanced over at her, aware that she was looking out the window and wouldn't notice. His eyes narrowed. She seemed paler than before, and again he felt that he'd been wrong to bring her here, to Caroline's house.

It wasn't long before they pulled into the driveway. Luke shut off the engine, conscious of the waiting emptiness in the large house in front of them. Silently he damned Alicia's stubbornness. He should have left her home and come alone.

In an abrupt movement, Alicia flung open the car door and climbed out. She still had not uttered a word.

He hurried around the car and caught hold of her arm. "Listen to me," he said in a steadfast voice. "If you start to feel dizzy, I want you to promise you'll tell me. Okay?"

She nodded, her blue eyes luminous. "I promise. And thank you, Luke. You're a very sweet man."

The last three words echoed in his head as he unlocked the front door and led the way into the handsome, marble-tiled foyer. It was an imposing house, complete with a curving staircase grand enough for Scarlett O'Hara to sweep down. A huge chandelier hung directly above their heads, its crystals dangling in precise geometric formations.

He watched her move forward, her face tight and still with suppressed emotion. She didn't speak. Instead, she wrapped her arms around herself and walked into the formal living room with its white leather furniture and brass-and-glass tables and exotic ferns growing out of Oriental pottery.

Turning toward him, she said, "It looks like something out of *House Beautiful*."

"Not the best place for a kid," Luke murmured.

He followed her from room to room, his gaze on her face as she took in the fancy kitchen, the ornate dining room, the library stocked to the ceiling with impressive-looking tomes.

She went over and read a few of the titles. "What in the world are we going to do with all these books?"

He shoved his hands into his back pockets. "Rice University is willing to take most of them. You can look to see if there's anything you want."

She shook her head. "No. Let's go upstairs."

The entire second floor had been Ronnie's domain. Luke had already emptied out the child's bedroom, but Alicia still hesitated there, surveying the designer wallpaper and the thick blue rug with an unreadable expression in her eyes. Nothing remained, not even a scrap of paper or a piece of Lego.

"Well," she said at last, her tone bleak, "I guess the only thing you need me to do is to go through Caroline's personal items."

They returned to the master bedroom suite, which they had all but bypassed on their tour of the first floor. Before,

Alicia had only glanced in, but this time her steps did not falter.

Luke lingered in the doorway. "I left some empty boxes in the garage. I'll go get them."

As if she hadn't heard, Alicia stood very still. "I can smell Caroline's perfume," she whispered. Jerkily, she brought her hand to her mouth. "Oh, God, Luke, I don't know if I can do this."

He reached her in three steps, his arms going around her just as she started to shake. "Sure you can, sweetheart. It's not easy, but you're one heck of a strong woman. If you don't know that, I do."

He pressed her against him, watching their reflection in Caroline's gilt mirror as her feminine warmth soaked through his shirt to his skin. She felt so small, so fragile, like a dainty spring flower fighting for its place in the sun.

"Strong," she repeated brokenly. "I don't feel that way."

"Do you want to leave? We can go right now if you want."

"No. I want to do what I came to do. It's just that I've spent my whole life being jealous of Caroline, and look at this!" She made a small, convulsive movement. "This is all I have left and... I can never make it up to her now."

Frowning, he lifted her chin. "Why would you be jealous of Caroline?"

"You really don't know?" Her eyes locked with his. "No, I suppose you don't. You knew Caroline, but I grew up with her." She drew a deep, ragged breath. "When I got A's, she got A pluses. I never had a date the whole time I was in high school—Caroline had boyfriends from the time she was thirteen. Caroline's room was always neat—mine was a mess. Caroline's teeth were straight—I wore braces. Everything Caroline did was right. Everything I did backfired. I lived in her shadow and I hated it."

"So that's how you got the idea she was perfect." He stroked a hand down her back. "Did she try to make you feel bad, honey?"

"No. That's why I feel so guilty. It was my parents who made me so aware of...my deficiencies." Her voice shook. "Caroline was like them, I guess, and I wasn't. She was intellectual and ambitious and single-minded. They were thrilled when she said she wanted to go to Harvard Law School. They used every penny they had to send her there."

"And left you with nothing."

"Not nothing," she corrected. "Just no choices."

Luke knew what she meant. She'd had to attend the college where her parents taught because she'd been able to get her tuition free and live at home. It had been one of the reasons she'd used to justify her decision not to come with him to Houston.

"Did you ever tell them it bothered you?" he asked.

He felt her shrug. "They wouldn't have understood. Especially my mother. She and I don't talk. Not about anything important, I mean." She pulled away with a shaky smile, then startled him by rising up on tiptoe to kiss his cheek. "Thank you for listening. Why don't you get those boxes, and I'll see what needs to be done."

Alicia had a box half-filled with memorabilia when she came across the snapshot. It had been taken at Caroline's wedding, but it wasn't one of the formal wedding pictures. No, it must have been taken by one of the guests at the reception, copied and sent on to Caroline and Richard as a gift.

She cupped it in her hand, her heart pumping in double time as she stared at it. The bride and groom were dancing and smiling. Just to their left and a little behind, Alicia and Luke were also dancing, gazing into each other's eyes with rapt, starlit expressions. Luke was holding her very close, even closer than Richard held Caroline.

"What's that?" Luke had just come into the room.

"A photo. From the wedding."

"Let's see." He walked over and took the picture from her hand. His face remained inscrutable as he studied it. "It seems like a long time ago."

No, she thought sadly. It seems like yesterday.

"I keep remembering how happy my mother was that day," she said. "She adored Richard, you know. He was everything she wanted for Caroline. They were so perfect for each other."

Luke handed back the photograph and sat down on the edge of the king-size bed. "Caroline was a good woman with a lot of positive qualities, but she wasn't perfect, Alicia. Between marriage and her career and being a mother, I think she bit off more than she could chew."

"How do you mean?" Alicia lifted her head.

"She and Richard were having problems," he answered, his eyes fixed on her face.

"What kind of problems?"

"This vacation they were on, it was sort of a last-ditch effort to save their marriage. They were both unhappy. Caroline wanted a divorce. Richard wanted to hang on for Ronnie's sake. It was pretty messy."

Alicia shook her head in disbelief. "That can't be. Caroline had a wonderful marriage."

"No," he said with quiet adamancy. "She didn't."

Alicia absorbed this for several seconds, trying to reconcile it with the image she carried of her sister. "She never told me," she said. "I can't believe my mother knows, either." Feeling weary and confused, she took one more look at the picture, then dropped it into the box.

"Come here." Luke reached for her hands and drew her up from the floor. "Don't look like that. I wouldn't have told you except for this thing you have about Caroline. You need to see her realistically."

Somehow it seemed quite natural to allow him to settle her onto his lap. It also seemed natural to rest her arm along his broad shoulders and to gaze straight into his dark, smoky eyes. As for the kiss, she couldn't have said which of them initiated it. It simply happened, a spontaneous coming together that was as magical as music and as basic as breathing.

Closing her eyes, Alicia lost herself in his taste, in the eager, sensuous slide of his tongue against hers. She let sensation take over, welcomed the urgent stroking of his hands on her body as though it were happening in a dream.

"You're so beautiful," she heard him murmur, his voice raw and brimming with tenderness. "So incredibly beautiful and sexy."

Sighing his name, she slipped her fingers under the front of his T-shirt, trailing them through the bramble of hair on his chest as she caressed the hard male muscles beneath. At the same time, her other hand drifted up the smooth, warm flesh of his back, explored the ridged muscles there with a sense of rapturous wonder.

He was doing the same to her, aggressively pushing aside the thin layer of her cotton top, finding and unhooking the front clasp of her lacy bra. And then his hands were on her breasts, and a few seconds later his mouth. Pleasure unlike anything she had ever known bloomed within her. A low moan rose in her throat as she arched back against his arm.

"Oh, sweetheart," he panted. "Alicia, stop me now or...or I swear I won't be able to stop at all."

Dazed, she opened her eyes and blinked. With a jolt of dismay, she remembered where they were. "Not here," she gasped. Her hands flew to her clothing, her bra, as she tried to cover herself. "Luke, we can't—not here."

He caught hold of her wrist. "Hey," he said hoarsely, "it's all right. Don't be embarrassed, honey. I'd lay bets they wouldn't have minded. But you're right, this isn't the place. When we make love, it's got to be somewhere you feel comfortable."

"When we make love," she faltered, rather stunned at his assumption that it was such a sure thing.

"Maybe 'if' is a better word. Maybe you won't want to after..." He halted as she climbed to her feet and turned away from him to refasten her bra. Into the silence that followed, he said, "I need to tell you something about me, Alicia."

There was a queer note in his voice, so queer she gave him a sharp look. "What's the matter?"

"There's something you don't know. At least, you might think you know, but you don't." His tone was stiff, defensive, as though he expected to be ridiculed.

And at once she knew. "Does this have to do with your reading?"

He got up and went to the window and stood with his back to her for what seemed like a long time before he spoke again. "I'm not illiterate," he said at last. "I'm dyslexic."

She looked at him, at the proud, straight lines of his back. "Dyslexic. You mean—"

"I mean I've got a learning disability. That's why I can't read to Ronnie. And why I can't enter numbers onto a spreadsheet. My brain is different somehow. It gets things mixed up."

Despite his matter-of-fact delivery, she sensed his underlying frustration. And more. She felt his pain and mortification as surely as if it were her own.

"And you think that might matter to me?"

"Doesn't it?" He swung around, his eyes drilling into her with fierce intensity. "Let's face it, you didn't like the fact that I didn't go to college. Your parents thought I was a loser. That's the reason you didn't marry me, isn't it? Because you and your family thought my business would fail. And then you'd have been stuck with an unemployed, uneducated bum for a husband."

"No!" She stared at him, aghast. "I never thought that! And I still don't. Luke, how could you think I would be so shallow? I have nothing but admiration for you. Look at what you've been able to accomplish, for heaven's sake! Look at your prosperous business and lovely home." Without hesitation, she took his hand, lifting it so she could brush her lips across his knuckles. "You've got nothing, *nothing* to be ashamed of! You should be proud of yourself. You've succeeded wonderfully with everything you've set out to do."

"Not everything," he countered. Still, the expression on his face had lost its grimness. Instead, he appeared rather wondering, as though he couldn't quite believe what he was hearing.

"Lots of people are dyslexic," she added. "I don't know much about it, but I do know that. Wasn't Einstein dyslexic? I bet you're a genius, too."

He smiled crookedly. "Yeah, right. I'm a genius at screwing things up."

Again, she understood what lay beneath his words. "It was hard, wasn't it?" she asked him in a gentle voice. "Growing up with this problem?"

He met her eyes. "It was pure hell."

"Maybe you'll tell me about it?" She gazed up at him, wanting to hear it all, how he'd suffered, how he'd triumphed. For this, she felt certain, was the key to that secret corner of his soul, the one to which he'd denied her access all those years ago.

"Yeah, maybe I will," he agreed, still looking down at her in that odd, thoughtful way. "Maybe I will."

Chapter Ten

"Don't let him get it, Aunt Alicia! Throw it really high!"
Ronnie waved his arms and bounced up and down in the
grass, his face aglow with childish glee.

"Go ahead and try," Luke warned them in a teasing tone,
"but I'm gonna get it this time. No more Mr. Nice Guy."

Alicia readied herself, trying to ignore the fact that the
monkey in the middle looked distractingly gorgeous. Wearing a pair of low-slung cutoffs and the most wicked grin she
had ever seen, he stood between her and Ronnie, hands
raised and ready to intercept the ball. Beneath the light
matting of chest hair, his bare torso glistened with perspiration. His eyes held a definite glint as she prepared to hurl
the ball.

"Get ready, Ronnie. Here it comes." She arced the ball
high, but not too high for Ronnie to catch.

Luke leapt up, pretending to miss. With a moan of
disappointment, he rolled across the grass and landed at

Ronnie's feet. "Foiled again," he complained. "You're just too good for me."

"Sorry, Uncle Luke," Ronnie gloated.

The little boy shot a conspiratorial grin at Alicia, and she grinned back. In the five days since her accident, her relationship with the child had taken a giant step forward. In some mysterious way, her injury had been the cause, for it had triggered in him an almost obsessive concern for her health and well-being. He was constantly checking the stitches in her arm, constantly asking her how she was feeling.

Moreover, he had developed an interest in her idea. Each day after school, Ronnie had gone to the kitchen table after school, forehead furrowed with concentration as he sketched and colored the illustrations for the story he'd decided to write. The words hadn't come yet, but the pictures were stories unto themselves, betraying the child's fear, pain and anger at the senseless tragedy that had altered his young life.

Clearly, too, Ronnie's pictures of Luke demonstrated how much he idolized his uncle. Not that Alicia hadn't observed this for herself. Each night when Luke came home from work, he and Ronnie did "guy" things in the backyard—wrestling or pitching a baseball or kicking the soccer ball around. Alicia would listen to Ronnie's joyful shrieks with a tug at her heartstrings, knowing a male role model wasn't something she could offer him. Yes, she could participate in their play, but that didn't change the fact that she hardly had a backyard, much less a man in her life who would do such things with the boy. With a sigh, she discounted Nick Easton. As good a friend as he was, she knew they were drifting apart.

She had never intended to stay in Houston this long, never planned to leave the matter of Ronnie's future unresolved all this time. Again and again, she had started to discuss the matter with Luke, but he seemed to want to avoid the subject. In fact, it almost seemed as though he wanted things to go on as they were—the three of them together.

Which was impossible.

For that to happen, Luke would have to ask her to marry him. Even more importantly, he'd have to say that he loved her. And she'd have to believe, really *believe* that he meant it, that he loved her as much as she loved him. That he wasn't just saying the words to make her happy—

"Look out!"

Taken by surprise, she barely caught the ball Ronnie had launched rather haphazardly over his uncle's head. For the child's entertainment, Luke repeated his previous performance and landed on his back at her feet.

"I thought it was going to hit you," he explained, scanning the length of her bare legs with masculine appreciation.

"Sorry, Ronnie, but I need to take a break." Tossing the ball aside, Alicia sank to the ground and flicked a piece of grass from Luke's shoulder. "Thanks. I was daydreaming."

"I could tell." He reached for her hand. He lay on his back, knees drawn up, his gaze resting on her face. "What's going on in that head of yours?"

She looked down at their entwined fingers. "I was thinking we need to come to some decision about Ronnie. Also, I've been meaning to tell you that I've got to go back up north for a few days. My boss called today. There's a small crisis at work, but it can wait 'til after the weekend. I'll leave Monday and come back Friday." She paused. "If it's okay to come back."

"Why wouldn't it be okay?" Luke's thumb stroked across her palm. "Do you think I want to get rid of you?"

"Well, I can't stay forever."

She thought, even hoped, he might comment on this, but instead he said, "So what's going on? They can't run the company without you?"

"The project I was working on has gone into cardiac arrest. George, the fellow I left in charge, quit today. My boss wants me back to make the presentation to upper management."

His thumb swept across her wrist. Something in his eyes, in the insistent pressure of his fingers, told her he wanted her flat on the grass beside him. Her heart did a few rapid skips at the thought.

"Don't," she warned, and withdrew her hand.

Luke shot the child a glance, but Ronnie had wandered over to swing on a rope tied to the branch of a sweet gum tree. "Don't worry, Alicia. I'm minding my manners." His eyes skimmed her face. "You look tired."

"I am. I didn't sleep well last night."

"Lonely?"

"Yes," she confessed, then wondered if the admission was wise.

"Me, too." His mouth curved just a little. "One of these nights is going to be the right night," he said softly. "I'm just waiting for you to tell me which one."

"You mean you're not going to seduce me?" She tried to make the question playful, but she had a feeling she sounded breathless and unsure.

His eyes blazed, stoking an answering fire inside her, a fire that began in the pit of her stomach and moved outward, flashing through her nerve endings with the force of an inexorable current. "Do you *want* me to seduce you?" he asked huskily.

"I don't know." She moistened her lips. "I'm not sure about anything right now."

Still, the pull between them was so strong that she could not resist the urge to touch him. Forgetting Ronnie, forgetting everything but Luke, she reached out and smoothed her palm across his chest and downward across his taut, hard belly. She heard the sharp intake of his breath, felt the responsive shudder of muscle beneath her fingertips. Then he recaptured her hand and held it fast, effectively ending what she had not meant to start.

"Just let me know," he murmured. "When you decide, I mean. Or if you want me to seduce you, just flutter your lashes or something. I promise I'll catch on real fast."

She had to laugh, albeit shakily. "All right."

He pushed himself up to a sitting position. "In the meantime," he said, his arms on his raised knees, "how about if we plan a date?"

"A date?"

"You know, one of those old-fashioned, preplanned appointments men make with women they're attracted to? We get a sitter for Ronnie, you put on something pretty and I—"

"You put on something pretty, too?" she teased, her heart flipping back and forth like a whole netful of butterflies. The mere idea of dating Luke was very, very dangerous.

And totally irresistible.

He gave her a smile that melted her bones. "And I do my best to look like a guy who deserves to be with you."

"I don't know what to write." Ronnie stared at the picture he had drawn of his house, the elegant West University house with its landscaped lawn and three-car garage. In the driveway, he had placed his mother and father on one side of a sleek black car, and himself on the other.

Alicia studied it with him. "How about something about the way things were before? What you did every day, maybe."

Ronnie thought this over. "Like when they went to work and I went to school?"

"Yes, the everyday things."

It took half an hour for Ronnie to decide what to say. First he ate his after-school yogurt and pondered, then he penciled a few words, erased and almost gave up. But at last, with only a little help from Alicia, he wrote:

Once upon a time I lived in a big wite house with my mom and dad. Most of the time I waz hapy. Eksep sometimes when my mom and dad got mad.

"How's that?" He looked expectantly at Alicia.

"That's excellent, Ronnie." She hesitated. "Did they get mad at you, sweetheart?"

He shook his head. "Just at each other. They had lots of fights."

So Luke had been right.

Without prompting from her, he added more.

They liked to werk. They werked a lot. Somtimes they had fites. I went to kinnergardn and day kare. On weekens I went to see my Unkel Luke.

The next drawing was of Luke and Ronnie. Luke stood very tall and wore a cowboy hat and boots. Ronnie's head reached the top of Luke's hip.

Unkel Luke is lots of fun. He plays with me. He looks like a real cowboy but hes not. He is reel good at fixin things that are brok. He has a stoor. I like to go ther and play on the komputr.

"You really love Uncle Luke, don't you?" Alicia asked softly.

Ronnie nodded and bit his lip, obviously fighting a wave of emotion. "I loved Mommy and Daddy, too," he said in a trembling voice.

Alicia reached for him. "Go ahead and cry, honey. It's okay. Don't try to hold it back."

As his face scrunched up, she lifted him out of the chair and carried him into the other room. Together they sat on the sofa, Ronnie cradled on her lap, his body heaving with sobs that seemed dredged from the very center of his soul. He felt small in her arms—small and sweet and infinitely precious. And as she held him and comforted him, she had the oddest fancy that Caroline and Richard were in the room with them, watching peacefully.

A long, long time passed, and then he quieted.

"I love you, Aunt Alicia." The whispered words were almost too faint to hear, yet she heard them, not only with her ears but with her heart.

"I love you, too, Ronnie." She pressed a gentle kiss to his cheek.

"Will you stay here forever with me and Uncle Luke?"

The simple innocence of the question brought tears to her eyes. "I don't think so, darling. I wish I could. But I have a life up in Massachusetts. I have a home and a job and friends I have to go back to. I came to Houston to be with you for a while, but I can't stay forever."

"Maybe if you asked Uncle Luke, he would let you."

"Your uncle and I are friends, but not the special kind that wants to be together. He has his life, and I have mine." She paused. "I'd love to have you come and live with me, if you'd like to change your mind."

Ronnie was silent for a handful of seconds. "I don't want to hurt your feelings," he said at last.

"You want to stay with Uncle Luke."

"Are you mad?" he asked timidly.

Alicia let out a groan and hugged him, the light, gentle fragrance of his hair, of baby shampoo, reminding her how young he really was. "No, sweetheart, no. I could never be mad at you."

"I love you, but Uncle Luke needs me. He doesn't have anybody but me. He'd get lonely without me."

Alicia shut her eyes. "Yes, I'm sure you're right," she said, her voice hollow with resignation. "You and your uncle need each other. Maybe you can come and visit me instead. During one of the school holidays."

"Okay," he said. "You won't leave yet, will you?"

"Not yet, but soon."

He raised his head, his blue eyes anxious. "Will you stay 'til Halloween?"

"Oh, Ronnie, that's a whole month away. I can't stay that long."

"How long then?"

"I won't leave before you finish your story," she promised.

She then distracted Ronnie with a knock-knock joke, which led to a whole round of nonsense and laughter. And then the phone rang, bringing the excitement of an invitation to a Saturday-night sleepover at Brian's house. With the resilience of youth, Ronnie recovered his smiles.

Alicia only wished it were as easy for her.

Luke squirted shampoo into his hair, welcoming the stinging spray of hot water against his naked body. His day had been hectic and tiring. Thanks to a recent thunder-and-lightning storm, they'd had a run of repair jobs and service calls. When a telephone pole or a tree took a direct hit of lightning, the current could flash over into a nearby house, inflicting damage to anything with an electrical circuit. Appliances weren't designed to withstand a hundred million volts. Business increased accordingly. And customers got antsy because they had to deal with insurance claims.

But he was glad he'd been busy. For the past two days, his date with Alicia had hung in his mind, ever since he'd learned about Brian Redford's sleepover. Naturally he'd been smart enough to seize such a golden opportunity. Yep, tonight was the night. For the first time since her arrival, they would be alone from dusk until dawn.

Alone.

Possibilities streaked through his head, along with a current of awareness that could have melted a few wires. He shut off the water and stepped out of the tub, wrapping a towel around his hips as he eyed himself in the mirror. His face stared back at him, his anticipation visible, at least to himself. *Don't get your hopes up, pal. Or something else is bound to come up, too.*

As he reached for his razor, he recalled other dates and evenings with Alicia. He'd taken a fair number of cold showers during those long-ago weeks, but he'd understood and respected her wish that they not make love until after they were married. One corner of his mouth quirked. Maybe he wouldn't have been so understanding if he'd known that day would never come.

They were older now, more mature. She'd been married and divorced; he'd taken other women to bed. He knew a moment's regret that Alicia had not been his first, and the feeling expanded when he remembered he had not been her first, either. Had that jerk she'd married treated her gently? Had he been attentive to her needs, sensitive to her inexperience?

The thought stayed with him as he dressed. And when he went downstairs to wait for her, to pace the floor and imagine what the evening had in store for them, she surprised him by being there ahead of him.

He halted in the living-room doorway. "Hi," he said, his eyes trailing over her. God, she was gorgeous. She was wearing a white dress, probably cotton, with some sort of gold embroidery around the neckline and sleeves. The fabric clung to her figure, molded her breasts and hips and thighs in a way that sent sparks flying through his bloodstream. She also wore lipstick and mascara, just enough to show that she wanted to look her best for him.

"Hi," she answered, her smile rather shy.

Talk about déjà vu. She had smiled exactly like that the evening of their first date, and looked just about as virginal. He had taken her out to dinner, some Italian place, and to the movies. What had they seen? He'd forgotten long ago, probably because his attention had been focused on the girl at his side rather than on the screen. He remembered they'd gone to a diner afterward and sat for hours over coffee and doughnuts talking about everything and anything. Except, of course, the things he hadn't wished her to know.

A decade later, it still didn't seem quite right to take her out to dinner in a pickup truck, but she hadn't minded then, and she didn't seem to mind now. She climbed in with her usual aplomb, arranged the folds of her skirt and smiled at him as he shut her door. He walked around to the driver's side, wishing she would slide over and sit in the middle the way she used to do.

He'd selected an Italian restaurant, a place called DiStephano's that Joey and Nora had recommended. A dark-haired waiter gave them a table along the wall, near a bearded guitar player strumming music from *The Godfather.*

"It's not as fancy as I thought it would be," he commented, glancing around at the restaurant's creative decor.

Alicia followed his gaze to the painted scenes of Venice above their heads. Her smile widened as she noticed the lines of laundry strung between a pair of wooden balconies. "It's charming, Luke. I can pretend I'm in Italy."

He looked at her curiously, hearing the wistfulness and longing in her voice. "Is that something you'd like to do? Go to Italy?"

"It's not something I'm likely to do," she said with a resigned shrug. "I always imagined traveling with my husband and children, but Kenny hated flying, so Europe was out. And now, well, I've used up all my vacation days and then some."

"How come you never had kids?"

She looked down, her face clouding. "Kenny didn't want them."

But she obviously did, which was a revelation in itself. However, since the subject distressed her, he let it go and steered the conversation back to travel. Tonight he was at ease, free of the choking inhibitions that so often leashed his tongue. Why this was, he didn't know. Maybe it had something to do with hope. Because he had found it again, that seductive emotion, and it was giving him new access to old dreams. It allowed him to envision a future for himself, a future that included Alicia and Ronnie and maybe other children, even grandchildren.

While the guitarist performed songs like *"La Dolce Vita"* and *"Torna a Surriento"* softly in the background, they sipped Chardonnay and spoke of places they yearned to go—places like London and Lucerne, Capri and Rome. And all the while, Luke's senses were growing more acute, his perceptions intensifying to the zenith of their potential. The pulse at the base of Alicia's throat, the rise and fall of her breasts, the faint outline of her nipples against the front of her dress—he absorbed it all. Amid the smells of flowers and food, he picked up her faint, feminine scent, a unique blending of perfume and the dizzying heat of her body. He could hear every guitar note, every fluctuation in Alicia's voice. He could taste every condiment, every herb that flavored the food. He could even taste her lips, though he knew this was a product of imagination and memory.

When the last plate was removed, he reached for her hand, studying the shape of her graceful fingers and the fine texture of her skin. "You got rid of your wedding ring," he said in a low voice.

"No, I still have it. It's a silly thing to keep, a ring from someone you don't love." Her head bowed a little, her golden hair falling forward to hide her expression. "Someday maybe I'll have the diamond reset into a pin."

He opened his mouth, then closed it again. He wanted to ask if she'd ever consider wearing his ring instead, but it suddenly seemed too soon, too wildly risky. So he brushed a finger over her palm and said, "You know what I'd like to do right now?"

She raised her head, the depths of her eyes reflecting age-old feminine knowledge. "The same thing I do, I imagine."

White-hot desire shimmered through him as he leaned forward, watching the way she blushed in the candlelight. He found that blush amazing and very sweet. *"Can* you imagine it?" he asked softly. "I can. I can imagine everything, every detail of how it's going to be for us."

"So can I." She whispered the words, but her eyes boldly sought his as though she found him as fascinating as he found her. "I've always wondered what it would be like," she confessed, "the two of us together."

Erotic images danced through his head, but he decided not to describe them to her, at least not now. Fortunately for him the restaurant was dim, and his pants had a pleated front, but that was all that saved him from embarrassment. "So tonight's the night?" he asked, praying he had not misread her signals.

Her fingers tightened on his. "If you want it to be."

On the drive home, he forced himself to stay below the speed limit, knowing it was foolish to rush, knowing the delay would only heighten the pleasure. In any case, Alicia had opted to sit in the middle this time, her hips snug against his, which was proving the sweetest of torments. His blood hammering, he steered with his left hand, his right arm draped around her shoulders.

When they reached the house, he shut off the engine and turned to her, seeking her eyes in the shadows. His impatience dismayed him. Each time he touched her, he felt like a clumsy teenage boy, filled with raging hormones and the grinding, relentless needs of male adolescence.

"Maybe I should have asked if you wanted to go to the movies first," he said with reluctance.

"What if I had said yes?" He could hear the smile in her voice, the breathlessness that told him where her interest lay.

"Then I would have done this," he said, leaning closer.

As his lips brushed hers in the darkness, he knew in the corners of his mind that it would be all right, that he possessed the control to harness his urges. And harness them he would, for despite the clamoring demands of his body, he meant to go slowly, to make their lovemaking last. He had waited ten years for this moment and he was going to savor every instant of it.

He ended the brief kiss and drew back, his breathing unsteady. "Let's go in, okay?"

"Okay." Her voice was as shaky as his.

He slid his arm around her waist, holding her close as they walked toward the front door. A mournful bark greeted them. Luke unlocked the door, shooed a joyful Daffy outside and held the door open for Alicia. As they stepped into the foyer, he saw her glance toward the staircase.

"Not yet," he said with tender amusement. "We've got all night, remember?"

How could she forget?

Alicia's heart thudded as he linked his fingers through hers and led her down the hall to the living room. She halted nervously while he strode over to his tape deck and popped in a tape. A moment later, the strains of a familiar melody reached out from the speakers to enfold her in memories. "Stairway to Heaven." She'd never have guessed he'd remember the song that had played when that wedding snapshot was taken. The first slow dance they'd ever danced together. The tune was engraved on her mind.

He turned back to her and held out a hand, a smoldering invitation in his eyes. Her nervousness died. Without hesitation, she walked into his arms, wordlessly melting against him with a sigh of sheer contentment. At last, at last, she was where she had wanted to be all these years. She had finally come home.

"I always think of you when I hear this," he murmured. "You and your dusky rose gown. Do you remember I said something about your pink dress? You looked at me with those big blue eyes and said, 'Actually, it's called dusky rose,' in that shy, sassy voice of yours."

She smiled against his shirt. "Shy and sassy are opposites."

"Maybe, but they describe you." He tipped up her chin with his hand, his gaze devouring her face as she parted her lips in mute enticement. "Let's take it slow," he whispered, and kissed the tip of her nose.

Clearly he intended to drive her crazy, for his hands explored her as they danced, heating her with tiny strokes and caresses. And while they swayed together, she fantasized about what was coming next. She imagined their clothes scattered on the carpet and the warmth of his mouth on her flesh. She imagined her own mouth on him. And she imagined his first intoxicating thrust and how it would feel to have the man she loved make love to her.

He was very aroused. She could feel him pressed against her, the telling size and stiffness of him. Beneath her cheek, his heart pounded. She thought of Kenny, who had only taken and never given, and felt an enormous tenderness toward this man who seemed determined to put her needs before his own.

"You were smart to say no to me before," he said huskily. "I wasn't in the right frame of mind. I would have rushed things, and that would have been wrong."

She kissed his chin. "Saying no wasn't easy. You're a hard man to resist, Luke Garrick."

As they drifted with the tempo of the music, he brought his mouth close to her ear. "Are you as turned on as I am, Alicia? Tell me how turned on you are."

"On a scale of one to ten," she murmured, "I think I just hit twelve. I never knew you could be such a tease."

His low chuckle ruffled her hair. "Baby, you ain't seen nothin' yet." His hand moved to unzip her dress.

She closed her eyes. It was like a dream, the way he eased the dress off her shoulders, the way it slipped down to puddle at her feet. The music finished, fading into another equally familiar melody. She realized he must have made this tape for her, filled it with songs from their summer of memories.

However, when Luke said slow, he meant slow. Their dance continued through several more songs, and though his hands roved, he made no move to take off her bra or panties. Instead, he whispered of fantasies he wanted to play out, sensual intimacies he'd been imagining during the past few weeks.

By the time he'd finished describing them, Alicia's whole body had turned to molten syrup. He'd touched her everywhere, thoroughly, except the one place she was dying for him to touch. And so, to urge him on, she put her hand on him, stroking in a way she knew would drive him over the edge.

His breath erupted in a harsh hiss, his body trembling just as hers had trembled. Eyes shut, he stood with clenched hands while she unbuttoned his shirt, then lowered the zipper of his pants. And then she caressed him with her finger, watching the convulsive tremors of his face as she spread a drop of his own moisture over his velvety, sensitive surface.

As she had hoped, his control snapped, and a low, deep growl issued from his throat. Without further delay, he began to shuck his clothes, all of them. "Where?" he grated in a thick voice. "Do you want to stay here, or go upstairs?"

Dazed by the exceptional beauty of his nude body, Alicia swallowed. "Here is fine," she murmured. "Anywhere is fine."

He laughed hoarsely. "I'll remember that."

Yet even when she lay naked on the rug, even when he knelt over her like some magnificent, hedonistic god, he did not hurry. He moved his lips over her as though they had a lifetime for this, tasting and teasing and showering her with kisses, exploring all her most secret places with his hands and with his mouth. And when at last his fingers parted the delicate petals of her flesh to stroke the bud of her female pleasure, she let out a moan of pure ecstasy.

"Do you like this?" he whispered. "Or is this better? Tell me how you like it, sweetheart. Help me make it good for you."

Curiously she didn't feel shy now. She felt empowered, voluptuous, like a woman who had never had a moment's doubt about anything. And so, without embarrassment, she showed him her preference.

He was a fast learner. Within seconds, he had her writhing and gasping under his expert fingers. "Please, Luke, no more. Now...I need you now."

He paused only long enough to put on a condom. And then he came to her, seeking entry into her body, thrusting into her with all the urgency of his robust male lust. As she gripped his shoulders, he moved against her, his weight supported on his arms, his gaze pinned to hers just as his body pinioned her to the floor.

"Oh, Alicia," he uttered through clenched teeth, "I've wanted you this way for...so long...."

She gulped air, past the point of speech. With each long stroke, the exquisite tension was building inside her, spiraling higher and higher with his rhythm until at last it claimed her—*he* claimed her—in a volcanic eruption of red-hot, delicious sensation. As wave upon wave of liquid fire cascaded within, through and around her, she felt him give one final thrust. He collapsed on top of her with a loud groan, shudders racking his powerful body as he rested his head next to hers.

They lay still for almost a minute, their hearts thudding in unison as though connected. Then Luke lifted his head and grinned. "So did I seduce you or did you seduce me?"

She smoothed a hand over his hair, her breathing still a little quick. "Both, I think. How about an encore to help us decide?"

"Insatiable woman." His eyes crinkling with good humor, he lifted himself away from her, then rolled them over so that she was on top. "Give me a few minutes, honeybun. I'm thirty, not eighteen."

Alicia gazed down at him, studying the tiny age lines that framed the corners of his mouth. It seemed incredible that he could be thirty, that she could have missed so many years of his life. Where had all the time gone? A kind of sadness crept over her, but she shook it off.

"What about Daffy?" she asked. "I think I heard her barking."

"Let her bark. In a few minutes, she'll lie down on the porch and go to sleep."

"Speaking of sleep..."

"Are you tired?" His hands slid down to massage her bottom.

"Tired of being alone," she answered huskily, and kissed the base of his throat.

Long minutes passed, minutes in which she fulfilled a few of her own fantasies. Skillfully, hungrily, she used her feminine talents to arouse him, to return him to the very pinnacle of pleasure. And when the final moment came, when he could no longer withstand her assault upon his senses, he drove himself into her once more, fiercely, with a potency that carried her along with him on the highest crest of the wind.

Chapter Eleven

Alicia gazed out the window of the plane as it descended toward Houston Intercontinental Airport, her fingers clenched around a handwritten note. She must have reread it fifty times by now, and each time she felt a little guiltier.

> Darling,
> I apologize for not being here now that you finally made it back to Boston. Unfortunately, I'm heading out to the West Coast for the week and won't be back 'til Saturday night. A family matter that couldn't be ignored, I'm afraid. You can imagine how unhappy I was, knowing I would miss seeing you. It's been hell having you gone all these weeks—I don't know how I survived. Please come back soon.
>
> Love,
> Nick.

The note had been delivered to her condo, an hour after her arrival on Tuesday, and had been accompanied by a dozen long-stemmed red roses.

Confusion sifted through her, joining the guilt. How could she have been so wrong about the state of Nick's sentiments? Then again, how could she have known? He'd never called her darling before, never behaved as though she mattered to him in any way beyond friendship. To make matters worse, what romantic feelings she'd had for him had died a swift and painless death during their separation.

Shaking her head, she tucked the note back into her purse. Perhaps she should have canceled her return flight and stayed on through the weekend, but she had promised Ronnie she would be home today. Anyway, she wasn't ready to face Nick yet. She'd left a message for him on his answering machine, said all the appropriate things. She hadn't lied to him, hadn't led him on. But she hadn't been cool to him, either.

As the plane's wheels touched the runway, her thoughts flew to Luke. Within minutes she would see him again, and her heart raced as she pictured the meeting. Would he embrace her? Would they kiss the way teenagers did, regardless of watching eyes? She would if he would. She wouldn't care if people noticed.

At last the plane came to a halt and the seat-belt light went off. Alicia rose and gathered her belongings, her adrenaline level rising with her.

Trying to stay composed, she emerged from the tunnel into the terminal and scanned the crowd for a tall figure in a cowboy hat. He'd hardly been out of her mind all week. She'd carried him in her head while at work, while out to lunch with the girls and during the evenings when she had stopped by to see Gail. Most of all, she'd thought about him at night when she lay by herself in the queen-size bed she'd once shared with Kenny. She'd pretended Luke was there with her, beside her, inside her, even though it had made her ache.

He wasn't here.

Certain she must be mistaken, she searched the crowd again. All around her, other couples and families were reuniting amid noisy exclamations and laughter. But there was no one here for her.

No one.

Swallowing her disappointment, she started along the corridor. First Nick, and now Luke. Wasn't she first priority with anyone? Immediately she squelched the self-pitying thought. Nick had had a good excuse, and so would Luke.

Down in baggage claim, she waited for the conveyor system to spew forth her suitcase, wondering how much it would cost to take a taxi as far as Luke's house.

"I see her!" squeaked an excited voice in the distance.

Alicia swiveled in time to see Ronnie and Brian push their way through the turnstile. Ten yards behind, Sharon Redford hurried after them, an apologetic smile on her face.

"Sorry we're late," she explained as she huffed up. "The traffic was worse than usual. Luke asked me to tell you he'd see you later. Two of his employees called in sick today, so he couldn't get away."

Relieved by the simple explanation, Alicia thanked the other woman for coming to her rescue, then turned her attention to Ronnie. "Hey, sweetie, I missed you."

Ronnie hesitated only an instant, then flung his arms around her legs. "I missed you, too," he said emotionally.

Alicia bent down to hug him, a tightness in her throat. When she straightened, she reached over to ruffle Brian's hair. "So what have you two been up to?"

While Ronnie and Brian chattered about Power Rangers, Alicia's suitcase slid down the chute and chugged toward them. She stepped forward and grabbed it. Ten minutes later, they were driving along the airport exit road in Sharon's Bronco.

"So how'd it go?" Sharon inquired.

"The presentation went very well—so well that my boss is willing to let me take a little more time off. Unpaid, of course. I'm lucky she's been so understanding."

"Hmm. What about you-know-who?"

"Ronnie?"

"No, silly. I mean the big feller. Anything new cookin' in that direction?"

Alicia gazed out the window. "I'm not sure," she said in a quiet tone. "That's one reason why I came back. To find out."

"Oh, really." Sharon cast her a speculative look. "Did your no change to a yes? Or shouldn't I ask?"

Alicia felt herself blushing. "Maybe you shouldn't ask."

"Okay." Sharon gave a small chuckle. "We had your guys over for supper last night. Luke seemed a little preoccupied. I thought maybe he had you on his mind. By the way, I've got that contest information you asked about. It's in the folder by your feet. There's one that might be suitable for Ronnie since he's such a budding little artist. It's called the National Written and Illustrated By... Awards Contest For Children. The other two are interesting, too."

While Sharon talked, Alicia listened with only half an ear. She hoped she *had* been the reason for Luke's preoccupation. She wanted him to have missed her as much as she'd missed him. Surely he had. No man could make love the way he had and not feel something very powerful for the woman involved. Logic told her he must love her, just as she loved him.

But neither of them had said the words aloud.

It hadn't seemed too important at the time. In fact, she hadn't even noticed the omission until afterward when, sated and exhausted, she had lain in Luke's water bed and listened to the sound of his breathing. He'd fallen asleep first, but she had stayed awake for another hour, dreamily reliving every exquisite moment of their lovemaking. The photograph on his dresser hadn't even bothered her, not when the length of his body pressed against hers. Whoever the woman was, she was clearly not a current element in Luke's life.

The morning after had not been awkward. They'd made love again, not in the bed but in the shower—a hot, hard, erotic joining unlike anything she'd ever experienced. He hadn't said the words then, either. And like the night before, it hadn't seemed to matter.

But now, when she didn't have the afterglow of his lovemaking to reassure her, it did matter. And it made her uneasy because this was what had corroded their relationship the last time around. Her doubt that he loved her. His failure to say those three simple words.

What made her even more uneasy was that as soon as Ronnie had come home, the moment they were three again instead of two, Luke had seemed to withdraw. He had been agreeable and courteous, yet he hadn't done any of the little things she might have expected. There had been no surprise kisses in the hallway, no physical contact, no secret visits to her bedroom. In short, he'd behaved as though they hadn't made love. And so, out of pride, she had done the same.

Time was running out.

If he wanted her, if he *loved* her, he had better say so soon because her boss wasn't too happy about Alicia's continued absence. In fact, Phyllis had made it very clear that her forbearance would not last much longer.

"Hey, wake up." Sharon's voice roused Alicia to the fact that they were pulling into Luke's driveway. "You've been in outer space for the past half hour," her chauffeur teased. "You didn't even hear the kids singing, did you?"

Alicia shook her head sheepishly. "Sorry, I didn't mean to be such poor company. I've got a lot on my mind."

"I'll bet. Give him a smooch for me, will you? Jim would kill me if I did it myself. By the way, the kids want to know if Brian can stay and play for a while. Is that okay?"

"Sure. Come on in, guys."

Inside the house, she kicked off her shoes, smiling as Daffy and the children raced up the stairs to Ronnie's room. Massaging the back of her neck, she wandered down the hall to the kitchen and fixed herself a tall glass of ice tea. She took a small sip, reflecting how strange it was that this place felt so much more like home than her condo. Turning, she was about to go into the living room when she noticed the blinking red eye of Luke's answering machine. Her pulse leapt. Maybe he had left her a homecoming message. She walked over and pushed the button.

"Luke," said a woman's voice. "Hi, surprise, it's Christina! Guess what, I'm in Houston. Remember that conference I told you about? I decided to come after all. It's this weekend, at the George R. Brown Convention Center. Anyway, I'm staying at the Hyatt, room 1123. Call me, okay? Let's try to get together while I'm here. Tonight would be best for me if you can manage it. I'm really anxious to see you. Love you. 'Bye."

The message ended.

Alicia stood frozen for an instant, then her hand moved to press the Save button. The answering machine belted out a few beeps and whirs, then subsided into unsympathetic silence.

So. Christina *was* a current element in Luke's life. She was a real, live, flesh-and-blood woman. She also possessed a voice as wonderful as her face—soft and clear and low.

Alicia walked numbly into the living room and sat down. What should she do? That was the first thing to be decided. Should she let Luke know that she had heard the message? Or should she pretend to know nothing about it?

"Damn him," she muttered aloud. It felt good to say that, so good that with all the force she could muster, she punched one of the sofa pillows. "Damn him for doing this to me. I don't deserve to be treated this way."

Anger and resentment sizzled through her, like alcohol in her blood. Why was he keeping this woman a secret? There could be no good reason, none at all. Except that he thought it was none of Alicia's business.

She remembered the night she'd first realized that Kenny was cheating on her. He'd come home late, half-drunk and reeking of another women's perfume. And sex.

She hadn't handled it well. She'd hurled accusations at him, demanded to know whom he'd been with. At first, he'd refused to answer, then he'd lied to her, claiming he'd been out with the guys. He'd said she was imagining things, suggested she was paranoid. It was what he'd said every time after that until the day she had filed for divorce. Then he'd suddenly turned honest.

Well, Kenny had been a bastard, but he'd taught her a few lessons. Accusations didn't work. Demands for the truth didn't work. Men revealed things when they wanted to and not before. Hadn't Luke reaffirmed that simple verity? He'd told her about his dyslexia when he was damned good and ready. Not a decade ago when they were engaged to be married. Not when he'd asked for her help in his store.

And so it would be with Christina. There would be no point in asking. He would say she was just a friend. No one important. *You're imagining things, Alicia.* She'd heard it all before and she couldn't bear to hear it again.

Clutching a pillow to her chest, she sank back against the sofa cushions. Her battered pride just wasn't up to any more abuse. If he wanted her to know, then he'd tell her. If not, he wouldn't. It was as simple as that.

Luke locked up the store at six o'clock, impatience seething within him. He'd spent the last five days thinking about Alicia. Missing her, aching for her. Gathering the courage to ask her to marry him.

It had been hard enough the first time around, but at least then he'd been sure of her feelings. This time he wasn't. During their lovemaking, he'd almost been sure, but afterward, well, he hadn't known how to behave toward her when Ronnie was with them. She'd seemed to want him to keep his distance, and so he had. He didn't want to rush her or push her into something she wasn't ready for. Above all, he didn't want to do anything to jeopardize the progress he'd made in his courtship.

If only he understood her, he reflected. But women weren't like circuit boards; they didn't come with a schematic. The flow of their thoughts didn't follow a predesigned route. Compared to the complex workings of a female mind, resistors and capacitors and diodes were child's play.

As he drove home, he tried to remember the carefully laid-out speech he'd concocted. When he'd thought it up at three in the morning, it had seemed a heck of a lot easier to say. The words had poured through his brain, along with the courage to speak them. But now his heart was pounding.

He felt a bit silly, getting all worked up about a simple marriage proposal. It reminded him of that song from *Camelot,* the one where King Arthur trembled and hid from Guinevere, or so the singer claimed. Luke's mouth twisted. Maybe this was something all men shared, this fear of rejection that made it so hard for a man to ask a woman to spend the rest of her life with him. He tried to envision some of the guys he knew proposing to their wives. He pictured shy, introverted Dave Thompson popping the question to his Suzanne. Man, that was a tough one. Far easier to imagine the indomitable Suzanne doing the popping.

When he pulled into the driveway, he broke out in a sweat. Telling himself he was an idiot, he reached over and switched the air-conditioning to max, letting it blow over his face and neck for a few moments. Then he got out of the truck and went into the house.

He paused in the foyer, listening for sounds that would tell him where Alicia was. All he could hear was Ronnie and a friend—probably Brian—whooping it up above his head.

"Alicia?" he called out.

As if on cue, she appeared at the head of the staircase dressed in jogging clothes. "Hi," she said far more coolly than he expected. While he stared at her in confusion, she bounded down the stairs and headed for the front door. "I'm glad you're here—I wanted to get some exercise before supper. Keep an eye on the kids, okay? Sharon's coming for Brian in half an hour. See you in a while."

The door thudded shut.

Left alone, Luke stood very still, his hat in his hand, his ego somewhere around his knees. Damn it, he knew she was wacky, but this sure beat all. He'd thought she'd be glad to see him.

Daffy trotted down the stairs, tail wagging, her adoring brown eyes fixed on his face. Luke squatted down and scratched her ears, and received an enthusiastic lick for his efforts.

"Thanks," he grumbled. "At least somebody's happy to see me." Still grappling with his disappointment, he gave Daffy a final pat and rose to his feet. "C'mon, let's go see if you've had your supper."

In the kitchen, Daffy went to peer into her dish. She gave it a tentative lick and looked plaintively at Luke.

"Okay, okay." He scooped two cups of food from the bag in the laundry room and tipped it into the dog's dish. As he set the measuring cup in the sink, the blinking light on the answering machine caught his eye.

Scowling, he got himself a cold beer and took a long swig before he walked over and punched the button. "Luke," began a familiar voice. "Hi, surprise, it's Christina..."

He listened to the entire message, conflict brewing inside him like a storm. Ah, jeez, what timing. Of course he wanted to see Christina, but it was Alicia's first night back. These past few days of aching and emptiness had nearly driven him mad.

On the other hand, it might be best to put off the marriage proposal for a day or two. He couldn't pass up an opportunity to be with Christina; she was too important to him, too necessary. And since Alicia didn't seem to consider a reunion with him to be a big deal, maybe she wouldn't mind if he went out for the evening.

As for his offer of marriage, he was beginning to think that caution would be the best policy. A smart man would wait to see how the woman behaved before he took the plunge. Yes, that's what he'd do. He'd let a day or two pass, wait for just the right moment, the right setting, the right mood. Maybe another dinner date would be a better time to spring the big question.

Next he debated whether or not to tell Alicia about Christina. Something inside him resisted. Explaining Christina meant explaining a whole lot of other things he didn't like to talk about. Nobody knew about Christina, not even Joey.

On the whole, he'd prefer to wait until he was sure of Alicia—sure of her love, her loyalty, her understanding. Then he'd share Christina with her.

After she agreed to marry him.

Despite the comfort of Ronnie's company, the evening seemed empty without Luke. Alicia tried to block him from her thoughts, but that proved impossible. She kept getting flashes of him with Christina, their two dark heads bent close in laughter over a romantic dinner in some dimly lit restaurant. And it hurt. It was too much like the old days when she'd endured endless evenings at home, not knowing where her husband was, knowing only that he was somewhere with the despicable Tracy.

To make it worse, she had to conceal her pain from Ronnie. For his sake, she had to be strong. She had to watch his face as he worked on his story, composing heartrending sentences about how his parents had died, how he had cried, how Luke had comforted him. After a while, they put the pages away and got out a board game, which they played until bedtime.

After Ronnie went to bed, Alicia returned to the living room and scanned the *TV Guide,* hoping to find something to distract her. She settled on an old rerun of *The Music Man* and stretched out on the sofa. She soon found herself empathizing with Marian the Librarian as she warbled her way through the song "My White Knight." Marian only wanted a man who would love her, someone honest, quiet, straightforward and gentle. Alicia knew just how Marian felt.

Halfway through the movie, the phone rang.

"Alicia?" queried the voice at the other end of the line.

Alicia's heart sank. "Hello, Mother. How are you?"

"I'm well as usual, thank you. I haven't heard from you lately." The statement rippled with accusation.

Stifling a sigh, Alicia carried the receiver into the living room. "I haven't had much news."

"Well, I still like to hear from you." Her mother then launched into a monologue about her grandchild. "I thought you intended to bring him up here. I can't understand what you're waiting for."

Alicia twisted the cord around her finger. "The plan has changed, Mother. Ronnie's going to stay here and live with Luke. He's settled in school now and made new friends. It seems to be for the best."

"That's ridiculous. How can it be for the best? The child needs a mother. What kind of father can that man be? He isn't even a blood relative."

"Blood has nothing to do with it. Luke will make a splendid father. Ronnie won't lack for a thing."

"Except a mother," her mother said tersely. "Do you think this is what Caroline would have wanted?"

"Yes," Alicia replied, "I do." As she spoke the words, full acceptance of their rightness bloomed in her heart. "Ronnie wants to stay with his uncle. They have a strong emotional bond. Yes, I do think it's the right choice. I believe it's what's best for Ronnie."

There was a short silence. "Then why are you still there? I hope you're not doing something you'll regret."

Like what, Mother? Sleeping with Luke? Or falling in love?

"Don't worry about me. I know what I'm doing."

She could almost see her mother's skeptical expression. "I hope so. I trust you learned something from that nasty business with Kenneth. What about Nick Easton? If you aren't careful, you'll lose that one, too, and he's worth keeping, unless I miss my mark."

Like a fish, Alicia thought without humor. Reel him in while he's still hooked. "Please don't get your hopes up, Mother. Nick and I are just friends."

"A clever woman could change that. You've got to be practical, Alicia." When Alicia said nothing, her mother sighed. "Well, lollygagging around Houston isn't going to help matters. You'll be lucky if you still have a job when you get back."

"My job is fine and I'll be going back soon. How's Daddy?"

For a while the conversation strayed to less personal matters, then Alicia mentioned the box of Caroline's things.

"Yes, of course I want to see what's in it," Mrs. Brant said in an altered, rather shaky tone. "I—" She sniffed and broke off. In the background, Alicia could hear her blowing her nose. "I do want to see. Alicia..."

"Yes, Mother?"

"You and Ronnie are all I have left. I may not have said it well, but... I don't want to see either of you hurt again."

"Please don't worry, Mother. I'll be fine, and Ronnie's in good hands."

"He's my only grandchild. It doesn't seem right that I never get to see him."

"You could visit him here."

"With our teaching schedules, that's difficult. And you know your father doesn't like to fly. His asthma always flares up. The air on those planes is so unhealthy."

"When Ronnie comes north to visit me, I promise I'll bring him to see you. He and I have gotten to be great friends."

By the time she hung up the phone, Alicia was too drained and tired to enjoy the movie. She switched it off, looking across the room, where Daffy was sleeping behind the overstuffed chair. "Hey, girl, do you need to go out?"

Daffy did. When the dog had disappeared into the back-yard, Alicia took a seat at the kitchen table and flipped through the pages of Ronnie's story. He had made a lot of progress, written far more than she'd expected. As Mrs. Glover had suggested, he was extremely bright. She wished she could stay to help foster that brightness. It was going to be very hard to leave him.

When Daffy returned, Alicia locked the doors, wondering how late Luke would be. She certainly wasn't going to wait up for him like some lovesick fool. If he wanted their relationship to go anywhere, he was the one who was going to have to make the next move. Not that it looked as if that were likely to happen. For the first time since her return, that fact struck home.

On impulse, she went to the phone and dialed Nick's number. "Hi, Nick," she said to the answering machine. "Just wanted to say hi. I know you usually check your calls, so wherever you are, I hope you're thinking of me. I miss you. The separation has been difficult for me, too." She paused, wondering if she had just made an irrevocable mistake. "Call me when you can," she finished lamely. "'Bye."

Somehow that made her feel better. And after all, saying you missed someone wasn't a declaration of love. Nor was it cruel or misleading or wrong.

Clinging to that thought, she went up to bed.

It was past one in the morning when she finally heard Luke. He was hushing Daffy, whose sharp woof had woken her from a dreamless sleep. Alicia lay very still, her heart pounding as Luke's familiar footsteps climbed the stairs.

When he paused outside her door, she came close to calling out to him. Her pride stopped her. What if he had just come from that woman's bed? What if he reeked of her perfume, smelled of her body?

While these unpalatable thoughts passed through her head, he continued on down the hall to his room. His bedroom door clicked shut.

Alicia rolled over and scrunched her eyes shut. But the tears still escaped, slipping down her cheeks to dampen her pillow. Maybe for once her mother was right.

Chapter Twelve

The doorbell rang shrilly, setting off a cacophony of howls from Daffy. Luke screwed open an eye and glared at the clock on his bedside table. To his surprise, it told him it was past ten in the morning. Damn, he must have been exhausted.

Memory quickened within him as he rolled over and stared at the ceiling. Alicia was back. He hadn't proposed. Nothing had been resolved between them.

When the doorbell rang again, twice in a row, he threw off the sheets and reached for his cutoffs. Man, had he been having dreams. Glorious dreams, erotic dreams, and all of them about Alicia.

Wondering why she hadn't answered the front door, he hurried downstairs, cursing under his breath as he stubbed his toe on the stairs. "Damn it, Daffy, stop that!" he snapped. "Quiet! Sit down!" He yanked open the door and stared at the man who had just started to walk back to his car, a black Lincoln Continental. "Yeah?" Luke said churlishly.

The man turned around, regarding him with one arched and very elegant brown eyebrow. "Is this the home of a Mr. Luke Garrick?"

Luke disliked him on sight. The visitor was cool, impeccably attired and clearly well-to-do. None of this gave Luke the least clue as to what the guy was doing in his driveway, but he didn't much care. Nor did he feel like being polite.

"*A* Mr. Luke Garrick?" he responded with sarcasm.

The man smiled. "Forgive me if that sounded rude. I only meant . . . are you Mr. Garrick? I know the address is right, but—" He broke off as though to say more would be indelicate.

Luke had a sudden vision of himself. When he first crawled out of bed, his hair had a tendency to stick straight up. He was also unshaven and his eyes felt gritty. Worse, he had on nothing but a pair of frayed shorts, whose zipper— he was afraid to glance down—he was pretty sure was only partway pulled up. No wonder the guy seemed dubious; he must look like some barefoot derelict on a street corner.

Luke shoved a hand into his pocket, then jerked it out again when it occurred to him that he might put stress on the zipper. Hoping to set the other man at an equal disadvantage, he widened the door so that Daffy could sidle out.

"So who wants to know?" he inquired as his faithful dog galloped over and shoved her nose into the visitor's crotch.

The man handled himself well. Instead of stepping back, he stood very still, then slowly put out his hand, giving Daffy an alternative to sniff. Like a true lady, she took the proffered bait, shifting her attention to the long, manicured fingers. Her tongue slurped out. After a few seconds, the man transferred his hand to her ears, a tribute Daffy accepted with a smug look.

"The name's Easton," the man said, his eyes fixed on the dog. "Nick Easton. I'm looking for Alicia Brant."

Luke felt as if a sledgehammer had just plowed into his stomach. For at least ten seconds, his brain went blank. "She's mentioned you," he said at last.

"Then you must be Luke." Easton walked forward and extended his hand—the same hand Daffy had just finished licking. "It's nice to meet you at last."

Easy, Luke warned himself. This guy's not competition, despite the expensive wheels. The car, he now realized, was a rental. He shook hands, but found he couldn't smile. "When did you get here?"

"Last night, actually. I wanted to surprise Alicia, but it was too late to call so I took a room at the Marriott." Easton cast a curious glance over Luke's shoulder. "I take it she's not here?"

Luke wished he could say she was. He wished they'd just finished making love when the doorbell rang. He wished she'd come down the stairs right this instant wrapped in his bathrobe and that Easton would see and realize he was not wanted.

"I don't know. I just got up." Too late, Luke realized that made him sound like a couch potato. "If she was here," he said curtly, "she'd have answered the door."

"Of course." Easton flashed another smile. "Any idea where she might be?"

"She might be anywhere. I was asleep when she left."

"Would you mind checking to see if she left a note?" Looking apologetic, Easton added, "I've come rather a long distance to see her, you understand."

"Yeah, sure. Come on in," he added, his tone rather grudging.

"Thank you." Easton followed him into the house and down the hall to the kitchen. "Nice place," he remarked.

Luke shot him a suspicious look, but there was no trace of condescension in either his tone or his expression. "Thanks." On the kitchen counter lay a sheet of paper. He picked it up, observing that she'd printed rather than written the message, but in his current state of mind he knew better than to try to decode it. Instead, he pretended to read it, then passed the note over to Easton.

Easton scanned it. "Well, if she left at nine, she ought to be back soon, don't you think?"

Luke shrugged. "It could be awhile. I'll tell her you stopped by."

"Would you mind if I waited?"

Damn right he minded. He didn't want the guy in his house any longer than necessary. But common courtesy precluded his saying so; after all, Easton had done nothing to warrant such rudeness. Even if he had come to court Alicia, Luke knew she wasn't interested. At least he didn't think she was. Then he recalled her odd behavior last night, and a new seed of doubt sowed itself in his mind.

"Suit yourself," he said with coolness. "You can have a seat in the living room while I, uh, finish getting dressed. Put the TV on if you want."

Easton thanked him and went into the next room.

Luke departed for the upstairs bathroom. Shutting the door, he risked a glance in the mirror. Lord, he looked awful.

Keeping an ear out for Alicia, he splashed cold water onto his face, combed his hair and shaved. Then he went and put on a clean shirt and his newest pair of jeans. As he tucked in the shirt, he noticed that a missing button had been sewn on. He paused, staring at it with surprise and gratification. That was just like Alicia, to do something for him and never mention it. She'd ironed the shirt, too, he realized. What a sweetheart.

His sweetheart. *His* woman.

A surge of primitive possessiveness rushed through him, altering the tenor of his thoughts. Easton would be a fool not to want her; pure common sense told Luke it was why the man was here. Easton was his foe, his rival, and the knowledge filled him with the barbaric urge to go down and beat the fellow's face into a pulp.

"Yeah, right," he muttered beneath his breath. "That would sure win me a lot of points with Alicia."

Still, the primeval desire to lay claim to the mate he wanted, to do physical battle against his adversary, did not abate. The mere idea that Easton might have touched Alicia, kissed Alicia, ignited a red haze of anger in his head.

Fingers curled into fists, he stalked back down the stairs, determined to be no more than civil. To his annoyance, he found Easton poking through his CD collection. "Looking for something special?" he asked through gritted teeth.

Easton glanced over his shoulder, unfazed by his host's tone. "Not really. I was just curious to see what you had. It's an interesting assortment. We share a liking for Rachmaninoff, among others. 'Prelude in C-sharp Minor' is one of my favorites." He straightened his posture, adding cordially, "The cabinet was open so I didn't think you'd mind if I took a look."

"No, I don't mind." For a moment Luke couldn't think what else to say. "Would you like something to drink?"

"Sure." Easton grinned.

Ah, heck, no wonder Alicia liked the guy. Easton was nice. Luke could feel his antipathy thawing as he led the way back to the kitchen.

Nice or not, he wasn't going to let Easton steal his lady. Alicia was *his,* damn it. However, beneath this conviction ran a chilling wave of uncertainty. After all, if it was Easton she wanted, there wasn't a lot he could do about it, was there?

Alicia smiled and thanked the young man who'd loaded her groceries into the back of the Silverado. Gallantly claiming that it was his pleasure, he winked at her and swaggered off.

Amused, she slid into the driver's seat and started the engine. "Still like 'em?" she teased Ronnie, who had stuck his feet up on the console, the better to admire his new Nike athletic shoes.

"They're awesome!" he assured her. "Totally radical. Can I call Brian when we get home?"

"I don't see why not."

As the busier streets gave way to rural country roads, she wondered whether Luke was up yet. It was unusual for him to sleep past eight, but he had a valid excuse. He'd been working long hours the past few weeks, too long, perhaps. And he had gotten in so very late last night.... At once she walled off that line of thought. What Luke did was his business and none of hers.

Still, she couldn't help wondering how he'd behave today, whether he'd tell her anything about his evening, about Christina. She didn't expect it. He hadn't last night, had he? Just as she'd predicted, he'd said he had to go see a "friend" who was in town on business. He'd even looked a bit furtive, as though he'd known he had something to hide.

She hadn't quizzed him about it. That would have been foolish as well as demeaning. Nor would she ply him with questions today. If he wanted to tell her, he would.

Her jaw lifting to a proud angle, she pushed down on the accelerator, as though by pushing it she was letting off steam. Too late, she saw the nail-studded plank in the road. She felt the tire bump over it with a thud. She pumped the brake, slowing the vehicle just as she would have done on an icy surface.

"What happened?" Ronnie asked. "Why are we stopping?"

After the truck came to a halt, she glanced at him and sighed. "It's okay. I ran over a piece of wood, that's all."

Climbing out of the vehicle, she walked around to check the right front tire. Unfortunately, it had sprung a leak. Air was hissing out at an alarming rate.

Her spirits sinking as fast as the tire, she walked back to retrieve the plank and tossed it into the back of the truck. Lord, what would Luke say? What a dumb thing to do. If she'd only been paying attention, she could have avoided this. Kenny would have skinned her alive, told her how stupid she was, how incompetent.

"We've got a flat tire," she told Ronnie. "But we're almost home so we can walk." She looked up and down the empty country road, but no white knight loomed on the horizon. "Uncle Luke knows how to change tires. Don't worry, all right?"

"Okay." Ronnie looked relieved.

Alicia turned on her blinkers, shoved all but one of the grocery bags inside the front cab and locked the doors. She then took the last bag of groceries, the one with the ice cream and cold cuts and started down the road. Ronnie trudged happily at her side, humming the Power Rangers theme song under his breath.

Twenty minutes later, they reached Luke's driveway and saw the Lincoln. Alicia's steps slowed. "I wonder whose car that is," she said, unnerved to discover that Luke had a visitor. What if it was Christina? If so, she couldn't go in there. She just couldn't, not like this, looking all hot and sticky and mussed. She hadn't even washed her hair this morning.

"Come on," Ronnie urged. "I want a drink."

Alicia shifted the bag of groceries from one arm to the other. "Okay," she said in a weak voice, "I'm coming."

Her heart thumped as they entered the house. This was going to be the bitter moment of truth, the closing act on her own fruitless fantasy. She was finally going to get to meet the woman with the violet-blue eyes.

As they walked toward the kitchen, she heard Luke's voice. "Didn't put him in until the top of the eighth inning."

Alicia took a deep breath, moved forward . . . and almost dropped the groceries in astonishment. "Nick!"

The two men were seated at the kitchen table, each of them nursing a can of soda.

"Surprise," Nick said with a smile. Rising, he came over to her, his intent blue eyes scanning her face. "Luke invited me to wait for you. I didn't mean to shock you."

Gathering her wits, Alicia shook back her hair and set the bag on the kitchen counter. "No. I mean— No, I'm not shocked. But I am surprised. What in the world are you doing here?"

"I wanted to see you," he explained, "so I canceled my flight to Boston and booked one to Houston instead. I thought we could go out to dinner or something." He paused. "I got your messages, by the way. All of them."

"Who's he?" Ronnie demanded.

Flustered, Alicia introduced Nick to Ronnie, then turned to face Luke, still seated at the table. So far as she could see, he hadn't moved a muscle. His face was a mask, his eyes unreadable. "There's a little problem with the truck," she said nervously.

"What kind of problem?"

"I, uh, ran over something in the road. The tire went flat. I left it a half mile or so down the road."

Frowning, Luke rose to his feet. "You're not hurt?"

"No," she assured him. "I didn't run into anything. There's no damage to anything but the tire. I'm sorry. It was such a stupid thing to do—"

Luke came over to her, ignoring Nick as though he wasn't there. "Don't apologize, Alicia. It wasn't stupid. It was an accident. As long as you and Ronnie aren't hurt, that's all that matters, okay?"

"Okay," she agreed, her eyes searching his. "The rest of the groceries are still in the cab."

He nodded. "I'll take the van and get them. Then I'll take care of the tire."

"I'll pay for the repair," she offered.

He gave her a level look. "No way," he said, and walked out of the room.

Nick regarded her with quizzical amusement. "Did you think he was going to beat you? You looked almost scared."

"Well, Kenny would have thrown a fit. I guess I'm used to temperamental men." Feeling foolish, she started to unload the bag of groceries.

"I see." Nick came over and slid his arms around her waist. "I hope you're not including me in that statement."

"Of course not." Alicia glanced around for Ronnie, but he had disappeared. Turning, she began, "Nick, I *am* glad to see you—" His hungry mouth silenced her.

It was not the first time they'd kissed, but it was the first time she'd been so conscious of his passion. Without question, his ardor had increased during her absence. Out of politeness and affection, she responded, but her heart wasn't in it. It was a nice kiss, a pleasant kiss, delivered with polish and skill. It simply did nothing to fire her blood.

"I have a room at the Marriott," he murmured. "Come back with me for the afternoon."

"Nick, I can't."

"Why not?" He skimmed his lips along the line of her jaw. "I've missed you so damn much, Alicia. I didn't think I needed you, but I do, I do."

Grabbing the ice cream, she moved out of his arms, her face hot with embarrassment and distress. "Of course I'd love to spend time with you. It's just that I've promised to take Ronnie swimming. And besides, how would it look? I have to set a good example."

Nick lifted a brow. "No one would know what we were doing. Certainly not the child."

"I can't break my promise to Ronnie," she pleaded. "He's been through so much. You can understand that, can't you?"

"Yes, of course I can." He was silent for a moment. "Dinner then. We'll make an evening of it."

"All right. Dinner would be lovely."

"Would six o'clock be too early?"

She gazed at him, at his tender expression and beautiful, grave eyes. What a truly good person he was, always so gentle and considerate and courteous. As her mother had pointed out, she could do far worse than encourage this man.

"Six o'clock would be perfect," she said.

Luke loaded the remaining groceries into his van and climbed inside, hoping Easton would be gone by the time he got back. But the Lincoln still sat in the driveway, looking as out of place as a yacht in a swimming pool. The muscles in his jaw tightened. The guy wasn't the turkey he'd been expecting, but just the same, he didn't want him as a house guest.

He wished now he'd had the sense to kiss Alicia before he'd left; that would have put a roadblock into whatever plans Easton had in mind. On the other hand, if she'd pulled away, it would have been damnably embarrassing.

Easton and Alicia were still in the kitchen when he walked in. Ignoring them, he dumped the first two bags onto the table and went back for the other two. When he returned the second time, Easton was helping Alicia put the food away.

Luke gritted his teeth, wondering if there was any polite way he could throw the guy out of his home.

"Do you need any help with the flat?" Easton inquired. "I'd be happy to lend a hand."

Luke looked him up and down. "You're not exactly dressed for that kind of work."

"True, but it doesn't matter. If you need help, just say so."

Luke couldn't deny that Easton had a kind of unpretentious appeal. If the guy hadn't been sniffing around his lady, he would have liked him. Perhaps it was Easton's straightforward approach, his failure to look down his nose at someone who was quite clearly not of his world. But he *was* after Alicia. Luke could see it in his eyes.

"No, thanks," he replied. "I can handle it."

"Okay." Easton shrugged. "By the way, I was wondering if you could suggest a good restaurant. I'm taking Alicia out to dinner tonight, and we'd like some place... romantic. You know what I mean. A place with atmosphere. And fine dining, of course."

Oh, of course, Luke thought with fury. A place where the entrées started at twenty dollars, a place with candles and white tablecloths and waiters in tuxedos. *A place where you can impress the hell out of my woman while you play footsie with her under the table.*

"Sorry," he said brusquely. "I only eat at McDonald's."

"Luke!" Alicia cut in, sounding rather shocked. "That's not true. What about that lovely place we went to—"

"I don't think that's the kind of place your friend has in mind," he interrupted. "Why don't you look in the phone book? I've got to get that tire changed and get to work."

Alicia took a long, hot shower, hoping it would ease the knot of tension that had been building inside her all day. It didn't. When she stepped out onto the fluffy blue bath rug, her insides were roiling as much as ever.

As she toweled her damp hair, she wondered why she felt so hesitant about going out with Nick. It wasn't as if she and Luke had made a pledge to each other. No promises had been exchanged, no permanent commitment mentioned. And there was no way she could have turned Nick down, not after he'd come all this way just for her.

No, she was doing the right thing, and if Luke didn't like it, well, that was just too bad. After the way he'd dashed off to be with Christina, he had no justification for his surly behavior.

Still, when she slipped into her newly purchased black dress a short while later, it was Luke's reaction she envisioned, not Nick's. Back in Boston, she'd chosen it specifically with Luke in mind. Maybe it was foolish to wear it now, for the wrong man, but it might be the only chance Luke ever had to see her in it. And she was determined that he should, even if it was only a brief glimpse as she walked out the door with her hand on another man's arm.

Sliding her feet into black high heels, she studied herself in the mirror. She wore only earrings; the dress required no other jewelry. In length, it came only to midthigh; its sleek lines clung to her figure, accentuating her curves. Two thin straps held up the bodice, whose scooped neckline exposed enough cleavage to bring a blush to her cheeks. Yes, without doubt it was a dress designed to allure the most jaded member of the male sex. Her pulse raced as she pictured Luke's face when he saw her.

She glanced at the clock. Five-forty. As always, Nick would be punctual; she had a little time to kill. She swallowed hard. All right, then. It was time to go down.

Her heart in her throat, she descended the stairs. Luke and Ronnie were in the living room watching TV. Holding her breath, she moved down the hall until she reached the doorway, but to her surprise, Luke was alone.

"Where's Ronnie?" she asked, grateful to have something innocuous to say.

Luke turned his head. And stared, though not in the way she had hoped. "What the hell are you wearing?"

Her head held high, she took two steps into the room. "It's a new dress," she said, spinning once around. "Don't you like it?"

"You look like a hooker," he said roughly.

Blood drained from her face. "What an awful thing to say."

"You asked, didn't you?" He sprang to his feet and walked toward her, fury and black lust blazing in his eyes. "You call that a dress? It looks like lingerie to me, Alicia. But I'm sure you know that without me saying so. Easton's a lucky man. I got the virgin, he gets the vamp."

Her mouth opened and closed, but no words came out.

He came closer, his eyes trailing over her in an almost contemptuous manner. "I guess the Lincoln did the trick, eh? It sure beats a truck any day of the week. I bet the guy can even read the menu on his own." He reached out and fingered one of her shoulder straps. "Well, enjoy your fine dining experience. But then, it looks like you plan to."

"How dare you?" she choked out. "You're not my... my—"

"Lover?" he taunted.

"You have no *right!*"

An unpleasant smile twisted the corners of his hard mouth. "No," he agreed. "I guess I don't."

"What's the matter, Alicia?" Nick reached across the table to cover her hand, his handsome face concerned.

She shook her head. "Nothing."

"Come on, tell me. You've been looking down in the dumps ever since we left the house."

She poked her filet mignon with her fork. "Tell me something."

"What?"

"Does this dress make me look like a hooker?" she asked bluntly.

To her chagrin, he burst out laughing. "No, of course not. It makes you look sexy and sophisticated. Where did you get that idea?"

She looked down, reluctant to answer.

"Did Luke tell you that?" The amusement faded from his voice.

"Yes."

He sighed. "What gives with this guy, huh? He's been giving me the evil eye ever since I got here. Now he's giving you a hard time, too."

"He and I were once engaged to be married."

"Good Lord, why didn't you tell me?"

"I didn't think it mattered. It was all so long ago."

"It appears to matter to him." Nick paused, his expression serious. "Does it matter to you, Alicia? Do you still love him?"

"Of course not," she lied. "Anyway, he's got a girlfriend. I don't know why he's acting this way. Maybe he's just trying to protect me. I suppose he thinks all college-educated men are like Kenny.''

"He didn't go to college? No wonder you didn't marry him.''

Without a moment's hesitation, she leapt to Luke's defense. "That had nothing to do with it! Luke had a very good reason for not going to college. He has dyslexia, badly. He was undiagnosed for years and it was hard on him. It still is.''

Nick's brows snapped together. "That is tough,'' he acknowledged. "I'm a bit dyslexic myself, though I learned to compensate for it at an early age. I still want to kick myself sometimes when I make a mistake.''

"Then you can understand,'' she retorted. "Anyway, college doesn't make the man. A man's true worth comes from within.''

"So why didn't you marry him?''

She sighed. "Because I didn't think he loved me. And because he wanted me to quit college and come down here to Houston with him. He didn't understand how important it was that I get my degree. At Kessler College, I didn't have to pay tuition because of my parents. I couldn't afford to transfer anywhere else. He either couldn't understand, or didn't want to. So we broke it off.''

"It seems like you're totally incompatible.'' Nick sounded relieved. "Unlike you and me.''

She raised her head.

"You know,'' he went on in a casual tone, "I asked you out tonight for a special reason.'' He reached into his pocket and drew out a small, black velvet box, which he set on the table between them. "I bought this while I was in L.A.''

"Nick, I—''

"Don't say anything yet. I want to tell you something.'' He cleared his throat, his eyes locked with hers. "Since Lynn died, I haven't been feeling very much. I wasn't happy or sad. I was just empty, just floating along. Existing. Then I met you, and I started to feel again. Just a little at first. Anticipation. Pleasure. Attraction. That surprised me, because I'd thought I'd never want to touch another woman. But I wanted to touch you.'' He reached for his wine and took a sip. ''Then you went to Houston. I thought I'd forget you, but instead I thought about you all the time. I missed you more than I thought possible. And I began to realize that I had fallen in love with you.''

''Oh, Nick.'' Dismay tightened her throat.

''I'd like you to marry me, Alicia.'' He picked up the box and handed it to her. ''And this is a token of my esteem.''

Somehow her hands accepted it, though her numbed brain whirled with tumult. With unsteady fingers, she lifted the lid and found a magnificent diamond solitaire ring winking up at her in the candlelight.

''Nick, it's beautiful,'' she said helplessly. ''But...''

''But?'' He cocked an eyebrow.

''I'm just not sure I'm ready to be married again,'' she floundered. ''I don't know what to say.''

He gave her a considering look. ''I see. Then you need time to think it over.''

''Yes,'' she said, seizing on this with gratitude. She closed the box and set it back down onto the snowy white tablecloth. ''This is so unexpected. You see, I thought we were only friends. I mean, we'd spent time together, but I hadn't anticipated this at all. I need time.''

''Then you'll have it,'' he said quietly. He reached over and touched her cheek. ''Take as much time as you need.''

Chapter Thirteen

Later, when they walked to the door of Luke's house, Alicia did not invite Nick inside. Nor did he ask to come in. After all, he, too, had seen that the lights were still on. However, he did kiss her again—a hard, swift kiss that, had it come from Luke, would have rocked her all the way to her toes.

"Good night, Alicia," he whispered. "I'll be in touch."

After he had driven away, she entered the house, her nerves jangling with anticipation. It was foolish to think Luke was lying in wait for her, like a wolf ready to pounce, but she could not shake the feeling.

Pausing in the foyer, she considered going straight to her room, but that seemed the height of cowardice. It would be better to face Luke now, to smooth things over while Ronnie was not around to witness their discord. Squaring her shoulders, she left her shoes and purse by the foot of the stairs and headed for the living room, where the soft strains of classical music gave away the wolf's whereabouts.

She halted in the doorway, taken aback to find him stretched full-length on the sofa, an empty glass and a bottle of Jack Daniel's on the coffee table beside him. His eyes were closed. His face looked as pale and drawn as if he were ill.

"Luke?" she said, moving toward him in concern.

He opened his eyes and looked at her, his eyes glittering like cold, gray ice. "Where's your friend? Didn't you invite him to come in and party with us?"

"Luke, are you drunk?"

"No such luck." His brooding gaze wandered over her, but at least he made no further comment about her dress. "Are you?"

"Don't be silly. I wouldn't do that and you know it."

"Right now I feel like I don't know anything about you." Something akin to pain crossed his face, then he shrugged and sat up. "Did you have a good time with Nicky?"

"I wish you wouldn't call him that. It's very childish of you to keep insulting him. I think you'd like him if you gave him half a chance."

Luke's laugh was hollow. "Oh, I like him a lot. He's a super guy. We have some major things in common."

"Even more than you know," she said on impulse. "Would you believe he's dyslexic, too? Not as severely as you are, apparently, and he learned to compensate for it when he was young. But he sympathizes with what you must have gone through—"

"You *told* him?" The words sliced the air, his voice laden with unmistakable fury. "You told him I was dyslexic?"

"Well...yes," she admitted, her stomach clenching as she realized the enormity of her mistake. "I mentioned it. I'm sorry, I didn't mean to upset you. It came into the conversation quite naturally—"

He rose to his feet, his face more dark and ominous than any wolf's. "Oh, it's natural for you to broadcast my personal concerns, is it? Did you tell him we slept together, too? Did you tell him what it felt like and how many times we did it?"

Shocked, she took a step backward. "Don't be absurd! I wouldn't dream of telling him something like that. Maybe I shouldn't have mentioned your dyslexia, but Luke, honestly, Nick understands. Anyway, it's not as though I told my mother—" She saw his expression and broke off, knowing she had just compounded her error. "Luke, that's not what I meant. I wouldn't care if my mother knew. I'm not ashamed of you."

"Is that so?" he said with terrible sarcasm.

"Yes, it's so! Look, I think you *are* drunk. I apologize for what I did, but I think we should discuss this in the morning when you're sober." With a heavy sigh, she added, "I've made the decision to return to Boston within the week. Tomorrow we'll need to start preparing Ronnie. Good night."

She started to turn away, but a strong hand closed on her arm and whirled her around. "Not so fast, sweetie pie. You started this, now you're going to stay here and finish it."

"Let go of me."

"When I'm good and ready. First I want you to sit down and tell me your definition of the word 'prepare'. I'm real interested to hear it."

She found herself deposited on the sofa, trapped by the wall of male muscle towering over her. She tilted her chin at him. "I mean Ronnie has to be told, that's all."

"So," he said, his fists on his hips, "you're saying you're just going to walk out on that kid. I can't believe this."

"I thought you'd be pleased! You wanted him to stay here. You don't seem surprised, so he must have told you he'd decided to stay and that I had agreed."

"He told me. What I can't believe is that you're going to walk out of here like he doesn't even matter to you."

"Of course he matters to me! It tears my heart out to leave him. But I have to do what I think is right."

Luke's lip curled. "So you managed to stay here just long enough to make him love you, and now you're going to take yourself off for the rest of his life. Do you really think you helped him, Alicia? Did you think he needed to lose another person?"

"Yes, I think I helped him. At least I . . . I tried."

Oh, God, maybe Luke was right. Her intentions had been good, but maybe all she'd accomplished was to pave the way for more pain and loss in Ronnie's life. Nearly blinded by tears, she tried to rise, to get away, but Luke thwarted her attempt with his body.

As if to twist the knife, he leaned over her, his hands framing her shoulders where he gripped the sofa back. "Maybe you tried, but I think you did more damage than good. You sashayed down here, Miss Eager-Beaver-Do-Gooder, ready to sweep Ronnie off to Boston. You took over his life and mine, fired my cleaning lady, sweet-talked us all, seduced me and now—"

"How can you *say* that?" A solid wave of fury slammed into her, lending her the physical strength to thrust him back a whole step. She leapt to her feet and pushed him again as hard as she could. "It wasn't like that and you know it! Why are you trying to hurt me?"

He looked stunned, as though her questions had hit some invisible target. "I don't know." He shook his head as if to clear it. "I'm sorry. I'm such a damned jerk. I shouldn't have said that. Any of it. And before, what I said about your dress ... that wasn't true, either. I'm sorry. I didn't mean it. Your dress is beautiful.'' He paused. "Like you.''

"It's okay,'' she said, dazed by this about-face. "You were upset about Ronnie. I'm sorry I pushed you.''

He shoved a hand through his hair, his expression rigid, his eyes focused on some point behind her head. "Alicia, we need to consider the other option.''

She froze. Her heart buffeted against her rib cage while she waited for him to continue.

"I think Ronnie should live with you.''

Her throat closed, her breathing shut off as she fought the urge to sob aloud. For a crazy instant, she'd thought he was going to propose. And like a lovesick fool, she'd been ready to accept.

"Think about it,'' he said tonelessly. "You're the one with the education. You can help him with his homework, help him learn to read. Look at this story you've got him working on. I couldn't have done that with him. I wouldn't even have thought of it. I don't think I'm cut out to be a parent. I'm a loner, Alicia. Not a ... a dad.''

Amazement wiped away other emotions. She stared at him, knowing the magnitude of his proffered sacrifice. Ronnie's words circled back to haunt her. *Uncle Luke needs me. He doesn't have anyone else.*

"No,'' she said, shaking her head. "No. Ronnie belongs here with you. I love him, but you love him, too. Your bond with him goes back to the time he was a baby. I think we both know it would be wrong for me to take him. I think I knew it from the start, but I was stubborn. I thought—'' She swallowed hard. "I guess I thought I could make a differ-ence. I wanted to do something for Caroline.'' She drew a breath. "But you're wrong, Luke. You'll make Ronnie a fine father. The very best.''

He made no answer. He gazed at the floor, his face set in
a peculiar expression, as though he was waging some great
internal battle with himself. "Alicia—"

"Luke—" she began at the same instant.

Their eyes connected.

"Go ahead," he said. "What were you going to say?"

"Well..." She licked her lips. "I wanted to tell you
that... Nick asked me to marry him tonight."

A gamut of emotions flashed across Luke's face, then
vanished, too fleeting to be identified. "And of course you
accepted him," he said, his tone lifeless.

"No, as it happens I haven't. But I'm considering it." Her
fingers curled into fists at her sides, her nails digging deep
into her palms as she waited for him to respond.

To her dismay, he went and poured himself a generous
portion of whiskey. Lifting it to his mouth, he said very
dryly, "I guess he liked the dress," and drained it in a single gulp.

"Aren't you even going to ask why?" she demanded in
frustration.

"Oh, I know why he liked the dress." Without expression, he appraised her with seeming indifference. "I bet his
designer pants were on fire all evening."

"Damn it, Luke, don't be like this! If you're mad, then
say so."

He set down the glass with a loud thunk. "Why should I
be mad? It's your life, Alicia. If you want to marry Easton,
go ahead. I won't try to stop you, even if I think you're
making a mistake."

"So you think I shouldn't marry him."

"What difference does it make what I think?"

"I thought you might care," she said in a low voice. "I
thought you might be concerned about me."

He raised a hand, pressing his fingers to his forehead as though it hurt. Then he dropped his arm and looked at her again, anger reanimating his narrowed eyes. "Damn it, I can't play these games with you. You want me to tell you not to marry the guy? Fine. *Don't marry him.* Go back to your condo and your high-tech job and your lonely bed. Is that what you want me to say?"

"I don't know," she said miserably.

"Okay, that's not good enough." He raked a hand through his hair, looking harassed and savage and scornful. "Then how about this for a laugh? Marry me instead."

"What?" she said, her voice faint. *Not like this. Oh, please, God, not like this.*

"I said, marry me. It'll solve all our problems with Ronnie, won't it? He's torn between us, and this way he can have us both. And it's not as though I can't support you. I don't have the kind of money Easton has, but you won't lack for anything. I happen to own a lot of land." His hands spread in a sweeping gesture. "You said you liked this house. Then stay here and live in it with me. We already know the sex is good. We can have all the children you want, brothers and sisters for Ronnie. I'll even put in a pool if you want. Anything. Just stay here with us. For Ronnie's sake."

Alicia stood very still, her insides cramped with anguish, unshed tears burning her throat. How could this be happening? Nick's proposal had been so gentle and loving. Luke's was flung in her face like a gauntlet.

Slowly, distinctly, she said, "I can't marry you for Ronnie's sake. Let's face it, Luke. You had what you wanted from me. All these years... well, we've both been curious about each other. Now we know what the sex is like. Yes, it was nice, but that's not enough to base a marriage on." She drew a shaky breath. "Nick loves me. His first wife died three years ago from breast cancer. He went through hell with her and...I don't want to be the one to cause him more pain. I think I'm going to accept him. As for you and me, well, it didn't work between us the first time, and it's not working again. So let's just go our separate ways and get on with our lives.''

A muscle jerked at the corner of his mouth. "Fine," he said very flatly. "If that's the way you want it."

So this was what defeat felt like. It made her feel old and tired, bereft and desolate. Hopeless.

With an inward shudder, she turned and walked away from him, but in the doorway she stopped and forced herself to look back. "I'll find you another housekeeper before I leave."

He didn't so much as glance at her. His head was bent, his stance rigid and immobile as a rock. "Don't bother," he rasped. "Just go, Alicia. And have a good life."

He'd blown it all, done everything wrong. No woman with integrity or pride could have accepted the proposal he'd tossed out. Luke knew that. He'd known it even while he was forming the words, but he'd gone ahead and blown it anyway.

The night stretched before him like a road without end. He didn't even try to sleep. He just stayed where he was, slumped on the sofa with his feet on the table.

And let the pain eat him alive.

He thought about getting loaded but decided against it. He'd had enough whiskey to blur the edges and more wasn't going to make him feel anything but worse. As it was, he felt like a fifty-pound weight rested on his chest.

Again and again he went over the scene in his head, trying to remember exactly what he'd said to her, exactly what she'd said to him. The confrontation came back to him in bits and snatches, mixed up like pieces of a puzzle. He'd said things to hurt her, horrible things. He'd insulted her, insulted Easton.

Why had he tried to hurt her? Even now, he didn't know. He'd wanted to protect her, love her, heal her. Instead, he had lashed out like some half-crazed animal with its leg in a trap.

Aren't you even going to ask why?

Her question drifted through his head, floating in a sea of disconnected phrases. At the time, he'd known she wasn't referring to her dress, but he'd chosen to misinterpret her question. Now he wondered what she'd meant. What had she been saying? It had been just after she'd told him that Easton had proposed.

He couldn't remember.

No, wait. She'd said she was considering Easton's offer. She'd also told him why. She was marrying the man because she felt sorry for him. Because she didn't want him hurt again. Luke's insides twisted. Damn it, what about *him?* How come Easton's suffering was more important than his?

Maybe she didn't even know he was hurting.

Maybe he should have told her he loved her.

Those words had never been easy for him to say. Long ago, Alicia had said them to him, but he didn't think he'd ever said them back. He'd wanted to, but he hadn't been very good at communicating his deepest feelings. He still wasn't.

I love you.

Only a few people besides Alicia had ever said those words to him. His real mother. Ruth and Walter Garrick. Richard. Ronnie. And, most recently, Christina. Important people, special people. Yet sometimes that other period of his life—the years when he'd known no love at all— caught him in such a stranglehold that he couldn't speak.

He remembered the first dour set of foster parents, Mr. and Mrs. Schmidt. He'd been six years old and aching for his mother, plagued with nightmares and trying not to cry. He'd tried to offer his love to Mrs. Schmidt. He'd whispered, "I love you," into her ear one night when he'd soiled his sheets and she'd gotten up in the night to change them.

And she'd answered, "Don't be silly. Now go back to sleep, and let's have no more accidents."

He'd not said the words again until his adoptive mother, Ruth Garrick, lay dying in her bed. Oh, he'd shown his love for her and for Walter in other ways. He'd expressed that love by legally changing his surname from Larney to Garrick when he was fourteen, and in a thousand other ways before that. But never in that one special way. And when he'd finally done it, when he'd finally said the words, Ruth had smiled, patted his hand and whispered, "I know, dear. I love you, too."

So the words weren't hard to say. He knew that. After all, he'd been saying them for years to Ronnie. His lips knew how to form the syllables, just as his heart understood their meaning.

Three simple words. Why hadn't he said them to Alicia?

Because his worst fear had always been that they wouldn't make any difference.

Alicia zipped her suitcases closed and glanced around the room that had been hers for the past few weeks. The bed was made, the drawers and closet empty. She'd left nothing. The room looked just the way it had when she'd first walked in. Her presence had been easily erased.

Four nightmare days had passed since her showdown with Luke. They'd barely spoken since then, even though she'd wrapped up a few items of business at his store. The guys there had bought her a gift, a selection of bath soaps and lotions picked out by one of their wives. Dave had given her a small bracelet. Woody had given her a hug.

She'd said her goodbyes to Sharon's family yesterday evening, and to Joey and Nora the evening before. Joey would be returning to work in November, so Luke would be on his own until then. Joey had told her not to worry. Luke had said he could manage.

True to her word, she'd helped Ronnie complete his contest entry and made sure he got a copy of it into the mail. He'd worked so hard on it, given so much, and she wanted him to keep the original. Despite what Luke had said, she believed the project had done Ronnie some good. Ever since he'd started on the story, he'd seemed less rebellious, less inclined to shut himself up in his room to cry. The temper tantrums had tapered off and so had the nightmares. Even Mrs. Glover had noticed a difference, for she'd sent home a note stating that Ronnie's behavior had improved.

This morning's parting with Ronnie had been excruciating, and she preferred not to think about it. Ronnie would not be accompanying her to the airport since her flight left while he was in school. All in all, he'd accepted the news of her departure rather well, though when she'd first told him, he'd burst into tears. Later, he'd given her one of his dinosaur pictures to post on her refrigerator. He'd also made her promise to write to him, and he'd promised to come visit.

But now the worst moment had arrived.

Nauseous with dread, she set her luggage outside the bedroom door and went back for her cosmetic case. Footsteps approached from the direction of Luke's bedroom.

"Are you ready?"

She steeled herself to turn and look at him. Framed in the doorway, he stood tall and remote, impassive and unreachable. The tender and passionate man who'd made love to her was gone, and in his place she saw a stranger.

"Yes," she said bleakly.

Without comment, he carried her suitcases down the stairs. Alicia followed in silence. At the foot of the staircase, Daffy ambled up, her tail wagging, her liquid eyes bright with pleasure.

"Goodbye, Daffodil. Be a good girl." Alicia set down her things and hugged the collie, her throat aching with the need to cry.

But she didn't. On the way to the airport, a curious calm settled over her, as though she had stumbled into the quiescence at the center of some great hurricane. Neither pain nor joy nor sorrow could touch her here, in this anesthetic void, and she welcomed it.

As they neared the terminal, Luke finally spoke. "Do you want me to come in with you?"

She shook her head. "There's no need."

More silence.

He pulled in at the passenger unloading area and shut off the engine, but instead of getting out, he just sat there. Unperturbed, Alicia reached for the handle of the door.

"Wait." Luke's voice was abrupt.

"What is it?" She didn't look at him; instead she stared at the dashboard. Ronnie had written his name in the dust.

"You said Easton loves you. What would you say if I told you . . . I love you, too?"

Her heart leapt, plunged, then settled back into its state of icy detachment. "I'd say you should have told me that a long time ago. If it's true."

"You think I'm making it up?"

As though they were discussing two other people, she considered the question. "I think you wouldn't know love if it hit you in the face. I've already been married to a man who said he loved me, then showed me otherwise. Nick won't do that." She paused. "With Nick, I'll be safe."

She turned away, opened the door and got out. Several seconds later, Luke did likewise. He removed her suitcases from the back of the truck and carried them over to the baggage check-in line. For a few throbbing seconds, their gazes met.

Neither of them said goodbye.

Chapter Fourteen

Alicia tucked a file folder under her arm and walked briskly down the corridor toward her office. The morning's presentation had gone so well that her boss had commended her afterward, hinting that Alicia's annual evaluation would be very favorable. If Phyllis had her way, Alicia would be getting an advancement in labor grade as well as a substantial and long-overdue raise. This news, plus the advent of a four-day weekend, should have put Alicia into a celebratory mood. But it didn't.

"Hey, Alicia, have a good holiday!"

Alicia spun around and smiled at the male co-worker who had addressed her. "Same to you, Sam. Happy Thanksgiving!"

She waved to two more acquaintances and entered her office, dropping the folder onto her desk with a sigh. Sitting down, she kicked off her heels and massaged her aching feet. Then, for the umpteenth time since she'd received it, she reached for her purse and withdrew Ronnie's last letter.

It was a simple letter, full of innocent chatter. He told her he was doing well in school. He'd been invited to Tara's birthday party. Tara liked him now. He thought she was okay. Daffy was fine. He was fine. Uncle Luke was fine. Brian was fine.

But it was the end of his letter that caught at her heart.

I miss you a lot. At nite I think of you. So duz unkel Luke. I know cuz I asked him. I wish you were here. So duz unkel Luke. I love you. So duz unkel Luke.

love Ronnie

"Oh, you're still here. I thought Phyllis might let you leave early."

Alicia glanced up to see a friend, Janet Jewell, lounging in the doorway. "She did. I was just about to pack up. What about you?"

Janet grinned. "I'll be bailing out in half an hour. You going to visit your folks?"

"Yes." Alicia grimaced. "I'm dreading the drive, though. I hope the traffic around New York isn't as bad as last year."

"It will be," Janet predicted. "You'll get stuck for hours on the George Washington Bridge."

"Thanks, I really needed to hear that."

"Well, at least it's not snowing. Give me a call if you change your mind. You can always come and have turkey with me and Pete. Pete's brother will be there. You know, the unmarried one with the Mel Gibson eyes."

Alicia couldn't help but smile. "I wish I could, but my parents are expecting me. They'd be hurt if I didn't go."

After Janet left, it seemed a lot quieter. Voices and laughter rippled in the distance, but they were far away. The silence in Alicia's office pressed against her like a living thing, pushing her spirits down into the same black pit she'd existed in for the past two months. Outside, the sky was overcast, which did nothing to improve her mood.

Sighing, she slipped her shoes back on, picked up her purse and coat and locked up her office. As she headed for the elevator, a part of her wanted to run back and take Janet up on her offer. Thanksgiving with her parents was bound to be painful, especially since this would be the first time they'd all been together since the funeral. Besides, she just didn't feel like she had a lot to be thankful for this year, and she doubted her parents did, either.

The southward drive to New Jersey proved as trying as she'd feared. Although the highways weren't slick, they were choked with vehicles; everyone in the world seemed to be traveling somewhere, everyone was in a hurry, and the result was chaos. As the miles and hours slid by, Alicia tried not to dwell on the knowledge that the two people she most longed to see wouldn't be there to greet her at the end of her journey. She played the radio, sang along with the songs she knew, tried to cheer herself up. But to no avail.

When at last she pulled into her parents' driveway, it was nearly eight o'clock, a good hour later than she'd hoped to arrive. Sadness overwhelmed her as she shut off the engine and gazed up at her childhood home, a small white colonial illuminated by lamps at either side of the blue front door. The sight revived so many memories—memories of Caroline, memories of Luke—but she pushed them aside.

Somehow they'd all get through this holiday, then she'd go back to Boston and go on, just as her parents would go on. Life didn't stop because people were unhappy. She'd found that out for herself.

Stiff and weary, Alicia climbed out of the car just as her mother emerged from the house. The wind whipped Alicia's hair as she locked the car door and walked up the sidewalk to meet her mother. As always, the two women made an awkward attempt at an embrace.

"Mother, you shouldn't be out without a coat. How are you?"

"I'm fine, dear, but you're later than I expected. We've held dinner for you."

"My suitcase—"

"Your father will get it. Come along. You must be famished."

Once inside, in the brighter light, she could see that Caroline's death had taken a visible toll. Her mother looked older, the lines in her face much deeper than they had been before. Her father, too, appeared to have aged, for he seemed grayer, more tired and stooped.

"Hello, Daddy," she said as he helped her off with her coat. "I'm sorry I'm late. I hope you weren't worried."

"We always worry about you, honey. How was the drive?"

Familiar smells and sights engulfed her as they led her toward the dining room. She was home. And yet she wasn't home, really, for her soul had moved on to another house, a house she might never set foot in again.

To her relief, neither parent mentioned Caroline or Richard, either during the meal or afterward when they'd gathered in the den. Instead, her mother spoke of her Latin students, her father of his physics textbook. Content to listen to anything that did not hit a raw nerve, Alicia relaxed, curled in one corner of the sofa with a glass of wine at her elbow.

In due course, her father excused himself and retired to his study, leaving her alone with her mother. Alicia braced herself for the inevitable barrage of questions. Her mother didn't disappoint her.

"I haven't heard you mention Nick Easton lately," the older woman remarked the moment her husband was gone.

Alicia reached for her wine. "That's because there isn't anything to say." She took a sip and set down the goblet. "I haven't seen him in weeks."

"That's a pity. I was hoping something would come of it."

"I'm sorry, Mother."

"I suppose he met someone else while you were gone. That's the way of men, I'm afraid. Out of sight, out of mind. You ought to have realized that."

Nettled, Alicia retorted, "As a matter of fact, he didn't forget me. He even flew to Houston to see me."

"Then what went wrong? What did you do?"

Too tired and depressed to be diplomatic, Alicia's temper flared. "I didn't do anything! It's just that he asked me to marry him and I turned him down. Naturally, things have cooled between us."

"You turned him down? But why?"

"Because I don't love him. And because—" Alicia couldn't stop her reaction; all of a sudden her throat worked and tears stung her eyes. "Because I'm in love with someone else. Someone you and Daddy wouldn't approve of."

She didn't know why she'd blurted that out. She never confided in her mother. Never. The only possible explanation was that the confidences she'd shared with Sharon had somehow eased her into the habit.

"Luke Garrick," her mother guessed with a sigh. She gazed at Alicia, her blue eyes sorrowful. "I was afraid this would happen. Alicia, how can you make the same mistake twice? The man isn't your intellectual equal. If you'd married him—"

"He is *so* my equal," Alicia interrupted fiercely. She straightened her spine, her hands clenched into fists. "If I'd married him, I'd have been happy. I'd probably have children right now and a real home instead of all this emptiness—"

"He doesn't have the education that you—"

"So what? Just because he can't conjugate Latin verbs or derive Schrödinger's equation doesn't make him a lesser man. Do you know what dyslexia is? I've been reading about it lately because I found out Luke is dyslexic—not just a little bit dyslexic, but a lot. And yet you should see what he's made of his life! You should see his store and his home. You should see him with Ronnie. Your grandson adores his uncle, and with damn good reason. Luke is worth a million of Kenny, and I wish—" Wetness escaped her eyes to trickle down her cheeks. "I just wish you c-could...see that..."

Her mother rose and moved across the room to the sofa. "I'm sorry, dear. I didn't mean to make you cry." A few seconds slipped by, then the older woman's thin arms enfolded her daughter.

Neither of them spoke. Alicia accepted the embrace, her cheek pressed to her mother's shoulder while she struggled to regain her composure. The scent of gardenias drifted to her nose, conjuring up long-ago memories that made her want to cling to her mother and weep.

After what seemed like a long time, her mother said, "I do know what dyslexia is. I've had dyslexic students. Many of them are embarrassed about their disability and don't want people to know. They're afraid people will think they're stupid."

"That's Luke," Alicia whispered. "But I shouldn't have told you. He wouldn't want you to know."

"It's better that I do," her mother said dryly. "The question is how are we going to fix matters? I take it things aren't working out between the two of you?"

"No, but he and I...we're past fixing."

"Nonsense, where's your Brant determination? Think of Caroline. What would she have said? Give up? Don't aim for what you want?"

Reflecting that she'd already aimed and missed by a mile, Alicia gave a watery smile and said, "Mother, did you know Caroline was having marital problems?"

Mrs. Brant's sigh ruffled Alicia's hair. "Oh, yes," her mother said heavily. "And it devastated me. She told me she wanted to be more like you. You had the strength to go through with a divorce, and she admired that. She had a tremendous admiration for you, you know."

Stunned, Alicia lifted her head. "No, I didn't know. I always admired *her.* In fact, I thought she was perfect."

"I loved her dearly, but she wasn't perfect. None of us is." Her mother hesitated, seeming to struggle within herself. "Alicia, if I've ever made you think I wasn't proud of you, I'm sorry. I was bitterly disappointed about Kenneth, and I know I said things that weren't tactful. I thought you'd brought your problems on yourself by neglecting your husband for your work. But Caroline made me see that it wasn't your fault." She paused. "I've wanted to apologize for a long time, but . . . I didn't know how."

Alicia gazed straight into her mother's blue eyes. She'd come this far; she might as well be completely honest. "Yes, I thought you weren't proud of me. I even thought—" She stopped and drew a breath. "I thought you loved Caroline best. I've spent my whole life trying to earn your love and Daddy's. Do you remember Great-Aunt Louisa? When I was eight, she told me that I had been an accident. You and Daddy had only wanted one child, but I came along anyway. After that, I always felt like an outsider."

Her mother looked horrified. "Oh, Alicia, I could wring that old woman's neck! What a thing to tell a child! Of course we wanted you. It's true you weren't planned, but when I found out I was expecting, I wanted you, and so did your father. And we've always been proud of you. Sometimes we haven't understood you, but we've always loved you, and not a bit less than Caroline. You never had to earn our love, darling. You've always had it." Her expression grew stubborn. "And if Luke Garrick is the man you want, then you have my full support. All we have to do is figure out how to bring the thing about."

Surrounded by the aroma of freshly baked pumpkin pie, Luke lay on his side and aimed his flashlight into the dark recess at the base of Sharon Redford's dishwasher. He didn't know much about dishwashers, but it shouldn't take long to find out what was wrong. As long as it had wires or mechanical parts, he could figure it out. He'd had that ability for as long as he could remember. He only hoped the problem was something simple because a replacement part might be hard to track down on the day before Thanksgiving.

"I can't thank you enough," Sharon was saying. "The perverse thing just knew I was going to have company, so it decided to break down. My mother and stepfather are coming. Nancy's bringing her latest young man, and Michael's invited his new lady friend. Counting you and Ronnie, that'll be eleven people! I need my dishwasher if I'm going to stay sane."

"I'll do what I can," he answered, glancing up at his distraught neighbor. "I owe you. You've done a heck of a lot for me and Ronnie."

One hand holding a can of diet soda, Sharon dragged over a kitchen stool and perched on its edge. "I just wish I could do more," she said with a sigh.

"Why?" he asked in amusement.

"I don't know. I always want to set the whole world right for everybody. Have you heard from Alicia?"

Luke's hand tightened on the flashlight, but he didn't look up. "Ronnie had a letter from her last week. She's heading down to her parents' house for the holidays."

Nearly a minute of silence passed before Sharon cleared her throat. "Forgive me if I'm out of line, but it seems like you miss her an awful lot."

"Yeah, I miss her," he admitted after a few brittle seconds.

"For a while there I thought maybe the two of you were going to, you know, get together."

Luke set down the flashlight and sat up, gazing miserably at his open toolbox. "That's kind of hard to do when she's getting married to someone else." Somehow he kept his voice neutral. Part of him desperately wanted to drop the subject, while the other part vibrated with the need to talk.

"You mean Nick Easton?" Sharon sounded surprised. "She's not marrying him. Didn't you know that? She turned him down weeks ago."

Alicia wasn't going to marry Easton. Luke's breathing stopped while he rolled the news around in his mind, trying to take it in. She had turned Easton down. Nice, safe, charming Nick Easton with his expensive clothes and high salary.

"No, no one told me," he said at last. Attempting nonchalance, he added, "Any idea why?"

"I don't know. I expect she didn't love him." Sharon sipped her soda, watching him with shrewd eyes. "My best guess is that she's in love with someone else."

"If you mean me, I don't think so."

"What makes you so sure?"

Embarrassed, he only shrugged. He couldn't tell her of that bungled proposal. Nor could he tell her that he'd declared his love only to have it thrown back in his face.

"Has it occurred to you," Sharon said in a careful tone, "that part of the problem might have been Christina?"

His heart gave a queer, sideways lurch. "What?"

"I said—"

"How do you know about Christina?" His whole body had gone stiff, even his lips, so that he could barely form the words.

"From Alicia. You didn't know that she knew?"

"No. No, I never mentioned Christina to her. Not once."

"You've got the woman's picture in your room," Sharon said gently. "You could scarcely expect Alicia not to notice."

He shook his head, feeling like a damned moron because he hadn't thought about it. It had never even occurred to him that she would think that he and Christina... Oh, God. "She should have asked me, damn it!"

"I agree. *I* would have, but Alicia's different from me. She holds things in. She keeps to herself. And she's proud. A bit like you, isn't she?"

Luke's thoughts whirled. Maybe Christina wasn't the reason Alicia had turned him down, but she must have colored Alicia's perceptions of everything he'd said and done. All at once, he remembered the message on the answering machine, and comprehension struck with the force of an electric shock. She must have heard it. He remembered how funny she'd acted when he'd walked in the house her first night back. Nothing had been right between them from that moment on.

He expelled a long, harsh breath, but his chest still felt tight. How could he have been so stupid, so foolish? Of course, if she'd seen the picture, she'd leap to the wrong conclusion. He couldn't blame her. Christina was a beautiful woman.

But when had she seen it? When she'd slept with him, the lights had been off. And in the morning, she had been making love with him, not exploring the surface of his dresser. "I didn't think she went in my room," he muttered.

"She did your laundry, didn't she? Didn't she have to go into your room to put it away? Didn't she change the sheets on your bed? I seem to remember her telling me she was doing those things for you. Very wifely, I thought it."

He gave a choked laugh. "You must think I'm pretty dumb."

"Of course I don't." Sharon's tone was kind. "Jim doesn't always notice the things I do for him, either, but that's all right because I point them out." She tilted her head, regarding him with open curiosity. "So aren't you going to tell me?"

"Tell you what?"

"Just who the heck *is* Christina anyway?"

Luke closed his eyes. "She's my sister," he said in a hollow voice.

Alicia removed her gaze from the stained-glass windows of her parents' church as the minister invited the congregation to bow their heads in silent prayer. She shut her eyes, enjoying the low, soothing organ music in the background. Peace seeped into her soul. She was glad they'd decided to attend the Thanksgiving Day service.

Her head bowed, she prayed for her parents, for Caroline and Richard, for Luke and Ronnie, then for herself. She would try to be a better daughter, to be more patient. With a sense of wonder, she recalled last night's conversation. She still couldn't quite believe her mother's change of attitude. Losing Caroline had changed her mother, made her more open-minded. In the end, they had talked until midnight.

They had reminisced about Caroline, wept together and comforted each other, finally taking a step toward healing their scarred relationship.

Alicia linked her fingers and turned her thoughts to the source of her heartache. According to Ronnie's letter, Luke loved and missed her. She hadn't dared to believe it. When she called on the phone, it was Ronnie she got. When she wrote to Ronnie, it was Ronnie who wrote back. In all these weeks, Luke hadn't made any effort to contact her... but then she hadn't made any effort to contact him, either.

Perhaps it was her tranquil surroundings, or perhaps it was the lingering effects of last night's conversation with her mother. Whatever the case, she felt stronger, more able to cope with the knowledge that she'd been unfair to Luke. She'd wanted him to say he loved her, but she'd been afraid to say the words herself. She hadn't asked about Christina because she'd measured Luke by Kenny's yardstick. And when he'd finally told her he loved her, she'd done the unforgivable: she'd told him he couldn't love.

But he could and did love. He loved Ronnie. He'd loved Richard. And he loved *her*, too. The truth hit her square between the eyes, clearing her vision so that for the first time she saw the situation as it really was. Of course Luke loved her. Everything he'd done, everything he'd ever said, even in anger, should have made her realize. The tenderness of his lovemaking showed it. His behavior toward Nick showed it. His actions when she'd been injured showed it. A hundred other examples flitted through her head. The simple truth was that Luke was better at showing than telling because— again realization struck—he was as afraid of rejection as she was.

For an instant, she despaired. Then she opened her eyes and looked around and felt a blaze of new hope. Anything was possible. Mistakes could be forgiven. The moment she got back to the house, she was going to call Luke.

The decision made, she closed her eyes and offered up one more prayer, a prayer of gratitude and thanksgiving. And as she did so, she felt bathed in sunshine, as though the golden warmth of a summer's day had somehow crept into the church.

On the ride home, Alicia gazed out the car window, rehearsing what she would say to Luke. It wouldn't be easy, but she would find the words. She would tell him she loved him, she needed him, she wanted to come back to Houston and be his wife.

"Whose car is that in our driveway?" Mrs. Brant asked suddenly.

Alicia glanced around, and her heart almost stopped beating. She didn't recognize the car, but the tall figure leaning against it was achingly familiar. So was the little boy sitting on the hood. "I can't believe it," she whispered.

"It's Ronnie!" her mother exclaimed. "Look, Edward, it's our grandson! And that's Luke!"

"Yes, Margaret, I see," replied Alicia's father, his voice just a little uneven. He pulled into the driveway next to the subcompact rental car and shut off the engine.

As her parents hurried from the Buick, Alicia found she couldn't move. Even her brain felt paralyzed. Outside the car, her father and mother exclaimed over Ronnie and pumped Luke's hand.

Ronnie broke away and pressed his face to the window glass. "Aunt Alicia, Aunt Alicia, I'm here to visit you just like I promised! I flew in an airplane!" Somehow she got the door open. However, instead of letting her out, Ronnie hurled himself into the back seat and flung his arms around her neck. "I missed you so much," he said in a small voice. "Writing letters isn't the same."

Alicia hugged him tight. "I know what you mean. Nothing is as good as this, darling. I'm so happy to see you. And so surprised!"

From the corner of her eye, she saw her mother say something to Luke and embrace him. Then the car door widened again, sending another sweep of chill air rushing inside.

"Come on, squirt. Let your aunt out of the car."

"Okay." The child climbed out and began to dance around the driveway.

Thunder roared in Alicia's ears as, attacked with something akin to stage fright, she looked down at Luke's boots. Her gaze traveled up, past a pair of long, jean-clad legs, past a black leather jacket, to the beloved face shadowed by the brim of a cowboy hat. His gray eyes gazed into hers, and in their depths she saw an echo of her own uncertainty.

He held out a hand.

Heart hammering, she accepted it and stepped out onto the blacktop. For a moment, neither of them moved a muscle.

And then they were clinging to each other, their mouths fused in a greedy kiss that seemed destined to last a lifetime. At the perimeter of her awareness, she knew that her parents were discreetly urging Ronnie toward the house, but right now she didn't care if the whole universe stood witness to their joy. All that mattered was that Luke was here, in her arms, melting against her, his strong, hard body pressed against her own pliant one. He had come for her, he was here, he was hers, and nothing else mattered.

"Oh, Luke," she gasped, bright stars rocketing in her head. "I was going to call you. Today. As soon as I got inside the house." Her fingers threaded through his black hair, her voice shaking as she confessed, "I couldn't bear it any longer. I couldn't bear to lose you a second time."

"You haven't lost me. I'm right here, and I'm not going anywhere without you." He crushed her against him, his mouth raining kisses over her face and eyelids and hair. "Oh, Alicia, I've been such a fool."

"No, I have. Luke, I love you."

"I love *you*." His hands cupped her face, his thumbs sculpting her cheekbones as he looked straight into her eyes. "Sharon said you knew about Christina. Alicia, she's my *sister.*"

"Luke, you don't have a sister.'

"Yes, I do. I just never told you." He glanced around, his expression wry. "Is there somewhere private we can talk?"

"The house? Or if you'd rather, we can go to the park."

"The park, unless you're too cold."

She smiled up at him. "I actually feel pretty warm right now. I think that kiss singed a few of my nerve endings."

"It was supposed to." His eyes gleamed, then he shook his head in amazement. "This feels like a dream. Do you know how hard it is to get tickets the day before Thanksgiving? I just sat in the airport and prayed for a miracle, just a couple of no-shows so we could get on that plane. And the miracle happened. I guess the man upstairs is on our side, Alicia."

"I think you're right," she said in a soft voice. "I think you and I are meant to be."

His arm around her shoulders, they wandered down the sidewalk toward the little neighborhood park that served as a playground for local youngsters. For a while, they spoke only of their love and need for each other, then Luke broached the subject of his sister.

"You know my dad ran out on my mom, and my mom died when I was six. Christina was just a baby, about one and a half. I remember I loved her very much and felt very protective toward her." He sighed. "I always let you believe I didn't have any relatives. Well, that's not true. My mother had a sister living in California. Aunt Gertrude came to the funeral, mainly to look us over.''

"Look you over?" Alicia glanced at him with a frown.

"She and my mother hadn't spoken in years. Aunt Gertrude thought my mother had married an uneducated loser and expected the offspring, as she called us, to be as disappointing as my father." When he paused, Alicia could sense the turmoil within him. "My aunt sat me down at the kitchen table and quizzed me about my letters and numbers. She wanted to find out if I was smart enough for her to bother with. Needless to say, I didn't pass her test. She humiliated me. She told me I was as slow-witted as my father and that she wouldn't take me to live with her. She took Christina but sent me out to foster care. I never saw my baby sister again until three years ago, when I hired a P.I. to track her down.''

"Oh, Luke." Alicia stopped dead, her eyes brimming. "Oh, Luke, that's horrible. How could your aunt do such a thing?"

He shrugged. "That's just the way she was. Anyhow, when I contacted Christina, I found out she didn't even know I existed. My aunt had never told her she had a brother. So it took a while, especially since she lives out of state. We've found opportunities to meet and get to know each other. It was tough going at first, but we've formed a bond." He cleared his throat. "This is hard for me to talk about, you understand? Even now, just thinking about Aunt Gertrude sends shivers down my spine.''

Alicia slid her arms around his waist, hugging him through the dual layers of coat. "Of course I understand. And I can't tell you how sorry I am that I rejected you. I thought you didn't love me. I didn't understand, but now I do and... and I love you even more, if that's possible.''

He smoothed back a lock of her hair, then pressed a kiss to her brow. "I should have told you about Christina. I meant to, after I gave you my ring."

She gazed up at him, tears blurring her vision. "Do you still want to give it to me?"

"Aw, Alicia, how can you ask that? I want you, babe. I've always wanted you." His voice cracked. "I've loved you ever since I first set eyes on you, and I never stopped loving you even for a minute. I apologize for that other proposal. I was hurting so damn bad I didn't know what I was saying. You should have picked up that whiskey bottle and bashed my head with it."

"I thought about it," she said shakily, "but I was afraid you'd get cut."

One corner of his mouth lifted. "It might have brought me to my senses." He slipped a hand into an inner pocket and withdrew a tiny white box. "All these years I've saved this. It's not much, just a quarter carat, but... at least I know it fits."

Her hands shook so badly she almost dropped the box, yet somehow she got it open. And there it was. The ring she had once worn rested, not on velvet, but on a layer of smooth white cotton. Yet this plain gold band with its tiny diamond represented the only thing she had ever wanted.

"What do you mean it's not much?" she said in a trembling voice. "You wonderful, foolish man, it's everything. It's beyond everything. It's precious. You're precious. Oh, Lord, I'm going to c-cry...."

Luke slipped the ring onto her finger, then applied himself to comforting her in the most effective and delightful way. This took several minutes, glorious minutes in which Alicia was hardly aware of cars driving past them on the street just a few feet away.

"Are you cold?" Luke murmured at last.

"Not a bit," she assured him with a tremulous sigh. "But I suppose we should go back. Mother planned dinner for two o'clock and I'm sure she needs help in the kitchen."

"Oh, yeah, your mother. How do you think she's going to like having me back in your life?"

"Don't worry. I think she's already accepted it." She bit her lip. "Luke, I told Mother. About your dyslexia, I mean. You've every right to be angry."

To her relief, he only made a slight grimace. "No, I'm not angry. How could I be? Do you realize that was the first time your mother ever hugged me?"

"Well, dyslexia is something she understands. What Mother understands, she can accept. Besides, she and Daddy just want me to be happy."

"I know someone else who's going to be happy."

Alicia's eyes widened. "Ronnie! My goodness, I almost forgot him! We've got to go back."

"That's okay," her new fiancé said smugly. "I was kind of hoping you had other things on your mind. Do you think your parents will let us share a room?"

"I doubt it. Not with Ronnie here."

"How soon can we get married, do you think?"

"As soon as we can get a license and arrange something with our minister. Unless you want a big church wedding, in which case it might take a while."

"Tomorrow wouldn't be too soon, if you want my opinion." He squeezed her hand. "Alicia, what about your job?"

"That's easy. I'll quit."

"Just like that? No regrets? You've worked hard to get where you are."

"Yes, but it's just a job to me, Luke. It's not part of me, not the way you are. I need to be your wife more than I need to be the manager of business systems development."

"There's something I haven't told you." He gazed down at her, his expression steady and filled with yearning. "Joey's decided to retire after all. Any chance you'd take his place?"

Her heart gave a leap. "As your full business partner?"

"As my partner in all things." Luke traced the curve of her lip with his finger, then bent and gave her a gentle kiss. "My partner in business and my partner in love," he whispered. "My partner for life."

"For life and for always," Alicia said mistily. "I couldn't ask for anything more perfect."

Epilogue

Late December
Venice, Italy

"I hope Ronnie isn't missing us too much." Alicia plopped down on the hotel bed and kicked off her shoes. "Maybe we should call him again."

Her husband slipped an arm around her waist and kissed her. "Don't worry so much. Ronnie's having the time of his life with your parents. Five days in Walt Disney World ought to keep any kid happy. Anyway, you called him when we got here, so he knows we're fine."

"I still can't believe he won the contest. By the way, did you ever figure out how he ended his story?"

"He twisted the facts a little, didn't he?"

"Well, he wanted a happy ending, and I didn't have the heart to tell him he couldn't have one. So I let him say that—"

"Aunt Alicia married Uncle Luke and came to live in Houston. Yeah, I know what he did. I thought it sounded like a great idea. I just didn't think it was going to happen."

"But it did." Alicia snuggled her head against Luke's shoulder and reached for his free hand, studying their matching wedding bands with a small, secret smile. "It was so nice of Joey to agree to run the store so we could have a honeymoon. I keep trying to decide which I liked better— Rome or Florence or Venice. Venice, I think. I'll never forget that romantic gondola serenade, no matter how long I live."

"The gondolier kept staring at you."

"It was your hat he was staring at. I hope you aren't going to be a jealous husband." She rubbed her cheek against his soft cotton shirt.

"Are you kidding? When have I ever been jealous? Only immature people are jealous. I'm just protective, that's all."

"Oh, good," she murmured. "Then it's okay to tell you I was pinched yesterday in Piazza San Marco."

"Ah, I think that was me," he said with a grin. "Sorry, but I couldn't resist."

Alicia rolled her eyes. "After what you said about Joey! And you aren't even Italian."

"That's what you think. One of my grandmothers was Sicilian."

"You never told me that."

"Why do you think I keep taking you to Italian restaurants?"

"Even so," she said with dignity, "being one-fourth Italian doesn't entitle you to pinch women's bottoms."

"Just my wife's bottom. And a very luscious bottom it is." He lowered himself onto the bed, exerting a firm pressure that brought her down with him. "All soft and round and cushy... Ah, babe, I love it." He kissed the tip of her nose, his hands cupping her derriere.

"So what else are you?"

"You mean besides hot?"

"I mean besides Italian."

"Mostly Irish, I think, with a bit of French thrown in for seasoning. Christina's putting together a family tree. She's the one to ask."

"I can't believe I didn't know that. There are still so many things we haven't told each other." She sighed with contentment. "So shall we go back out and do more sightseeing?"

"In awhile. That was a great lunch we just had, but now I'm ready for dessert."

"Insatiable man."

"I have to be to keep up with you."

"Moi?" She opened her eyes very wide. "I beg your pardon, but 'twas not *I* who woke *you* up at six o'clock this morning for a little hanky-panky."

"No, but 'twas you who said it was the best wake-up call you ever got."

Alicia blushed. "I don't recall saying that."

"You have a very selective memory, darlin', but that's okay because I remember everything." He began to stroke the curves of her back, his fingers playing little games with her spine.

"Oh, do you?" she inquired, her tone sweet. "And do you happen to remember what you said on our wedding night while I was fulfilling your erotic fantasies?"

He nuzzled her throat, his mouth warm and insistent against her skin. "I said, 'Alicia, baby, you are absolutely fantastic.' And you are, honeybun. And always will be."

"Hmm. Well, you do seem to have a good memory. Like I told you before, you're probably a genius. *I* think so, in any case."

"Of course you might be a little biased."

"Maybe, but did I tell you what my mother said?"

"I'd rather you didn't."

"It was very complimentary, Luke. Since she got all those pamphlets from the Orton Dyslexia Society, she's been dying to be helpful. She seems to think—"

"I know," he interrupted in a suffering voice. "She wants me to join a support group. She's all fired up about this re-mediation idea." Mouth quirking, he touched her cheek. "I'm not against it, Alicia. I think it's great that help is available. Heck, I'm willing to subscribe to their newsletter and go to their meetings. But right now, I've got other things on my mind. And the first of those things is..." Disentangling their assorted limbs, he went over and rummaged through his suitcase, then extracted a small gift-wrapped package. "I bought this yesterday while you were looking at postcards." He came back and sat on the edge of the bed, kissed her on the mouth and handed her the box.

Alicia tore off the festive paper and lifted the lid. Inside, a set of twin silver bells nestled against a bed of green velvet. She smiled and glanced up. "They're beautiful, sweetheart. Are we going to wear them?"

"Well, I'm not wearing *mine*. I like being able to sneak up and grab you."

She laughed. "Then I'm not wearing mine, either. So what's their significance, my darling husband?"

Luke's expression grew serious as he lifted one of the bells and gave it a shake. It had a light, silvery tinkle, like distant sleigh bells on the breeze.

"Any time I'm not telling you something you want to know," he said, "I want you to ring your bell in my ear. And any time you're not telling me something I want to know, I'm ringing mine in your ear. We're going to work on this communication thing, Alicia. I want us to keep our marriage strong."

"Oh, Luke." Moved almost beyond words, Alicia leaned over and kissed the hard plane of his cheek. "That's a splendid idea. I'm so glad you're my husband. I think I must be the luckiest woman in the world."

"I just figure a couple of paranoids like us need all the help we can get." Looking pleased, Luke set the bells aside and turned back to her with a lazy smile. "And I think this is an ideal time to do a little extra communicating," he said seductively.

A familiar shiver of awareness rippled through her as, one by one, he worked loose the buttons of her blouse. "Oh, you mean *that* kind of communication."

"Well, it is my specialty." He bent down to plant a row of kisses along the upper swell of her breasts, then moved slowly upward toward her mouth.

Alicia feigned a sigh of reluctance. "We really shouldn't be doing this, Luke. We *ought* to go out and do more sight-seeing. After all, this is our last day in Venice, and we paid an awful lot of money..."

"True," her husband agreed thickly, "and it's going to be a long while before we can afford to come again."

"You mean visit again," she corrected with mischief.

"Uh, yeah. Visit." He pushed her back down on the bed and covered her with himself. "Wicked woman. How did I survive without you all these years?"

"I don't know." She gazed fully into his eyes, her heart filled to the brim with happiness. "But I do know one thing. I love you with all my heart, Luke Garrick."

"And I love you, honeybun. With all my heart."

* * * * * *

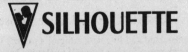

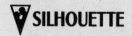

▼ SILHOUETTE

‹ SPECIAL EDITION ›

COMING NEXT MONTH

A MATCH FOR CELIA Gina Ferris Wilkins

That Special Woman! & The Family Way

This holiday was supposed to be exciting, but Celia Carson had no idea just how much adventure, romance and passion she was in for!

MOTHER AT HEART Robin Elliott

Man, Woman & Child

Tessa's late sister's baby was now her son and his happiness was at risk thanks to Tessa's desire for an arrogant, impossible man—a man who would never acknowledge this child as his...

FATHER IN TRAINING Susan Mallery

Hometown Heartbreakers

Sandy Walker needed a provider for her children, not an adventurer... She just wasn't prepared to talk a walk on the wild side with notorious bachelor Kyle Haynes.

COWBOY'S KISS Victoria Pade

A Ranching Family

Jackson Heller couldn't believe that his father had left this pretty city woman half his ranch! What had he been thinking of? What was Jackson going to do with her?

ONLY ST. NICK KNEW Nikki Benjamin

Taking a job in New Mexico Alison Kent had intended avoiding Christmas, but Frank Bradford and his motherless twins couldn't allow that. They wanted to give her a family for Christmas—them!

ABIGAIL AND MISTLETOE Karen Rose Smith

Could anyone understand and live with Abigail's secret? Was she brave enough to risk revealing her true self to Brady Crawford?

SILHOUETTE

Desire

COMING NEXT MONTH

THE DISOBEDIENT BRIDE Joan Johnston

Man of the Month

Zach Whitelaw wanted a bride to give him children. Rebecca Littlewolf wanted Zach and children, his children, would be a bonus—what could go wrong?

A CHRISTMAS COWBOY Suzannah Davis

Mac Mahoney was in trouble; he'd got snowed in with his ex-girlfriend and her five-year-old. The child was convinced that Mac was the daddy that Santa was bringing him...

OPERATION MUMMY Caroline Cross

Alex Morrison's three little sons had picked out the mother they wanted and they were determined to get Shay Spencer and their dad together. Alex couldn't fault their taste but he wasn't getting married again—ever!

CAT'S CRADLE Christine Rimmer

Dillon McKenna wanted a family and he knew just the right woman for the task. However, Cat Beaudine had already raised one family and thought once was enough. But once with Dillon wasn't anywhere near enough!

THE REBEL AND THE HERO Helen R. Myers

Strong, sexy Logan Powers was the kind of man that rebel Merri Brown could never understand. So she unwisely married someone else. But now she was back and the man she didn't marry still wanted her...

DARK INTENTIONS Carole Buck

Royce Williams had once saved her life, so Julia Kendricks was determined to help him when a tragic car accident left him blind. He couldn't recognise her so he need never know who she had been.

❤ SILHOUETTE
Intrigue

COMING NEXT MONTH

HOPSCOTCH Rebecca York

A 43 Light Street novel

Who was Jason Zacharias? That riddle was the key to Noel Emery's frightening predicament—being pursued by assassins! Her guardian angel was a seasoned veteran of murder…and he claimed to be her husband.

I'LL BE HOME FOR CHRISTMAS
Dawn Stewardson

Ali's 'dead' husband was alive, her son was missing and her mind was reeling. She turned to the one man she could almost trust—the single dad next door, crime writer Logan Reed.

BEARING GIFTS Aimée Thurlo

Just days before Christmas, little Amy Hawken's nightmare began—her mother was attacked and then framed. Bachelor J.D. Hawken would do anything for his special niece, and he was equally drawn to Mari Sanchez, Amy's godmother, now his cohort in both child care and crime solving…

BREATHLESS Carly Bishop

Second in the Pulse trilogy

It had been three long years since Zoe Mastrangelo lost her husband and child in a freak accident. Now her surviving daughter was in desperate need of a donor from her father's side. Zoe set off for Rafe's hometown, unaware she was in for a surprise…

♥ SILHOUETTE

Sensation

COMING NEXT MONTH

OUT OF THE DARK Justine Davis

Victoria Flynn didn't want to trust the dark and dangerous Texan who was too darn handsome for her peace of mind. But she was in big trouble and he owed her family.

Cole Bannister was prepared to help Tory find out who was out to ruin her reputation and her business, but he made it a rule never to get involved with his clients. *Rules are made to be broken...*

SIMPLE GIFTS Kathleen Korbel

He Who Dares

Rock O'Connor was a cop in Chicago and he'd seen things that had made him lose faith in people, whereas Lee Kendall was an eternal optimist who lived every second of her life to the full, thought people were fascinating and really believed in true love. But it was Lee that someone wanted to kill! Suddenly it had become vitally important to Rock that he solve this puzzle—before Lee got hurt. She might be about to break his heart, but at least she'd be alive!

MIDNIGHT STRANGER Diana Whitney

Ruth Ridenour was on the run, determined to keep her baby son safe. She met Garrett Kincade when he was wounded and fleeing from the corrupt but long arm of the local law. They were two fugitives, guarding secrets too dangerous to expose. No one knew where they were for the moment, but could true love really grow in such tense circumstances?

NO MORE SECRETS Linda Randall Wisdom

Security specialist Nikki Price had returned to Scott Carter's house because she felt she might have unwittingly betrayed him and his young daughter when she'd uncovered a traitor there five years ago. Now she needed answers. Their lives depended on them. But she'd broken the cardinal rule: NEVER FALL IN LOVE...

A year's supply of Silhouette Desires — absolutely FREE!

Would you like to win a year's supply of seductive and breathtaking romances? Well, you can and they're FREE! Simply complete the wordsearch puzzle below and send it to us by 31st May 1996. The first 5 correct entries picked after the closing date will win a years supply of Silhouette Desire novels (six books every month—worth over £150). What could be easier?

READER SERVICE
ROMANCE
RESIST
HEART
MEMORIES
PAGES
KISS
SPINE
TEMPTATION
LOVE
COLLECTION
ROSES
PACK
PARCEL
TITLES
DREAMS
COUPLE
SPECIAL EDITION
EMOTION
DESIRE
SILHOUETTE
MOODS
PASSION

M	E	R	O	W	A	L	R	L	M	S	P	C	O	S
	O		E	C	I	V	R	E	S	R	E	D	A	E	R
R	O					E		O	S	M	A	E	R	D	S
O	D	H	E	A	R	T		S		S		S	E	L	T	I	T
M	S			S	E		M	E	M	O	R	I	E	S	S
A	E			C	G			S	A		C			E
N	P	T		A		E	K		W		O	I		W
C			T	P	K	I	S	S	C			L	T	T	O
E			E		H		A	E	V	O	L		E	N	N
	A	E		U		M		P	R		T	E	I	M	O	E
	E	N		L	O		L	I		S	C		P	I	O
S	L	I			H	A		S		I	T		T	S	A
	P	P	A	R	C	E	L	N	E		S	I		A	S	Z
	U	S	D	B			I	D		E	O		T	A	I
O	O		O		N		B	S		R	N		I	P	S
	C		E	N	N	A	M	T	R	R	L	G	N	O	L	T
	O		E	M	O	T	I	O	N			O		N		I
N	O	I	T	I	D	E	L	A	I	C	E	P	S	K

Please turn over for details of how to enter...

How to enter

Hidden in the grid are words which relate to Silhouette and romance. You'll find the list overleaf and they can be read backwards, forwards, up, down or diagonally. As you find each word, circle it or put a line through it.

When you have found all the words, don't forget to fill in your name and address in the space provided below and pop this page into an envelope (you don't need a stamp) and post it today. Hurry—competition ends 31st May 1996.

Silhouette Wordsearch
FREEPOST
Croydon
Surrey
CR9 3WZ

Are you a Reader Service Subscriber?   Yes ☐   No ☐

Ms/Mrs/Miss/Mr _____

Address _____

_____

_____ Postcode _____

One application per household.

You may be mailed with other offers from other reputable companies as a result of this application. If you would prefer not to receive such offers, please tick box. ☐

COMP295
E